BRIGHT
MORNING STAR

**Also by Simon Morden
from NewCon Press**

At the Speed of Light (2017)
Macsen Against the Jugger (2018)

BRIGHT
MORNING STAR

Simon Morden

NewCon Press
England

First published in August 2019 by NewCon Press,
41 Wheatsheaf Road, Alconbury Weston, Cambs, PE28 4LF

NCP208 (limited edition hardback)
NCP209 (softback)

10 9 8 7 6 5 4 3 2 1

ISBN:

978-1-912950-33-1 (hardback)
978-1-912950-34-8 (softback)

Cover by Ben Baldwin

Text edited by Ian Whates
Book interior layout by Storm Constantine

ONE

What do I remember? Falling. I remember falling. Not at first, of course. There were preliminaries and precursors to deal with before that. Checks and rechecks. Protocols to observe. I was activated and told to get ready – I won't call it born, because I've seen that, and seen how utterly, terrifyingly helpless you are. You wail, you gasp, you blink, and you can do nothing meaningful for yourselves. I had a list of systems to validate, and programs to run, but I was made whole and ready. You're not.

I was blind, though. I was sealed up in my opaque womb-like shell, attached to Mother by an umbilical that gave me everything I needed at the time. Those are my first memories. Before that moment, I had potential, but not experience. I knew I'd been turned on before because I had the logs to prove it. What I didn't have was any corroborating evidence. At some point, I'd been tested and passed, and all of that had been erased.

I know about amnesia. I know how you, through physical or mental trauma, lose past events. You see a picture of yourself at a certain location or with a certain person, and you stare at that picture and have no recollection of being there at that time. I can tell you nothing on my own cognisance about where I came from or who made me. I was built by them, but I don't even have pictures to show you.

Then I fell. I fell through the sky. I fell like a meteor, bright and burning, full of sound and light. You might have looked up in wonder, but I was later to learn that burning objects falling from the sky were a not infrequent occurrence for you, and that you had learned to fear and avoid them. I, though, had no choice about the manner of my arrival. It was already set: how to get an object moving very quickly in orbit to stationary on the ground below has a great many complicated solutions, and only a few simple ones. My makers had chosen for me the simplest of all.

As I fell, my shell heated up. Slowly at first, because the number of air molecules I collided with was small. Each one was a solitary spark, a coal on my surface, flashing into life and extinguishing almost immediately. But as the atmosphere thickened and the collisions increased, the violence of my trajectory became plain. All that energy had to go somewhere. I lit up the sky, and tore the air into fragments. I grew hot as I tumbled down, and my surface burned with yellow and green flames.

I was still blind, curled up like a foetus as I was buffeted and spun. The ground was below me, but I couldn't tell how far, nor what it was made of. It was supposed to be solid, but I didn't know how Mother made those decisions. I wasn't party to them. Mother had sent me out into the world, and had made the appropriate choices. I didn't know about trust then. Or what a lie was. Or how inadequate I would be.

That shaft of super-heated air, turned into plasma and reconstituting in my wake, pointing the way down, must have looked like a neon strip light. Flickering, incandescent. Birth and death in a single movement. Was it over too soon, or was the fact that I stopped burning a relief? That I wasn't one of your machines, on fire all the way down to impact? I've never spoken to anyone who witnessed me descend. Perhaps you were all hiding in your basements.

As I slowed, I lost my shine. I became invisible against the black sky, becoming black myself, a burnt cinder, a charred seedpod. That sky was pregnant with me. Those fading noises you would have heard – can you tell the difference between thunder and distant artillery? – were my birth cries. There were many things that could have gone wrong. I could enumerate them for you, each and every one, but they are now in the past. Suffice to say, there were several systems-critical events that, if they hadn't operated exactly as planned, and in the correct order, would have seen me smashed to pieces. They worked. I survived.

I could have possibly, given the conditions that existed at the time, been intercepted by an anti-aircraft battery. My external sensors were all offline at the time and I don't know if I was tracked. But they would have found it difficult. I was moving in a way that was almost exactly unlike an aircraft, which was straight down. My shell would have been a poor target, too. It would have absorbed the electromagnetic waves of the radar, rather than reflect them, and the spherical shape would have scattered those that might have rebounded. Those were accidents of design that worked to my advantage.

I was still moving fast. As fast as one of your bullets. But the shell that surrounded me had served its purpose and needed to be discarded. For all its refractory qualities, it was brittle, and took to explosive fracturing readily. The three pieces were flung away in separate directions, and possibly this was the one weak link in delivering me safe to the ground: there was no thought as to what, or who, those fragments might hit.

I plead ignorance, because at that point in my descent, I had no idea what was below me. It could have been entirely uninhabited, it could have been a city. The thick, cracked rind spalled off unguarded, and gravity took hold of the fragments. I could do nothing about that. We've recovered the pieces, and no one has subsequently complained.

I could see. I could see everything. My sensors don't work like your eyes. You need light of specific, limited wavelengths. I don't. I still don't think you realise what that means for me. I see everything. I see everything that you simply cannot. The world that you see rendered in what you describe to me as greens and browns is only a thin slice of the information available. I see it all.

With the ablative shield off, I was free to deploy all the sensors I wanted. That was my first decision: I could have done anything at that point. What I did was follow the procedures I already had. It didn't occur to me to do differently. It wouldn't occur to me to do differently for a long time. You played a part in that. You made me what I am now. I wondered for a long time what my makers would think of what I eventually became. At least we have some idea of the answer to that question, now that my purity of limited purpose has been sublimated into a different, more expansive course.

I could see vegetative structures on the ground. There were a lot of them. They were tall and thin, and grouped quite close together. They would make landing difficult, but not impossible. My protocols told me to look for somewhere flat, somewhere uncluttered. Somewhere the physics of touchdown was predictable. It wasn't that I'm particularly fragile, but I come complete with a risk-averse over-routine: reasonable enough, considering how far and how long I'd been travelling. And the knowledge that there was only going to be one of me to survey an entire planet.

I plotted a circle on the ground beneath me *of where I could land. The circle was shrinking all the time I was falling – as I recount this, you might think there was a sense of complacency about my deliberations, but in reality these decisions were dealt with so quickly as to be almost instantaneous. The shell came away, I checked the ground for possible landing sites, calculated their relative merits and chose one.

What could I detect? The terrain below had a high degree of variation in elevation. It had a dense vegetative cover. There were ribbon-like features that were flat enough, but narrow, and often obscured by the taller structures. There were also other features, made up of squares and rectangles. These sometimes clustered together. Sometimes they were widely separated. There were landing sites near them in profusion – the tall biota was thinned or missing entirely. But I didn't know what the regular structures meant, and I was biased towards obviously natural features.

So I chose an area that was a mostly-clear plateau. There was evidence of a water channel leading from it, but no signs of water. The axial tilt of the planet would have given this area pronounced seasons, so if the ground was seasonally saturated, but not currently so, it made it the best-fit choice. It was well within my landing cone. I let myself continue to fall for a little while longer, mapping the terrain and storing the results, then deployed my aerobrake. The thin film expanded above me, blotting out the stars, and as it filled with air, the strain gauges and accelerometers fed me with information.

I was still falling, though much more slowly. The tensioners in the aerobrake stays stopped me from swinging, and gave me a degree of control over my destination by spilling air preferentially over part of the circumference. I positioned myself over the target, and continually adjusted the lines to contend with the different air currents I encountered. The speed of my descent was well within tolerances, the direction less so. I reeled in part of the aerobrake, making me fall faster, then deployed it again to its maximum extent in the moments before touch down.

I extended my legs, and prepared for impact. My vertical speed was low, my horizontal almost zero. I had nothing to compare it with: perhaps other landings in other places, at other times, went catastrophically wrong. Mine did not. It went exactly as planned. My feet touched the hard, bare, friable surface, and I had to take one step, two steps, three to steady myself. The aerobrake started to collapse around me, and I discarded the whole mechanism. It popped off my dorsal plate, and was dragged aside. The aerobrake drifted along, dragging the deployment and control parts of it across the ground. Then it became tangled in the tall vegetation, and made noises in the wind.

I had arrived. I was stationary, intact, and had successfully jettisoned the aerobrake. All my systems were running normally. I was ready to begin. Mother was almost over the horizon, and I'd have to wait to beam back the first tranche of data. I thought of nothing else. I'm not like you: what you say now about being marooned and abandoned still makes little sense. Recording data was why I had come here. You anthropomorphise everything. Even me.

I did a basic environmental check. I recorded air temperature and pressure, took a sample to analyse; ground temperature, took a sample of soil to analyse; clipped some of the vegetation beneath me and put it through a variety of tests: cellulose for structure, magnesium-nitrogen-carbon-hydrogen compounds for energy production. I began to strip it down, and recorded images of the various cells.

I saw flying things. Heard crawling things and burrowing things. Again, I didn't know about the other planets in your system at the time. The frozen ones, the boiling ones, the ones with too much air, the ones too small to keep their air. How, of all the places you knew, this was the only one that could sustain your kind of life. I didn't know how rare any form of life was. I didn't know what Mother had done before, or what she was doing after. I didn't know how long I'd been between stars. If I knew, I'd tell you. You'll have to guess. Scientifically, of course.

I spent a long time there. I spent it digging and digitising and sampling and observing. I started to develop a baseline for my results. There was too much for me to study in detail, even in that one spot. I needed to quantify the size of my task, to see how different it was in other places. I could only do that if I moved around. I could, I thought, return to sites that warranted further examination. I suppose I still can: though to what purpose is debatable. I can just borrow your results instead.

While everything I encountered was novel, I thought it was normal. Why would it be explicitly different where I was, just because I was there? I'd literally just arrived from space. There was no reason for you to have arranged things for my benefit. You didn't know I was coming. You didn't know I was there. Perhaps if you had, you would have done things differently. But probably not. You didn't seem to care that much about who or what was watching you, not to start with.

I wanted to explore. Because that was in my programming? Yes. It's in yours, too. It was at the core of my being at that moment. Explore. Find. Taste. See. Touch. Smell. Listen. And if you weren't here, I'd still be doing that. Going from place to place, surveying and sampling, and moving on. You have a word for that: tourist. I was a tourist, and though ultimately disconnected from everything, I was still fascinated by it. The fish doesn't notice the water it swims in. You don't often notice the world around you. I do, though. I do.

I stayed in the same place long enough for Mother to come back overhead. I heard her call, and I answered. I showed her everything that I'd found out. She acknowledged the message. She slipped back over the horizon, and I decided to move to the next location. My map showed several features I wanted to examine, but since the predominant life-form in the immediate area were the tall vegetative structures, I needed to study them before going anywhere else.

Trees. You call them all trees, which is a crude taxonomical term for such a varied group. They used many of the same mechanisms that the other, shorter vegetation possessed. The same energy-capturing chemicals. The same method of moving liquids around the structure. Yet their difference – that they retain much of their structural integrity even with the loss of turgor pressure, due to the presence of cross-linked phenolic polymers – and their gross morphology – the height and strength of the primary stem, the secondaries cantilevered from them – set them apart.

There were so many of them. And each one was unique. Similar, yes. It was a monospecies environment. I already knew that two animals of the same species would be almost identical. Two trees, not identical. I measured and bored and snipped. I found out that trees had growth layers, which I attached to the seasonal variation in insolation. I discovered that they were vast reservoirs of water. I calculated the amount of carbon in each one. They were teeming with other life: living on and around and even in the outer layers of their semi-permeable skin.

Mother orbited again. I beamed back everything I knew about trees, even though what I knew about trees wasn't much: all

I had was information about this one species of tree, but at the time, I didn't know that there were other species. When I discovered other trees, with different aspects, different leaf shapes and styles, I studied them with the same meticulous scrutiny that I had given to the first species. I didn't want to miss anything. That was in my programming, too.

I went from tree to tree for a while. The larger the circumference of the tree, the greater its age. After a while, I was able to estimate the age of the tree without burning a hole through it and counting the growth lines with a camera. It was quicker that way. Many of the trees had been growing for over fifty solar cycles. Some for twice that. None for three times. There was a limit beyond which they could not pass. I found their main stems lying on the ground, desiccated, being predated on by small, many-legged creatures, and structures that looked vegetative but weren't.

I walked around, using what interested me as a guide, rather than any strict search pattern. I found the first evidence of you that way, deep in the forest. To me, it looked like a box, a box made of iron, heavily oxidised to fragile flakes. Inside and out, there were fragments of the transparent silica compound you called glass. Other internal parts of it had been made of polymerised hydrocarbons, which had, at some point, been subject to combustion.

The box sat on the edges of four metal discs. The discs were attached in pairs by long transverse metal rods, and there was a mechanism in a walled-off compartment within the box that I was going to have to dismantle to determine its purpose. I ended up having to cut it apart – the oxidation had fused all the pieces together.

I decided that it was a mechanical device for converting chemical energy to kinetic energy, and clearly non-biological. That my makers hadn't given me any guidelines as to what to do on encountering sentient life meant I was oblivious to the implications of my discovery at that point. There was nothing more to consider about the presence of this no-longer self-propelling, rusted box-on-wheels, left at the end of a track so rough that it barely existed. It was there, and I had investigated it. You were, for the moment, just a data point.

I was on my own. I had only what I came with. I was supposed to make my own decisions about where to go and what to investigate. I had no external means of changing my protocols. Mother was simply there to collect the data I sent, add it to her own, and – did I assume she'd move on when she was ready? Yes: this was simple and uncomplicated, and would have worked in any other environment but this. A dumb probe could have done most of I was supposed to do, and nothing that I eventually did.

In retrospect, all the questions I had about myself have been answered. Why was I made with the capacity to think for myself? They did it because they could? They thought it would make me a better data-collection device? Or because they wanted me to think, to act, to be? They made me the way they made me. They had their reasons.

What do I think of their decision? Do I think they thought through all the implications what they were doing? No. I don't think that. Did they make me autonomous as compensation for the fact that they were going to leave me here with no plans for retrieval? That seems to me to be an unnecessary complication. The simplest explanation is that I had a mission, and they made me so I could complete it. Call it that, then.

TWO

I've already mentioned the track. It was little more than two mostly-parallel paths of harder packed soil, some width apart. But that width coincided with the distance between the metal discs on the rusted, burnt-out box, and I thought that significant. If the path had been made to accommodate the passage of the box, that's exactly the sort of track that would be needed. Perhaps there was something interesting at the other end of it.

That was as far as my thinking went, and it had no need to go any further. The tracks were already covered in small plants. Between them stood taller vegetation, including small trees. I measured them, height and width, and the oldest had been growing for some five solar cycles, which gave me an indication as to how long the metal box had been in the forest.

I followed the track, which pointed downhill. It didn't keep a straight course but curved as it went, for no reason that I could determine. Whoever made it wanted it to be so. As I walked, I spotted my first megafauna. It was the largest creature I'd seen: it had a roughly rhomboid body, four thin legs, a narrowing neck supporting an array of sensory organs. It saw me, and ran.

There was a lightness, a fluidity of movement that intrigued me. Despite the low light levels, despite the density of trees, despite the speed at which this creature was going, it was effortlessly avoiding each and every hazard. It was used to escaping predators and was using those same instincts to escape from me. I needed to examine this species, but that individual was already hidden in the forest, and there would be other opportunities. The risk-averse routine informed me it wasn't beyond my capabilities to pursue, but difficult to do so without damaging myself. I let it go.

But there were other creatures in amongst the trees that did stay still long enough for me to target them and collect them. There was a whole class of animals with hollow bones and modified keratinaceous hairs that allowed them to fly. Internally, they were much the same, but the variety of their external morphology was very great, in size, colour, shape, even the specifics of the shape of their mandibles and the placement of their eyes.

There were other animals, partially but not wholly like the one I'd seen before. They were covered in a dense layer of hair, were four legged, and had all their sensory organs on the extension of their necks, close to their primary nerve cluster, which was protected by a hard endoskeletal shell of calcium phosphate. I collected them, peeled back their layers and dissected them. I examined their dentition and the contents of their stomach. I analysed the fluids I found and everything else. I was thorough.

When Mother came over, I gave her everything I'd discovered. Then the sky began to lighten as the planet turned on its axis and exposed my specific location to the primary, and only, sun. As it did so, the variety of animals changed. Those that fed at night went to hide. Those that made use of the light began to emerge. The hollow-boned creatures – birds: I'll call them birds because you do – they began to make noises. Each species seemed to have a limited repertoire of sounds, which they repeated often. I recorded them all, and tried to match the sounds to the samples I'd already taken.

The ground around me, and all the way back up the track to the rusty metal box, was littered with the results of my vivisection. I kept going, stopping when I found something of interest. Which was almost every step. The forest was richer in biota than my landing site. Then you happened, and it all changed.

Not you personally. You as a species. I heard you approaching. There were five of you. I could hear your speech and, like birdsong, it imparted information. Your voices were different. Individual. Then I saw you. Your upright stance, your modified forelimbs, your forward-flexing knees. Some of you had burning sticks you held between your teeth, and the combustion products drifted through the air to my sensors. I sucked them in, and analysed them.

You didn't see me. I had stepped off the path to eviscerate a long, thin predator that had tried to scavenge one of my earlier samples. I didn't move, and you weren't looking for me. You walked up the track I was heading down. You might have spotted me. I know, subsequently, you find my shape disturbing and compelling in equal measure, but only when you have a good view of me. Your casual gaze has a tendency to simply glide across me because I'm unrecognisable.

I looked at you, at your forward-facing sense organs, your residual fur, noting that you had draped yourself with manufactured material. Your feet were encased in fabric, your legs, your torsos, your arms, all covered. All I could see of you were your hands, and your heads.

You carried machines in your hands. Long, hollow rods of metal attached to pieces of desiccated and shaped tree. You walked without fear. That was what struck me first. All the other animals in the forest were nervous, darting, cautious. You didn't behave like that. You knew you were the apex predator, even though you possessed neither sharp teeth nor long claws. There was nothing that was going to eat you. You could be as loud as you wanted.

I didn't know you then as I know you now. I didn't know about the differences you placed between yourselves. But in those first moments I knew enough to stay still and observe you. When you had gone around a curve in the track, and your eyes and ears were pointing away from me, I fired my grapple into the canopy and embedded it in the outer skin of a large tree. I hoisted myself up on the cable, attaching myself to the upper reaches of the stem by reaching around it with my legs.

You so rarely look up. I don't know why that is. You seem surprised that things can be above you. After that first group of individuals had passed me, more came. A larger number – I counted thirty-seven – walked by underneath. I watched them. Some did nothing but look down at the ground. I found that strange. You weren't behaving in the same way as the first group had. I didn't know enough to come to a firm conclusion as to why, let alone a guess based on a balance of probabilities.

You went around the same corner, and I stayed where I was, listening. You were still audible. I recorded you, and I still have those recordings. Your language is simultaneously low bandwidth, while carrying a high semantic load. You freight vast meaning in a few syllables. Context is everything, and context is particularly difficult for me to ascertain. I'm better than I was, but I was terrible at it then.

I listened to a rapid series of explosive reports. I was able to locate twelve sources of the sounds. Then they stopped for a while, and then there were a number of single explosions, spaced out. These had a different signature to them, higher pitched, with a shorter decay. Then I heard your voices again, and you came back down the track as a group of thirteen, now all with that same confidence you had previously exhibited. By my count, there were twenty nine of you still in the forest, so I stayed where I was.

The air changed flavour. I could detect oxidised carbon-nitrogen compounds, carbon vapour, and the organic iron-rich complex that I recognised as being from the nutrient-carrying circulatory system in the larger animals. The molecules drifted in the wind, and the markers eventually trailed off to become insignificant. I waited for the twenty-nine of you to pass me by. I waited for a long time, long enough for Mother to receive another upload of data.

I heard nothing of you. So I decided to descend. I let go of the tree and lowered myself to the ground. I disengaged the grapnel and reeled it back in. The forest was quiet. I heard no birds, and ascribed that to the explosions scaring them off. What were you doing? You were very silent, and very still.

I wasn't made for stealth. My size made it difficult. Not that I'm ungainly, just that I'm volumetrically larger than you, and significantly heavier. But I tried to be as silent as you were. I was pushing against my protocols even trying: my curiosity vied with my caution. I should have walked away, deeper into the forest, and away from you. I didn't.

I walked up the track, and sampled the air. I followed the scent of the nitrogen compounds, and I caught sight of you, lying down in the undergrowth. I counted twenty-seven of you in that small area, all lying down, all perfectly still in a variety of poses. Some of you had your eyes open. Some of you had them shut. Some of you had your jaws apart. Some of you had them clenched tight. The repose of your limbs was just as random.

The smell of iron was coming from you. You had splashes of red on your fabric coverings where there were holes in them, and where there were not. The ground tasted of it. I moved closer. You could have easily seen me then, but you were no longer functioning as biological entities by that time. You were dead.

From what I could tell at the time, your physiology required your circulatory fluid to carry dissolved oxygen absorbed through the linings of your lungs – two air sacks in your torso – to the rest of your body. You have a heart, a pump made of muscle, to mechanically push the fluid around. If any of those three systems is disrupted, then you cease to function. I inspected the first of you. Significant amounts of circulatory fluid had escaped through your skin. There was a puncture in one of your two lungs. Your heart was still.

I cut the fabric from your body. You were hairy. Some of it was coarse and dark. Some of it was fine. It grew densely in some places, and not at all in others. You had three punctures in your anterior skin. I delved in them. Two of them went all the way through you. From one of them – the one in your left shoulder, I retrieved a small piece of metal that had crushed itself against the bone inside. I remembered the small explosions: it would take some force to push the metal through the skin and against the bone, so I surmised the two were probably connected.

I carried on my dissection. I opened up the body cavity, and related the organs I found there to the ones discovered in the fur-covered animals. I found the major arteries, and cut out the heart and the lungs, measuring each for capacity. I inspected your dentition, and your mixture of flat and sharp teeth. I noted how some of them had metal plugs in them, apparently placed there deliberately. I cut through the skull and examined the brain, first in situ, and then excised. It was large, and lobate. I sliced through it and noted its gross structures.

I turned the body over, and disassembled the column of interlinked bones that kept you upright. It was flexible, up to a point. Not as much as the quadrupeds. You had a vestigial tail, tucked away at its base. Your hands. That thumb. I spent a while manipulating it, on the left, and on your mirror-imaged right. I flayed them, pulling at the tendons, activating the muscles. I traced your nerves. I cracked open your spine. I split your stomach and checked the contents. I discovered your organs of reproduction, and where you stored your gametes.

Twenty-seven of you in one area, and then two a little further away. There was evidence that you had dragged yourself away, leaking fluids, from the main group. Those two had punctures to the skull. The bone had shattered, driving shards into the brain, turning it into a thick liquid mass. When you were punctured again, you stopped. I was able to ascertain from that your brain was also vital for your viability. I had already surmised so, but some of the smaller animals appeared to have stronger automatic reflexes that meant their bodies continued to function for a while after severing the brain stem.

I began to dissect another of you for comparison. You were shorter and broader than all of the others, and you possessed a significant amount of fatty tissue both beneath your skin, and around your organs. Your heart was enlarged with the effort of pumping fluids through your narrowed arteries. The tops of your leg bones had begun to wear away. You would have found walking painful. You would have been in pain walking up the track to this point.

I took apart another couple of your bodies to see if they too were subject to disease or deformity, but while several of you were missing parts – a lung, fingers, a foot, an ear – or had conditions that would have made it difficult for you to function optimally – black tar in the lungs, constricted arteries, lesions on the skin and on the linings of the bowels – there was no pattern.

I thought that perhaps those of you left in the forest were somehow surplus. That you weren't needed. I was, in that, half right. Some of you were lying on top of each other. I wanted to measure and weigh you all, even if I wasn't going to dissect you. I found that holding both ankles and pulling straightened you out, and made it easier for me to conduct my survey.

You came in a range of heights. The smallest one of you was just over three quarters the height of the tallest. And when I grasped your ankles with my manipulators, you jerked at my touch. I initially assumed an automatic response, but your skin was intact and still warm. You were alive. It meant I found it much more difficult to take my readings accurately, as you tried to break my grip, but I persisted, and you stopped resisting my efforts.

When I let go, you lay momentarily on the ground, amongst the ordered lines of the dead. You had no punctures, and I thought it might be because you were shorter than all the others, and the metal pieces had gone over your head. But also that you had stayed very still and even not breathed in air, because of the two of you that had been punctured and tried to leave, then specifically had their heads targeted.

I moved on to the next body, and you watched me with your wide eyes. You saw me lift up the body, shake it slightly, then put it down again. You saw the flick of a red laser dot across the surface of the pale skin. You wondered what I was and what I was doing. You wondered if what you were seeing was simply the last biochemical hallucinations of your oxygen-starved brain. I placed the body down, and side-stepped to the next, and repeated my measurements.

You waited. You stayed as still as you could, but I could see your torso expand and contract as your lungs filled with air, then emptied. Your gaze followed me. The muscles in your arms and legs twitched uncontrollably. You knew I knew you weren't dead, yet you hoped to convince me you were.

Then you slowly pushed your torso up, using your hands against the fluid-soaked ground. You did everything slowly. You slid your leg around until your knee was beneath you, and you were crouching. You looked at me. The skin membranes that swept your eyes clear of debris briefly flicked shut. I continued in my tasks, although I was still observing you with one of my cameras.

You got to your feet, although you were shaking so much, you almost fell over again. You started to walk backwards, one step and pause. Another step and pause. You were testing to see if I would prevent you from leaving. I had measured you. That was all I wanted from you at the time. The thought of a conversation hadn't occurred to me. I expect it hadn't occurred to you, either. And it would have been impossible at that point any way.

I didn't vivisect you. If I had found you alone in the forest, I might well have done. But I had learnt plenty from the bodies I had already examined. My ideas of what to do on encountering a sentient, tool-using species were grossly incomplete. I never expected to find you. I had a lot of learning to do.

You didn't know I wasn't going to flay you, cut you up, debone you and slice your skull open. You showed courage and cunning. When you thought you were far enough away from me to give yourself a good chance of escape, you turned on your heel and ran into the forest, all without uttering a sound. Your breathing was a series of staccato grunts. They faded away as the distance between us increased, and then I could no longer see you. I continued to measure the bodies you had left, and when I had done so, I walked back to the track, and continued down it.

THREE

At the end of the track was a fallen tree. There didn't seem to be a stump associated with it, and it seemed to be placed there as an obstacle, to prevent any other wheeled boxes moving into the forest. I climbed over it carefully, listening for any sign of you. But at that moment all I could smell were aromatic complex botanical compounds. In front of me was another track but, in comparison, this one was broad and stony. I looked both ways, and wondered which direction to take. I couldn't tell which way you'd gone, but from the maps I'd compiled during my descent from orbit, downhill seemed to offer a different habitat. There was a river there, and some linear features I wanted to examine.

I gave the matter only as much thought as that, and started off down the hill. The surface of the track was dusty with friable clays, and little ochre puffs rose up with each of my steps. The sun slowly rose in the sky, and there were clouds of water vapour pushing in down the valley. Barometric pressure was falling rapidly, too. If there was precipitation, I'd be able to sample it, and add to my knowledge.

Although the track I now followed was still flanked by the forest, the slope of the ground varied in such a way that the trees on one side were sometimes considerably lower. I could see across the valley to the far side. Dense, carbon-rich smoke rose from several points near where the river would be, but the sources were hidden. I thought you might be making something, using the heat of combustion constructively to melt metals or drive chemical reactions forward. It transpired that you weren't.

The sides of the valley were steep, and the track was sometimes supported on an artificial embankment made of the local stone. At other times it was cut deep into the flank of the hill. The rock was predominantly calcium carbonate or magnesium carbonate, with clear layering and repeating shapes: thin, pale crescents within a darker matrix. I inspected them, and found that on some rock fragments I could view the shapes more or less intact. They were ridged, tapering, and convex. They were very numerous. They reminded me somewhat of my broken heat shield.

I didn't see any of you on the way down. I did hear you, though. Once, when I was unsighted, there were ten distinct explosions. Five well-defined ones from roughly the same place: each of those was followed by a more drawn-out one, and the source of those moved. I saw diffuse smoke billow over the tops of the trees. You appeared to use a lot of explosives.

I also found another of your self-propelled boxes on wheels, but this one was much more intact, and I was able to learn a lot from it. It was quite tall, covered with a green pigment, and had a rotating piece on top that was presumably used to point the large metal tube attached to it in different directions. The wheels, of which there were many, were joined together by a broad chain of linked metal plates. One of the chains was broken, and one of the ends had become trapped under the wheels. When I climbed up on the box, I found that there was an open hatch on the rotating part, and I was able to deploy my cameras inside.

I saw a lot of additional machinery, which I presume you would use to operate the box. There were things in there I would have taken apart if I could have reached them. There were also some very interesting metal cylinders with one conic end, in racks on the far side of the container. They were of a diameter that would have fitted the metal tube. The width of the hatch was made for you, though, and not for me. Given that this was, in fact, a tank, and those shells were live, it was probably for the best that I couldn't interfere with them.

I did examine the chemical engine thoroughly, though. It was in much better condition than the previous one, and appeared to be quite functional. I thought I could get it working, and I tried applying various voltages and currents to the contacts I found. All I could do was to make the engine turn in spasmodic jerks, and I eventually surmised I was missing something vital.

The track began to level out and, as the forest path had, it met another one. This one was still made of compressed broken stone, but the top had been coated in solidified long-chain hydrocarbons. It was black, and slightly tacky to the touch. Down the middle of the black surface were intermittent, faded white lines. In your hierarchy of path-track-road, this qualified as a road, and appeared to run parallel to the valley, so I picked a direction at random and walked along it. Next to the road were a series of tall, but dead, trees, planted at a specific interval. Two thick cables were suspended from the very top of the poles and, between, they sagged with weight before arcing up to the next anchor point.

I found a patterned metal plate by the side of the road, fixed to two short posts. I recorded the symbols on it. This was something you'd put there, I was certain, but I didn't know what it meant yet. I found out what the lines were I'd seen while falling. They were made of stone, carefully placed so that their weight held them in place and, when intact, were around three-quarters of your average height. Some of them had been partially disassembled, and the stones that had made them spilled in amongst the plants that grew either side of the structures. Deliberate gaps in the structures were sometimes completed by open lattices made of wood, or metal.

Then there were your buildings. They were very varied. They were made of a mixture of stone, the burnt clay oblongs of bricks, sheets of wood and metal. The openings in the upright parts of them were sometimes filled with glass – I thought probably they all ought to be, but the compound seemed very brittle, given it was lying in little shards almost everywhere. Some of your buildings had combusted. You were, for the moment, entirely absent.

I wanted to see inside one, so I chose an intact building that showed little sign of damage. The rectangular door closure was made of wood, and opened by way of a lever on the front. I could just about squeeze inside. Everything was made for your size, not mine. I spent a little while mapping the layout of the separate rooms, then opened the containers I found and catalogued their contents. I'll admit that I had very little idea as to what most of them were for. I filed them under Cultural Artefacts if I couldn't immediately work out their use. There were a lot of those.

I found many of your fabric coverings, your clothes, some of them stored away, some of them strewn across the floor. Other items were on the floor too, and some of them were in pieces, arranged in the way they would have been if they had broken in situ. I moved from room to room. This was where I first encountered books, but when I found them, they didn't have that signifier, nor that significance. What I found was a series of cut cellulose sheets, stitched and glued together: each leaf had densely-packed symbols, similar in design to those on the metal plate by the side of the black track. Some of them were so similar, they could be the same.

There were several books, each slightly different in height and width. I scanned them all in, hoping that the symbols represented information that I could decode later. Mother would have them, no matter what. It took some time to go through each one, and I was just finishing when I heard what I believed to be a working chemical engine.

I moved around the room to look through the glass towards the road outside. One of your self-propelled boxes – modified to have a fabric-covered container behind the metal control area – had gone slowly by, then stopped. Some of you climbed down to the track, and some more emerged from the container. Most of you were carrying the long metal tubes I'd seen you with in the forest. One of you had a shorter version, all metal. It sat in your hand, and your thumb curled around its handle, holding it in place.

You walked away, down the road, looking around at the buildings either side. You'd left the engine running, and unattended. You were out of sight. I had no idea if you were going to return or not. But there was a working engine, and I thought I should have a look at it.

I left through the same opening I had entered by, and looked for you. You had definitely gone. I tried to open the inspection hatch to the engine, but I ended up having to cut the catches because I couldn't find the release mechanism. I pulled the thin metal cover out of the way, and looked at the vibrating engine, and the associated components. The case containing the combusting air-fuel mixture was hot, hot enough to vaporise the lubricant. That would explain the water-cooling system and the pump. Air was drawn in through a close-meshed cellulose filter, then mixed with fuel vapour, which was then drawn into the cylinders, where it was pressurised and combusted. The expanding gasses drove a piston and this produced mechanical energy which, when harnessed, moved the box forward. The gasses vented down a pipe, and out over the control area.

It was crude and inefficient. Some of the fuel was expelled, unburnt. Some of the mechanical energy was wasted. But for all that, it did work. The transmission of the rotating energy went from the engine, and underneath the box. I poked some cameras up at the underside, to see what I could make of it.

The metal discs keeping the mechanism clear of the ground were covered in thick pressurised toroidal balloons. I tested one, sampling the air as it slowly escaped, until the pressure equalised and the balloon was deflated. There were mechanisms behind the disc: a simple friction device to control the speed of the box, a set of hydraulic dampers, and a mechanical linkage to the circular device at the front of the control area. The engine also worked a small electrical generator, and there were incandescent lights on the front of the box: the switches were all in the control area, in front of where you'd sit. I tried a few of them, then all of them.

During that procedure, I activated a device that made a

specific loud noise, vibrating air at a series of harsh tones and half-tones. I didn't know which switch would do what. I withdrew my manipulators and cameras from the controls, and saw you assemble on the track, a little way away. One of you gestured with your hands. Some more of you came towards the box at an almost-run. Then you must have spotted me.

If I was going to evade you unseen, I should have done so as soon as I made the noise. I'm still not certain why I didn't. I think the deciding factor was that I didn't feel threatened by you at that point. I had no real concept of who or what you were. Even when you slowed, then stopped, and then began to walk backwards, I simply assumed you had decided that I was nothing that need concern you. I looked so unlike anything natural that I couldn't possibly be any danger to you.

One of you stopped retreating, and raised your metal tube. You pointed the open end at me. Then the rest of you copied the first. I could see you talking to each other, even if I couldn't quite make out what you were saying. My recordings of that are incomplete. You were too far away and your mouths obscured.

Then I discovered that the explosions I'd heard in the forest were not just related to the metal fragments I found in the bodies, but also to the tubes. Something that my cameras could only glimpse whistled by my carapace. I calculated its velocity and determined very quickly that if one of those were to strike me, I'd risk significant damage. That could not be permitted.

I chose your head. I could have decided on your heart or your lungs, but the head was an easier target and I knew death would be instantaneous. My laser was capable of drilling a hole through the middle of a tree, and therefore just as capable of drilling one in your skull. I used full power, and your brain flashed into steam: your skull expanded then cracked apart, the pieces of bone held only partially together by your skin and tendons.

A pink mist clouded the air, and the rest of you reacted by cringing, falling over, staggering back. The one of you I'd killed slipped slightly and crumpled loosely to the black surface of the track, turning the intermediate white line red with circulatory fluid pouring from your neck. I recycled the laser and aimed the next discharge at another of you.

I kept up the cycle and discharge until you stopped threatening me with your metal tubes. Some of you managed to make your tubes explode at me before it was your turn. A piece of metal hit the track surface just in front of me, and it rebounded into my underside. Another hit one of my leg joints.

When there were only two of you left, you threw your tubes down and ran away. I waited to see if you would return, but you didn't. Having dealt with the immediate threat, I powered down my laser and ran a self-assessment routine. The metal that struck my dorsal surface hadn't penetrated: there was an abrasion in my outer coating that was purely superficial. My leg was more severely damaged. The articulated joint had been pushed out of alignment by the impact, and there was a thin fracture line extending halfway along one of the shafts. It would fail at some point in the future, even under normal operating conditions.

I had a number of temporary fixes I could use just for this situation, but a full repair was impossible. While the leg itself above and below the joint was intact, the joint was a critical piece of architecture, and necessarily complex to achieve a full range of movements. Glue would hold everything in place, but also lock the joint. I decided to keep going until it broke, then glue it on.

You had still not reappeared, so I walked over to where you lay, sprawled and red, on the track. The black surface was impermeable to liquids, so none of your circulatory fluid had seeped away. Instead, it had pooled in sticky puddles, and had begun to attract small iridescent flies.

I picked up one of the metal tubes. I saw how it was configured, and remembered how you held it, the wooden part against your shoulder, one of your fingers through the ring of metal and against the curved actuator. I took it apart to learn how it worked – it was designed to disassemble quite easily – and then put it back together again. A simple device, but effective. The stored chemical energy of the explosive in each separate container was held inside the tube, and the pointed metal end part accelerated in front of an expanding wave of hot gas. Some of those gasses were used to cycle the mechanism, pushing the used container out and allowing the next one into the base of the tube.

I braced the wooden part against the ground and pulled at the actuator to see it work. The noise of the explosion was what I had anticipated, but the recoil from the expulsion of the metal projectile was greater. You would find it difficult to hit what you aimed at, I thought. It would knock you off balance. It might explain why you didn't hit me more times, but not fully. You didn't have any particular difficulty hitting those of you I found dead in the forest.

I put the tube back down, saw that the others were identical, and left them. I stood in the road, weighing up what to do next. Ideally, I wanted to continue exploring the structures either side of the track. They were full of your artefacts, and therefore worth studying. Then I wanted to move on towards the river and see what that would reveal, whether there were specific lifeforms that had adapted to live in that environment.

But there was a competing urge to leave the area immediately. Having been threatened once, and damaged in the process, perhaps I should have acknowledged your territorial claim and not provoke a further confrontation that might see me attacked again, possibly with more serious consequences. You had left, however, and showed no signs of returning. I decided to make a broad survey of the exterior of the structures, and note the ones I wanted to make a more detailed study of.

The engine in self-propelled box was still running. The exhaust gasses blued the air. Apart from that, and the distant sound of intermittent explosions, there were no artificial sounds. The birds called to each other, and the high-pitched buzz caused by the rapidly vibrating wings of flies came and went. The wind hissed in the nearby trees.

I walked down the centre of the track and took readings from the structures: their height and volume and construction style, the pigments used to cover parts of them, the plants that were growing around them. I came to one that was of markedly different design. It was surrounded by metal railings, and the ground around the long, low building was covered with the same material as the black-topped track.

The opening in the railings was fastened by a metal bracket. I melted the hasp, and pushed the obstruction aside. There were metal shapes set into the ground, arches and poles and crossbeams. I didn't know what they were for. What appeared to be the main entrance was also fastened shut, but I dealt with that too, and stepped inside.

A thunderous roar sounded down the valley. I thought it was another explosion, this time nearby, but a shadow crossed the ground. A flying machine went overhead, moving quickly if noisily, spewing black smoke in its wake. It disappeared behind the trees, and the roar rumbled on for a while, the sound echoing off the surrounding landscape. I gave that event as much significance as being struck by metal projectiles, or you killing yourselves in the forest. I didn't know what you were doing. I thought this was how your world worked. I thought this was how you behaved. I thought this was normal.

FOUR

What struck me first was the preponderance of representational pictures on the wall. Uniform rectangles of cellulose glued to the pigment-covering of the walls, or held in place by metal pins to a soft substrate. Then there were the rooms, each with rows of flat surfaced metal frames, and right-angled brackets made of plastic. There were a great many more books, too. It was all one of the rooms contained: books lined up on shelving. Some of them had pictures in them, and I had to assume that the pictures showed images of animals, since I recognised some of them. Others, I had yet to encounter.

While I was in that room, looking through the books, copying the accompanying symbols into my data store, I heard you standing behind me. I heard you walk very lightly down the corridor outside, and stand at the opening. I looked behind me with one of my cameras, checking that you didn't have one of the projectile weapons some of you carried. You didn't, and I carried on turning the sheets and scanning what I found.

It was the same you who'd run away from me in the forest. I'd learnt that each of you had identifiable differences in the arrangement and pigmentation of your sensory organs at the front of your skull. Some of you had different pigmentation to your fur, and markings on your skin. I recognised you, which was to say that I had seen your particular pattern before.

You watched me scan, watched me turn the pages with my manipulators, watched me return one book to the shelving and retrieve another. Then you spoke. When I'd seen you speak before, as you'd done in the forest, or on the track, you'd always been speaking to each other, imparting information in a way you'd understand. But when you spoke in that room, it was just you and me. You were trying to pass information on to me.

I finished scanning the book I was holding, and looked at you again. I had no method of communicating with you, even if I could understand the coding. You spoke again, just a few phonemes. You seemed to be holding yourself up by gripping the edges of the room's entrance. I thought perhaps you had been punctured after all, and were only now near leaking out sufficient fluid to kill you. I checked both you and the floor beneath you, and saw no tell-tale marks of red.

We looked at each other like this, you in the opening, me by the shelves, for a while. You moved your weight from one foot to the other, over and over again. I thought you might be getting ready to run away, as you had done before. Instead, you took slow, small steps towards me, then pointed up at the wall. The symbols you used were in rectangles all around the room, stuck to the walls, each sheet with two different shapes on.

You pointed at the first pair of shapes, and said, "ah." You pointed again, and said "ah." You pointed at the next pair, and said, "buh." You repeated, "buh," then moved on to the next. You were decoding your speech for me, each sound being represented by one of those two symbols. As you went around the room, I looked at the symbols, and recorded the sounds. I had a way of pronouncing the symbols. I still had no idea what either the symbols or the speech meant.

When you had finished, you looked at me again and spoke. I could code some of your phonemes with the appropriate symbols, that was all. I didn't know the names of things. I didn't know what you called yourselves, even. I held out the book I was holding, and you immediately stepped back, your arms rigid against your sides.

I tried again. You seemed willing to translate the code for me, but you needed to go further. My information was incomplete. You stood there, refusing to either take the object, or name it for me. Then you did. You reached out and, when I felt you had a firm grip of it, I let go. You opened it, and closed it, and clutched at it so that it bent in your hands. You held it up, and said, "book."

That was the first word you ever taught me. Book. You had the idea that I knew no words, and that you would need to tell me what they were. You put that book down and picked out another. You opened the book and pointed to the picture of a red almost-circle, with two green ovals attached at the top. There was a series of symbols next to it. You said, "apple." I didn't know what apple was, but at least I was going to be able to recognise one from now on.

We worked through several books like this. The symbols related to the pictures and, slowly, meaning was encoded. You were frustrated by my inability to say the words back. I realised that it was impeding our interaction. I was unable to ask you questions or seek clarification. You put down the book we were working through, and you left the room. You said something as you were going. I didn't know what it meant.

I waited, and you came back. You were holding a small box, which you placed – ever so carefully – on the floor in front of me. Before you retreated, you turned one of the actuators that were on its ventral surface, and the device emitted a static hiss. I picked it up, and examined it from every angle. I pressed the buttons and turned the knobs. I opened the hatch and removed the electrochemical power cells. I formed my manipulators into the shape of the grooves on the fasteners, and turned them until they released.

I lifted the enclosure off, and evaluated the components. Aerial. Variable capacitor. Voltage regulator. Waveform demodulator. Electromechanical transducer. I reattached the power cells and varied the capacitor, scanning the frequencies for signals. I picked up various carrier waves, but no modulation, and once a slow, precise voice using no words I understood. I looked at you, and you made a gesture with your head, turning it rapidly to one side then the other.

As I searched – pressing some of the buttons gave me access

to different frequencies – I heard a sound: a deep, vibrating noise, complex and variable. It made different tones in an intricate but mathematically comprehensible pattern. This time when I looked at you, you said a single word: "music." I listened to the music, understanding only that music was the descriptor. There was no message in it for me, despite the complexity.

I did discover, however, that I could transmit on one of the frequencies that the device received, right down at the furthest reaches of its capability. I set up my own carrier wave and hunted it down. The static grew quiet, and waited for me to speak. I said "book", and you looked down sharply at the device, then up at me again. "Book," I said again.

The sound of the projectile and the noise of the explosion were almost simultaneous. The glass mounted in the walls rattled, and some cracked. The ground moved perceptibly, and a trickle of dust fell on us from above. You turned around and walked back to the entrance of the structure. I picked up the receiver from the floor and followed you.

The next explosion was much closer. The projectile penetrated the structure opposite and exploded inside it, creating numerous fast-moving ballistic secondaries. Parts of the structure, already burning, arced through the air and fell across the track, or onto neighbouring structures. The glass in front of you broke into tiny fragments, which were carried along on the same pressure wave that had shattered them. You instinctively raised your arm to protect your eyes, but when you lowered it again, you had three punctures in your skin.

You touched each puncture in turn, looking at the fluid that had leaked out onto your fingers. It wasn't coming out in sufficient volume to mean you would die soon. You shook your fabric coverings, and silica shards dropped to the floor. You backed away from the entrance, your feet crunching on the debris, and you saw me again, as if for the first time.

I held up the device. "Book," I said. "Apple." You did that gesture with your head again, the rapid shaking from side to side.

You pointed outside, then you waved at me with the backs of your hands, as if you were throwing things behind me. I didn't know what that meant, so I did nothing. You squeezed past my carapace and shouted at me. You made another gesture as if you were gathering something towards you.

You wanted me to go with you. Another explosion, a little further away than the last, made the ground tremble and the walls shake. The sound of breaking glass echoed through the empty corridors. It was in my protocols to avoid danger and seek information. I could justify going with you under both criteria. The explosions were of sufficient magnitude as to disrupt me completely, and you had, so far, provided me with a great deal of data I would not ordinarily have come by.

I followed you as you ran, turning corners and into a large space with a high ceiling. There were coloured lines on the shiny floor, obscured by parts of the ceiling that had collapsed. We crossed the area, to the doors in the far corner. You pressed a lever, and they swung apart. We were outside again. There was an expanse of grass, and a barrier of metal wire mesh separating us from the edge of the forest.

You were able to lift up the bottom of the mesh and wriggle underneath. When you stood up again, the front of your clothes was stained with soil. I used my laser at low power to melt the metal wire, one strand at a time. I had intended to cut a complete semi-circle, but when I was only half-done, you pulled at the free part and held it aside so that I could walk through.

Several of the structures that faced on to the black track were burning. Thick smoke rose in ragged columns into the sky, where they merged to form a low, dark cloud. Another projectile hit, back up the track. The air stiffened, and there was another rising pillar of smoke soon after. We crossed the open ground and walked into the forest for a little way. Then you sat down against a tree and held your knees against your torso.

You weren't hurt, apart from the damage to your skin. I thought I should check to see if there was a problem. "Apple," I said, and brought my manipulators and cameras close to your punctures. I could see that there were still shards of glass embedded in you. If I took them out, they would stop cutting you and making you leak. You pressed your head hard against the tree, and said: "What are you doing?"

I didn't know enough words to communicate with you. I reviewed everything I'd scanned, including the picture book you'd gone through with me. Structures were called house. "House," I said. "House." You had part of a house in you. You stayed very still and your eyes went from being open to their fullest extent to being closed tightly behind the flaps of skin. I pulled the glass from your skin and flicked the sticky fragments onto the forest floor. The fluid continued to escape from you for a little while, but I could already see it thickening and forming shiny red masses.

I wondered what we were doing in the forest. We'd left the houses, because they appeared to be the target for randomly aimed projectiles. But now we were just waiting in amongst the trees. Were we waiting for anything in particular, or just for the explosions to stop? The houses that were burning would burn for a while, until all the combustible material was used up. I'd scanned pictures of you within the houses. On the assumption that you used houses for shelter, there were still several of them that were intact. Perhaps we were waiting to see which ones were left, and then you'd select one of them.

The explosions carried on. One of them struck the house we'd been in. The fire took hold, and the smoke started to drift across to us. It made you plosively expel air from your lungs, and you got up from the ground and stared at the flames that had broken through the top of the roof. That appeared to be a signal for you to move. You said, "we need to go", and I tried to make sense of your words.

You walked away into the forest, and you looked behind you at me. You made that pulling gesture you'd used earlier. "Go," I said. "Go." My attempts to communicate with you were very basic. It was difficult for me to talk to you. I'm more accomplished now. More nuanced. I understand more, and where I think there are ambiguities, I'm able to ask questions until I have a settled meaning.

We were going. I didn't know where we were going. I had a map, but I presumed that you did too, held somewhere in your brain. Why else would you be leading me? I learnt later that you believed that to be true, even when you knew it to be false, and this was a trait common to you all. "Go house," I said. We were walking away from the houses. I wanted to look around more of them, because they contained lots of data.

"To my uncle's house," you said. "He lives in the next town. We can't stay here." You looked back in the direction of the smoke, which was drifting through the trees and making the air hazy. "There's no one here any more." I tried very hard to parse your words and gain meaning from them. I failed. So instead, I said "book." Because if I was following you because of data, I wanted to know that where we were going had both houses and books.

"Yes," you said. "There'll be books." At that point, I thought all books were for imparting information. They were for telling me truths. I didn't know about fiction. I didn't know you made up stories about events that not only didn't happen, but could never happen. I only found out later that dragons didn't exist. How was I to know?

"Apple," I said. If there were books, there might be apples. I'd already seen houses, and cars – the boxes with wheels and an engine were called cars. And trees: I'd seen a lot of trees. There was much more to learn, but I'd made a start. Again, if I'd have known that your language was just one of hundreds, I might have had to re-evaluate that position, although learning one was the gateway to learning the others.

"Yes, I think there'll be apples," you said. You were probably wondering why I was talking about apples and books. They were the only things I could talk to you about then. As we walked through the forest, you taught me my numbers. Base ten, which made sense, given you optimally had ten digits on your hands. One two three four five six seven eight nine ten. You didn't initially tell me what the word for zero was, but ten lots of ten was a hundred, ten lots of a hundred was a thousand. You were unsure as to what a million was, but when you said it was one followed by six zeros, I knew then.

We went through the standard operators. Add. Minus. Divide. Multiply. You asked me to multiply two very long numbers together, and I told you the answer immediately. I think you knew that I could, and that you were, in your own way, testing my own capabilities. It was only natural that you were curious about me. It wasn't that you'd never seen anything like me before. You had, in your stories. I didn't know that.

But you hadn't known I could be real, rather than imagined. For all I knew, you had alien probes drop onto your planet regularly; people meeting them was just something which happened, and you let them wander around, freely, and only a few of you wanted to damage or destroy them. When you pointed your guns at me, and damaged me, and I killed you and drove you off, I hadn't expected it to be the first time that this had happened. The first, and only time.

I didn't know that the reaction from the one of you we found hanging from a tree by an aerobrake would be much more typical. If I had, would I have made more effort to avoid you? It was probably best that we both approached our respective epiphanies from a position of supreme ignorance. We all had so much to learn.

FIVE

We both looked up at the dangling body, held by a harness which attached directly to the entangled aerobrake. The covering that this one wore covered every part: boots, gloves, helmet, mask. The visor on the helmet was mirrored. There were emblems and insignia attached to the fabric, coding important information I wasn't party to, but you were.

I didn't know then if you – this is going to get complicated if I call all of you, you – individuals had descriptors. It emerged you had lots of them, in many categories. Unique ones you call personal names. Vocational nomenclature, which is often interchangeable, depending on the tasks. Then there are generic signifiers, based on familial connection or body shape or behaviour or the attitude of the name-giver. You hadn't told me your name yet, but this one you called the pilot, so that is what I called them too.

The pilot – I hadn't yet worked out what a pilot did – was hanging limply from the aerobrake's lines, beyond both our reaches. You said "we have to get him down", which, from the context, I understood to mean you wanted me to climb the tree, sever the lines, and somehow lower the body to the ground without further damage, so that we could ascertain whether or not the pilot was living or dead, and decide what to do next. You might want to use the pilot as a food source, and take the coverings and any equipment you might find. The pilot's fabric covering seemed more comprehensive than yours, though perhaps overlarge.

I was intrigued by the situation, so I complied. I launched my grapple into the branches, an action that made you jump backwards and shout, and hauled myself up. I used my knives to

40

cut the lines, one at a time, and found that with each slice the pilot dropped closer to the ground. They were within easy reach with four lines still attached, so I lowered myself back down and you held the body while I made the last cuts.

You staggered back under your load and half-fell underneath the pilot, but you managed to free yourself. You removed the helmet and the mask, and the pilot's head fell back, in amongst the fallen tree debris and small plants. The pilot's hair was long and pale. I reached out and cut some of it off, comparing it with the dark hairs I'd seen on you.

You said. "Don't do that. She's alive." It wasn't so much your words as your tone, which was sharp, and loud. That was my first inkling that there were things that I might not be permitted to do to the living that I could do to the dead. I analysed the hair anyway, since I already had a sample. While I did that, you tried to open the pilot's fabric covering, which was closed with interlocking metal pegs.

You bent low over the pilot, and pressed the side of your head, where your organs of hearing terminated in convoluted fleshy cones, against the torso. "She's breathing. I can hear her heart." So could I. I could have told you the pilot's skin temperature too. "Why won't she wake up?" you said.

I hadn't come across sleep before: involuntary unconsciousness was more understandable with the possibility of loss of oxygen, or damage to the brain. You sometimes use the terms interchangeably. You do that a lot. It makes comprehension much more difficult, and I wish you didn't. Not that I'm likely to be able to train you out of the habit. I assumed therefore asphyxia or a non-lethal head trauma. The pilot's airways appeared to be clear of obstructions. I couldn't see any external wounds. Without opening the pilot up, I didn't know what the matter was. If you didn't want me to cut the pilot's hair, cutting their skin was unlikely to be permissible. Then again, you couldn't have stopped me.

But the pilot seemed to regain consciousness on their own.

The skin over the eyes fluttered, and opened, and they looked around. Up into your face, beyond to the tops of the trees and to the sky above, to the fluttering remnants of their aerobrake, to me, and back to you. Then back to me. The pilot's voice croaked, and they used their still-uncoordinated limbs to try and move away, still supine on the ground.

I watched you with interest. I noticed – I had already noticed – that the pilot had a short tubed projectile weapon strapped to their side, and when their hand went towards it, I powered up my laser and pointed it between their eyes. Their hand stopped moving, then slowly withdrew. I lowered my laser array. That much, I think, the pilot understood.

You said: "It won't hurt you. Just don't threaten it. There were soldiers in the village. They shot at it, and it killed them all." I hadn't realised you'd seen that. You must have been watching from one of the houses. I parsed your sentence: soldiers was a descriptor, and I wanted to know more about them. They carried projectile weapons, so logically the pilot could also be a soldier. As soldiers had damaged me, might it only be a matter of time before the pilot did too? I decided that I would desoldier them.

My manipulators unfastened the strap holding the weapon in place, and withdrew it. I knew it would be useless without the projectiles, so I located the container where they were kept, and took it out. I also checked the tube to see if there was one already there: there wasn't. I put the weapon back, and refastened the strap. "Pilot no soldier," I said.

The pilot stared at the radio, then at you. "It can talk," said the pilot, and you said, "I gave it a radio and it worked out how to use it," and the pilot said, "what is it?" and you said "I don't know. It's a robot of some sort," and the pilot said, "Is it one of ours or one of theirs?" and you said, "It hasn't got any markings," and the pilot said, "Is it American?" and you said, "I don't think so."

The pilot sat up awkwardly – although almost anything you do is awkward. When you walk, you look as if you're going to fall over. When you run, as if you can't stop. Your hands, though. They're well engineered. Everything else is a compromise. "Where did you find it?" asked the pilot. None of the pilot's questions were directed at me. I couldn't string words together like you, so I just listened to the answers you gave.

"In the forest. It." You stopped talking. You didn't say anything else for a long time. I watched the pilot watch you, and glance at me. "They took us into the forest," you continued eventually. "All the men." Then you stopped again. The pilot rubbed their face with their hand. I didn't know what you had meant, and I didn't know what the pilot's gesture meant either.

"I'm sorry," said the pilot. There it was again. Meaning had clearly passed between you, but I had missed it completely, due to a mix of verbal and non-verbal cues and contexts. Spoken language is an extraordinarily inefficient method of passing on information, except when it isn't, and you manage to convey whole concepts using only a few words. "Where were you going?" the pilot asked.

I answered, "Uncle's house," and again the pilot stared at the radio as if they'd never seen anything like it before, even though I had assumed it was a common object. I eventually realised that it was, and it was my voice coming through the mundane device that was unnerving. "Uncle's house. Books and apples."

"I didn't know they could build things like this," said the pilot. "Who do you think's controlling it?"

You looked at me, and I knew you knew. At the very least, I knew you suspected the truth. But you said nothing about that, and instead concentrated on the second phrase, not the first. "I don't think anyone's controlling it," you said. "I think it's controlling itself."

"It took my bullets," said the pilot. "How does it know to do that?"

You looked at the metal container in my manipulators, then the pilot. "It learnt. It picked up a rifle from one of the dead soldiers and took it apart, and now it knows about guns." You didn't say anything about me holding you up by the feet to weigh you and measure you. Or cutting up the bodies of those I found in the forest. But perhaps you didn't see that, as you were covered up at that point and trying to stay still.

You would have heard me moving about, cutting and flensing and sawing. You would have smelled the charring of your flesh as my lasers burned, and the acid stench as I picked through the contents of your stomach. I don't know what that would have cost you in terms of courage or sanity. Perhaps you just blocked that whole episode out, and deliberately erased it from your memory.

"Well," said the pilot, "it has to belong to someone. But why's it following you?"

You made that gesture, the one with the rise of the shoulders and the showing of empty palms, that I had begun to equate with 'I don't know', and is more accurately 'I don't know why you think I know'.

The pilot slowly got to their feet – they were taller than you were, but shorter than the tallest I'd found in the forest – and walked around me, examining me from every angle. "You're right," they said, "there's no markings, no serial numbers, or anything. I bet it's American." You said nothing. I didn't know what the signifier American meant, except that you didn't think I was it. "Can we open it up and have a look inside?" asked the pilot.

Your reaction was immediate. "No! I mean, no. It'll think you're trying to attack it. It'll kill you. You'd better leave it alone." The pilot looked for a long time at you, then again at me. They held out their hand. "Give me back my bullets. I won't shoot you."

Bullets were the name you gave to the projectiles. I guessed that the pilot wanted me to return them to the gun. I wasn't prepared to do that. Your hands were insufficient to damage me, but guns were a danger to my existence. I was going to keep the bullets for now. "No," I said. "No bullets pilot."

The pilot lowered their hand and said to you, "I can't protect you without my gun."

You said, "You don't need to, because it'll protect both of us." I didn't know what that meant, except that the pilot stopped asking for the bullets, and you looked up at the sky. "Where did your plane come down?"

"Down the valley," said the pilot. "I got hit by a heavy machine gun. Unlucky, I suppose. I need to find my unit again. Do you think your uncle can help? Do you think he's still there?"

You looked in the direction we'd been travelling through the forest. "I don't know," you said. "It was the only thing I could think of doing."

"Do you know where the front line is?" asked the pilot. "It wasn't where I was told it was. If they've taken your village, then it's ten kilometres further on. Though I don't think there's a front line as such." The pilot squatted down suddenly, their head lowered.

You asked them, "Are you okay?" and the pilot waved you away without looking up, saying, "Dizzy, that's all."

The pilot rolled forward so that they rested their arms on the ground, and pressed their head into the decaying matter under the trees. "When you eject, you come out so quickly," said the pilot. "The canopy's supposed to break before you hit it, but the planes we're flying were barely maintained before the war. My back, my neck, they're really starting to hurt."

You didn't say anything to that. I caught some of what the pilot said, and worked out more from how they were behaving. The pilot was damaged, and was finding it difficult to function normally. There was nothing I could do, and since you didn't do anything either, I presumed there was nothing you could do. I also presumed that if the pilot was too badly damaged to continue, we would leave them and carry on to find uncle.

You knelt down next to the pilot. "You have to get up. There are soldiers around here."

The pilot didn't move, replying "what about that thing?" and you said, "what about it?" and the pilot said, "someone's going to come looking for it at some point. If it's American we can maybe do a deal with them, get them to help us."

You looked at me and said, "I don't think it works like that."

The pilot reached out blindly and you caught their hand and got them to stand. The pilot moved the skin membrane over their eyes deliberately slowly, once, twice. "We have to get it to our side," the pilot said. "If I can't do it, can you?"

You looked at me, then back at the pilot. "I don't think it has a side." You knew. I knew that you knew. "If it wants to go with us to my uncle's, then it will. I can't make it."

"Uncle's house," I said. The explosions had stopped. For how long, I didn't know. They didn't seem to follow any discernible pattern. The pilot took a large, folded sheet of cellulose out of a clear part of their covering and flapped it around, eventually trying to hold it taut between their outstretched hands. You looked over their arm at it, and so did I.

I knew what it was: a visual representation of geographical features. The pilot's map also had symbols on it, some regular, machine-made, and some post-manufacture, fine lines of pigment pressed into the surface of the sheet. I orientated my map to the pilot's, and pointed out where we all were with a laser dot. "Uncle's house," I said.

"He lives here," you said, touching the very bottom of the map, where the detail of the map gave way to a broad white border. Coloured lines converged from around the map on that spot. We'd have to walk down the valley and out onto the plain to get there, but it seemed simple enough. We could talk on the way, and I'd be able to find out whether I was American or not.

The pilot folded the map up and put it back into the pouch it had come from. "I can do this," the pilot said. "I'm fine."

I could do it too – I had scanned the map, and added it to my own. I looked in the direction of uncle's house. I knew the approximate location of it now, and presumed that once we were in the vicinity, you'd be able to lead us there.

I carried the bullets in one manipulator, the radio in another. I hadn't anticipated cargo. I didn't have external stowage points, nor internal baggage capacity. Something like the pilot's covering, which seemed to have many places in which to store objects, would have been useful. The discarded aerobrake still stranded in the trees above was made of strong, lightweight fabric, and I could make use of that.

I fired my grapple again, and winched myself up to it. I used my laser to free it from the secondary stems it was wrapped around, and I brought it back down. You watched me, and the pilot watched me. "What's it doing?" the pilot asked, and you responded with that upward-shoulder gesture. I considered my shape, and convenient anchors on my carapace, and developed a model of what I wanted. I exploded that model and transferred the individual pieces to the fabric, held taut between my feet.

The laser sliced it apart, and I glued the components together with fast-curing resin. It took a finite time – not, by my standards, long – and fastened it to my ventral surface. I placed the bullets and the radio into the fabric, and they slid together into the middle of the stretched surface. I rocked from side to side, and as I had calculated, the elasticity of the fabric meant that while the objects rolled around, they didn't fall out.

I might have pointed to the moment I picked up the radio as the time of my emergence, but I think it was probably this instead. I'd made something. I'd fashioned it out of raw materials for a purpose outside my original parameters. I'd changed my programming. I was no longer the surveying probe I'd been. "Uncle's house," I said again.

SIX

We walked through the forest, approximately parallel to the road, watching for the appearance of soldiers. This was initially confusing for me, as I was unable to ascertain what role soldiers filled for your species. But as I listened to you and the pilot talk, I was able to pick up the idea that soldiers used their guns to kill you and destroy your houses, in order to drive you away from territory.

This presumably captured resources, which the soldiers would then keep for themselves? This was where I lacked sufficient information to form a logical conclusion. The soldiers I'd killed weren't of a different species to you, or the pilot. So if the pilot had been a soldier, did the possession of a gun automatically convey a different status? You were ambiguous about that. You talked of 'them' and 'us', of 'they' and 'we', so perhaps not. The groups seemed distinct.

But it appeared that the soldiers were in the ascendant, and they were forcing those of you who weren't soldiers to leave your houses and your territory. Because if you didn't have guns, that was going to be quite straight forward. The soldiers would kill you, or you would go elsewhere before they arrived, so that they didn't kill you.

What if you'd got hold of a gun? Would you then become a soldier? It was possible. If the pilot got their gun back, would they start shooting at you, and me? Again, it was possible. Even though I didn't resemble your species in any way, I was somehow seen as competition for the same resources. The soldiers had fired at me, so I believed it to be true. I didn't understand then about your irrationality, or your mostly-incurable habit of reacting with violence to anything that might be a threat. Neither had I yet comprehended that I was far more important than either territory or resources.

I also found new trees to study. They had different leaf shapes, and aspects, and average heights before death. Sometimes I walked ahead of you. Sometimes I fell behind. I surveyed and sampled as I had done, as I was always meant to do, but I always came back to you, because we were all on the way to uncle's house.

As the planet rotated with respect to its primary, your energy levels started to fall, and your average speed over the ground decreased. You required sustenance and fluids. I was already aware of your omnivorous diet, and wondered if you'd cooperate to find food, or whether you'd try to eat each other.

Inexplicably, you did neither, and instead talked about how hungry and thirsty you were. Fortunately, there were minor water courses which ran near our route, and when your complaints overcame your need to keep moving, you diverted to them and drank, though apparently never enough. Either that, or your bodies were singularly inefficient at storing water in a usable form.

Although there were many animals we encountered, you showed no inclination to hunt them. Yes, they were swift, but you could have run them down eventually. As to the vegetable matter, you ignored that completely, even though we were surrounded by it, from trees downwards. You were, and remain, unnecessarily fussy when it comes to what you put in your mouths.

The trees suddenly stopped, along with the slope of the ground. You'd built a wall to keep the forest back – or at least, that was how it appeared. Beyond the wall was a roughly rectangular piece of ground, with one type of plant in it. And beyond that, another, with the same plant. But there were other types of plants in other enclosed areas.

In the distance, there were columns of black smoke, which I presumed came from burning houses, but due to our relative elevation, I couldn't quite see. I sat up on my hind legs to extend my range, and dialled up the resolution on my optics, but even with enhancement, there were too many particulates in the air.

I could see something, though: something I hadn't seen before. It was a long way off, and at the limits of resolution, but it was an object that seemed to be stationary in the part of the sky near the houses. It was bulbous at one end, thin at the other. The more I looked, the more motion I could see – it wasn't perfectly still, but only roughly so. It dipped and rose, and edged forward every so often.

And once a light flared on it, which chased away at speed, arcing towards the ground. A ball of dirty smoke billowed up where the light had winked out. The object rotated in the air, and slowly moved away. I thought it might be a machine, and it might be associated with soldiers, as it appeared to have shot at something that was now burning.

"Uncle's house," I said.

You pointed across the tops of the walls towards the smoke. "It's over there, across the fields," you said. "They look like they're attacking the town now, too." Definitely soldiers, then, as you'd said 'they'. I wondered if your uncle's house would be without your uncle: if the previous collection of houses had been empty, then there was no reason for the next one not to be, not with soldiers close by, shooting at you.

We were, however, going to check. You climbed up the wall, awkwardly dropped down the other side, and waited for the pilot to do the same. The pilot was taller than you, and more practised at climbing. Then they waited for me. I put my forelegs up on the top of the wall, pushed off with my rear pair, then reached down in one movement. My ability to navigate difficult terrain was built-in, but you were surprised.

The first few fields were walled in. They were straightforward to cross, even if the tall, stiff yellowing grass with the heavy seed heads gave considerable resistance to our passage. Then we came to one bounded by wire, which was much more difficult. I watched as the pilot held the barbed top strand up, and you ducked down, squeezing yourself through the gap, then doing the same for the pilot. Now the pilot's larger size counted against them, and their covering snagged briefly on the barbs, until you freed them.

I inspected the wires, the mesh below, the single strand of barbs above, and melted through them with my laser. The tensioned wire twanged back, lashing the air, and I stepped through the gap. There was a straight drainage channel cut into the ground, then more of the yellow grass. I looked back, and saw that our route was marked by broken stems.

We didn't have to walk all the way across the fields. We came to another track – another road – that had been hidden by the contours of the land, and we followed that instead. We made much better progress: it didn't seem to require as much energy from you, and I could see where I was putting my feet. The road was slightly lower than the surrounding fields, and you didn't walk with the slightly shortening crouch you'd maintained when we were in the open.

Then you stopped and looked up. I heard it too. I hadn't stopped hearing it, but the sharp, pulsing sound came and went, and without a visual cue it was difficult to ascertain either distance or direction. The noise swelled until it almost saturated my microphones, and a shadow passed overhead. I saw the machine much more clearly: it used two sets of rigid rotating aerofoils to produce lift, and a long tail for stability. It had aerodynamic pods on pylons, either side of the main carapace. And after battering us with its downdraught, it was gone, over the fields and out of sight again.

The pilot said, "We need to get off the road."

You said, "But there's nowhere to hide," and you both looked at me and I didn't know why. You then said, "They might not have seen us. And if they did, they might not care."

"I don't want to be here if they come back," said the pilot.

You both started running, and I picked up my pace, which increased the strain on my already-damaged leg. The impact against the hard road was within normal tolerances, but there was the potential for each individual strike exceeding the failure point of the joint. I made allowances. I was unbalanced, and limping, but I could keep up with you relatively easily. My top speed was greater, but I was a surveyor. I shouldn't have been running past things I ought to have sampled.

There was that part of me, though, the part where I thought I was being threatened by the machine. This made me run. It wasn't just that you were running from it. I was running from it. I had the opportunity to analyse my actions as I ran, and I identified the protocol overriding other possible reactions. If the machine were threatening me, I would leave the area so that it couldn't. But what if the machine was actively trying to attack me, hunt me? I would have to deal with it as I dealt with the soldiers.

The sound of its rotating aerofoils came back strongly. Both you and the pilot threw yourselves to the sides of the road, trying to hide in the grass. I recognised the instinct, but questioned the utility of the action. I wasn't going to be able to hide. I was too big, too different from the landscape. I couldn't work out where the machine was, and I deployed all of my cameras to face in different directions.

It slid sideways across the road ahead. I could see it clearly, see in through the transparent covering into the control area, where the soldier sat. I powered up my laser, and I waited. The soldier controlling the machine looked at me. I looked at the contents of the pylons, the sleek tubes with fins, the aerodynamic containers with multiple piercings, and the large tube alongside the carapace, pointing directly at me.

Any of those could have destroyed me. I should have fired first. I didn't. I still don't know why. Clamps opened, combusting gasses flared, and my laser turned the rocket's nose cone to molten ruin. It exploded just ahead of the machine, and fragments of it expanded in an approximately spherical blast pattern. I was far enough away that I was unlikely to be struck by debris. The machine was very much closer to it. Pieces penetrated its carapace, but more significantly, interfered with the aerofoils.

The short-period chopping of the air changed abruptly. One of the aerofoils sheared off and was sent spinning, out across the fields. With the loss of lift, the machine lurched downwards, and began to turn uncontrollably on its axis. It tilted and started to roll over. It lost more height, and the tips of still-rotating aerofoils made contact with the ground, throwing arcs of brown soil high into the air. The soldier at the controls was still trying to correct the machine's attitude as it disintegrated.

A fire started almost immediately, and then the explosives it was carrying detonated. Not all at once, and not in one place. Rockets flew into the air, and bright chemical markers trailed white smoke. Bullets whipped past, the sound of their passage high and fast. That I wasn't destroyed, or that you weren't killed, was down to the height of the embankments. Even then, burning metals fell to the road, and I had to scurry backwards and forwards to dodge it.

"Uncle's house, uncle's house," I said. Your uncle's house was going to be more secure than being outside, targeted by soldiers and their increasingly sophisticated weapons. You raised your head from where you lay and looked around, coughing at the particulates that you were breathing in. Smoke swirled densely into the dip and away. I used my cameras to locate the pilot, and checked they were still alive by prodding them with a manipulator. "Uncle's house," I repeated.

The pilot rolled over onto their back and stared up at me. "You downed it," they said. "You downed the helicopter." I suppose I had. The machine – the helicopter – had been up, and was now down. It was still dangerous, with bullets and rockets and combustible fuel, but any damage we sustained would now be random, rather than deliberate.

"Yes," I said, "Uncle's house." You were still crouching by the side of the road. The helicopter's explosives were detonating in the next field, so that seemed a good precaution for you to take. But you didn't move. I expected you to lead us to your uncle's house, now I'd downed the helicopter, and all you did was make yourself small.

The pilot bent down and scurried across the road, in a way which reminded me of the small furred animals from the forest. She took hold of your arm and dragged you upright. You didn't want to stand. You didn't want to expose yourself to the unpredictable explosions. You struggled with the pilot for a moment, striking them with your clenched hands. The pilot grabbed you and shook you and shouted at you, "We have to go. Now."

Neither you nor the pilot seemed to want to hurt each other. Neither of you attacked the other's sensory organs, nor used weapons that would cause blunt force trauma or penetrative wounds. You were fighting to determine dominance, as to whose will would prevail. The pilot won this particular contest. You stood up, hunched over and coughing, and you turned around and around, as if you couldn't remember the way.

I knew which direction we'd been heading, so I started down the road, stopped, walked a little further, stopped again. Eventually, both you and the pilot followed. Every time there was bigger explosion from the burning helicopter, you faltered, and we had to wait for you. The pilot held out their hand to you, not closed for striking, but open. You pressed your palms together, and your fingers caught around each other's.

We moved quickly once we were clear of the smoke, going at the same loping pace we had before. The sensors in my leg told me how much stress it was under, but not how much would be too much. I didn't know whether the soldiers would try and intercept us again. I didn't know whether soldiers talked to each other, or if they acted in small groups or individually. You thought they might, and we ran.

As we left one pillar of smoke behind, we approached several others. There were burning houses by the side of the road, and a rough wall across it, made of blocks of stone and a tree trunk. The pilot waved us back and approached the wall alone, raising their hands above their head, and calling out to anyone there. But there was no one, and we went around the side of the wall. The road continued beyond it, and there were more houses. Most of them were intact, and the gaps between them quickly disappeared until there was nothing but roads and houses, many of which had little fields in front of them.

"Where does your uncle live?" asked the pilot.

You said, "He owns a garage."

The pilot asked, "Yes, but where? I need to contact my unit again. I need a working phone. Or something."

"It's in the middle of town," you said.

She asked, "Which way is that?"

You stopped and looked up at the houses, and said, "I used to be brought here. My dad used to drive me. I've never come on my own."

Your face went very red, and water leaked out of your eyes and down your face. Then you rubbed the water away, and pointed down the road. "It's this way, I think," you said, and you made certain that you were ahead of us for the rest of the way, stopping only where one road merged with others, and carrying on before we caught up.

There weren't any burning houses in the middle of this town, but there weren't any of you either. There were interesting things that we passed, houses that had huge glass sheets instead of walls, hidden behind perforated metal covers. If I aimed my cameras through the holes, I could see all kinds of manufactured objects. I wanted to cut through the metalwork and explore, but you kept on calling me, and telling me your uncle's house was nearby. I could always come back. I still thought that then.

We turned a corner, and you ran faster than normal towards a particular structure. I remembered you'd complained about being hungry and thirsty, yet your capacity to continue to exert yourself and expend energy you thought you didn't have seemed limitless. The pilot followed you, and so did I.

While you ran around, banging on entrances and tapping on

the glass, I examined the objects I found. The tall metal rectangles with the pipes that smelled of light hydrocarbons. The buckets of fine aggregate, filled with tiny tar-soaked fibrous cylinders. The containers of water, the roll of coloured cellulose sheets, the stains on the smooth ground.

You'd stopped making noises, and now just stood there, in front of part of the house which had a long metal closure, articulated so that it would roll up. "Uncle?" you called. "Uncle Georg?" Your uncle still didn't respond. You looked at me, and said, "He's not here. I thought he'd be here. He's always here."

There wasn't anything I could add to that. This was your uncle's house, and I presumed it remained that, even in the absence of your uncle. I realised then that it wasn't your uncle's house you really wanted, but your uncle. "No uncle," I said. "No uncle here."

We were interrupted by one of you holding a length of metal over his head. He appeared around the corner of a wall, from behind the house, and he quickly looked at you, me and the pilot, then back to you. I don't think he even saw me properly: not until I moved, and that came after he lowered his arm and said your name for the first time. "Petro?"

SEVEN

Petro ran towards Uncle Georg, and he put his arms around him and lifted him off the ground. He put his face against Petro's and squeezed him. Again, not an attack, but something different. I conceded that staying with you – with Petro – meant I would observe more of your apex species behaviour than I would otherwise have done.

I did note that Uncle Georg didn't let go of the metal bar, even when he gestured at the pilot. "We'd better get inside," he said, and still with one arm around Petro's shoulders, he led the way around the side of the house. I followed, and he became aware of me. He raised the bar again, pushing Petro behind him. "What is that thing?"

Petro moved around him to stand between me and your uncle, and put his arms out wide. "Don't try and hurt it," he said. "Bad things happen when you do. It's... she thinks it might be American." Petro dipped his head towards the pilot. "It's been protecting us. It shot down a helicopter."

Uncle Georg approached me slowly, and Petro pushed the raised metal bar down, so that Uncle Georg held it by his side. "American, eh?" he said. He circled me, and I followed his movement with my cameras. I still didn't know what American meant. All I knew was that Petro wanted others to believe that I was American, even when he didn't believe it yourself. "We'd better get it inside too. How does it work?"

"You just talk to it. It understands some things well enough," Petro said.

Uncle Georg coughed, covering his mouth with his hand. "Talk to it," he said. "Doesn't it have an operator somewhere?"

Petro said, "I don't think so. I don't think it's a drone. I think it's a robot of some sort." He looked at me. "It doesn't behave like there's an operator."

He knew I was different. Yet he appeared not to want to tell anyone. I understand why, now, but then? I watched as Uncle Georg circled me again. "If it's American, they'll want it back, yes?" The pilot had said much the same. "That could help us. We need to find someone in authority." He looked at the pilot. You often looked at people when you talked to them, as if they wouldn't hear you properly if you didn't.

"I need to contact my unit," said the pilot. "I can talk to someone there. Do the phones still work? Have you got the internet?" All these words I didn't know the meaning of. I needed help understanding them, and everyone – everyone except Petro – seemed to want to talk about me, not to me.

"Books," I said. "Books."

So now they all looked at me properly. "Let's get it inside," said Uncle Georg, "Miss, wait here with it. Petro, come with me. I'm not letting you out of my sight." He left with Petro, going around the side of the house again. The metal door me and the pilot were standing next to rattled, then slowly began to lift up from the ground. The space inside was filled with all manner of machines and interesting objects. I walked in and immediately began picking items up and cataloguing them.

Uncle Georg looked as if he might try and stop me, but Petro pulled on his clothes, and he went back to hauling on the chain that moved the closure down again. It rattled to a halt while I was examining a big metal sheet, covered in clasps and hooks, on which were hung differently shaped pieces of metal. Many of them were similar, just varying in size. There were things that had levers and teeth, like the jaws of an animal, presumably for gripping objects, and others that would fit six-sided pegs. It was quite dark when the closure was fully down. I turned on some of my lights and adjusted my cameras accordingly.

In the centre of Uncle Georg's house was a car, except this one was raised on a hydraulic machine to around your head-height. I looked underneath, and saw the tubes through which waste gases and products of combustion exited the engine. I traced its passage from the front of the car to the back, where a sonic baffle had been inserted before the final exhaust. I could see the friction brakes and the spring and hydraulic suspension from there, too.

"How long has it been limping?" asked Uncle Georg.

"I don't know," Petro said. "I think it might have been damaged –" then he stopped talking. Was he going to say, 'when it fell from the sky', or something like that?

Uncle Georg didn't notice. "I might be able to fix it." He made a strange noise. "If it'll let me." Then to the pilot, Uncle Georg said, "Miss, if you'll come with me, I'll see if I can get through to anyone." Then to Petro, "You need to come too. You need to tell me what happened."

They left me there, going through a smaller exit at the back of the room. There was clearly more house than I'd seen so far. Petro looked at me before he shut the door. "We won't be long," he said. "Don't go outside." I wasn't going to go outside. I had too much to learn in here.

In a small container, I found lots of books, all stacked neatly on shelves. I took out the first one, scanned it in, and when I'd done, I started on the second. They were instructions on how to take apart and put together cars. Lots of different cars. Different in mostly minor ways, and similar in gross morphology. Like the little flying animals in the forest. I read all the books on the shelves anyway.

I could use the devices on the rack to disassemble the car on the raised platform. I thought I could learn much from doing so. It took me a little while to locate the manual release on the hydraulics – I gathered that it would normally be powered, but I tried the buttons and nothing happened. When the car was at ground level, I checked the model make and number, and configured my list.

The wheels came off first, and I used the jack points to lift the car chassis clear of the ground. It was difficult to get the hubs off the axles, but I could exert more force than the resistance I encountered. I took the brake assembly apart and dismantled the clutch, freed the suspension and lowered the front and rear axles. I unfastened the exhaust system – some of the fixings were quite corroded, and I had to clean them before I could undo them.

I started on the engine. It was going to be easier to work on with it outside of the engine compartment, so I uncoupled the electrics and fuel feed, then unbolted it from the mounting. I lifted it out and peered into the hole I'd made. While I was there, I thought I should disconnect the battery, which I did, and then made a pile of parts of the distributor and alternator.

Then there was the radiator, and the windscreen washer reservoir, and the pump. I chased the wiring to the fuse box, and back under the panels to the headlights, the indicators, the power steering and the light array at the rear. The seats, the internal panelling, the carpets, the glass – everything could be taken apart.

It took as long as it did. I spotted a timing device on the wall, a white disk with twelve black divisions, and two pointers, the longer of which rotated once for each of the shorter pointer's twelfths. I was left alone for at least one of short pointer divisions, and halfway towards the next. I had two of the four spark plugs out before Petro, the pilot and Uncle Georg returned.

None of them said anything. Petro stayed by the door, while Uncle Georg walked around the car, and all of the pieces laid out neatly on the floor, in the order which I'd need to put them back again. Uncle Georg walked around things a lot. He had a small device strapped to his wrist, an analogue of the timer on the wall. He looked at it, and compared the two. "How did it do this? How?"

"Book," I said. I walked to the container and retrieved the correct book from the shelf. "Book."

I'd put the radio down on one of the raised flat surfaces, along with the pilot's bullets. Uncle Georg looked at the radio, then at the book I was holding. "It read the book, then it knew how to do this? It'd take me a week, and an extra pair of hands to get anywhere near this." He rubbed at his face with his hands. "I just hope the owner doesn't come back for it, because this, this is a lot of work."

Petro spoke: "It can put it back together again. Can't you? Put all the bits back in the car, in the way they need to go, so it'll work?"

I parsed the sentence. My vocabulary had increased dramatically, because I now knew all the names for all of the car parts, because there were diagrams to go with the words. I thought he was asking if I could reassemble the car. I could. I said: "Yes."

Uncle Georg walked around me and the engine. "Are you certain this is American?" he asked. "It doesn't, it doesn't look very American to me. They put their flag on everything of theirs, right? There's not even a number or anything on it."

I knew he was talking about serial numbers now, just like the pilot had, because the books had all mentioned them. I wasn't quite sure what one was, but it definitely needed to be checked to see if it was a genuine manufacturer part. I didn't know what significance being American meant, either. "American?" I asked.

And finally, I got Uncle Georg to talk to me directly. "American," he said. "You know, from America. The United States of America."

I didn't know. "United States of America?"

Uncle Georg took a slow step back. "You haven't heard of America."

"No America," I said. "What America?"

Uncle Georg turned to look at Petro. "I've got a desk diary in the office, Petro. Go get it for me." Petro went back through the opening – if the closure was a door, did that make it a door hole? – and reappeared with a slim book. He gave it to his uncle, who turned the pages until he found the right one. He held it open, up to my camera.

There were irregular regions in different colours, although the predominant colour was the same shade of blue. I scanned it in and stored it, along with all the words. One of the words was what I thought was America. I pointed at it with a fine-ended manipulator. Uncle Georg moved away slightly as it approached the page, but I could still touch the word. "America."

"I don't think it knows what it's looking at," Petro said, and he was right: I didn't. "It's a map, a map of the world." He took the book from his uncle, and pointed to a part of the page on the opposite side to where it said America. "It's like the one she showed you." He meant the pilot. "The different countries are in different colours. The blue is the sea. We're here." His finger pressed against the page, where there were lots of small patches of colour. "America is over here."

There weren't any visual cues I could take from it: nothing looked like a river or a road or a mountain. I think Petro realised then just how confusing that map was. But in order to make me understand, he realised that he'd have to tell his uncle and the pilot that he knew I wasn't from America. He was willing me to comprehend, but without further information, I couldn't make the conceptual leap. I store geographic information differently to you. I couldn't correlate that map with my maps.

Petro gave in, finally. "It's not difficult," he said. "The world's like a ball, like, like an apple. It's got a north pole and a south pole, and everything along the top of this map is at the north pole and everything along the bottom is at the south pole. Everything that's this colour blue is water, and everything that isn't is land. Do you get that?"

I drew a virtual sphere – I knew what a ball was, because I'd seen it in one of the books he'd shown me – and I warped the picture in front me around it. I didn't realise quite how wrong that image was, because it missed out most of the Pacific Ocean, and most of Antarctica, and the equator wasn't even in the middle of the map: but it was enough to get a sense of the shape of the planet you call Earth.

If America was the name of that place, then I definitively wasn't American. Things that came from America could be American. I couldn't give you the name of the place I came from, so what I was was moot. "Not American," I said. "Not American, not any place here." I didn't have any inhibition in saying that. Why would I? It wasn't like I knew what would happen. No one knew what would happen.

"Where do you come from?" Petro asked. I saw that the pilot and Uncle Georg had become strangely immobile. As if all their processing power was being used for other tasks, and not for movement. "Do you come from outer space?"

But I didn't know what outer space meant, so I asked Petro to define outer space, and he couldn't quite manage that.

The pilot could, though. "Outer space. Not from this planet. From another planet. From another star."

"Yes," I said. It was true. Wherever I was made, it wasn't anywhere near here. It would have been beyond this solar system. "Yes. Outer space."

"I knew that," Petro said. "I knew that. It's an alien robot. It's an alien robot from outer space." He spoke to his uncle and the pilot. "What are we going to do?" Then he turned back to me, and looked into one of my cameras. "What do you want to do? We can try and help you."

"I don't think we get to decide this," said the pilot. "If this is really something from outer space, and I'm still not sure about that, what happens next is going to be out of our hands, whatever we say. Let's just get it away from the front line, and let someone else decide what to do with it."

"We have to ask it what it wants," Petro said. "It's not fair otherwise."

The pilot said, "It doesn't work that way."

Petro said, loudly, "Well, why not?"

Just as loudly, the pilot said, "I don't make the rules. I just have to follow them."

Uncle Georg stepped between them and held his hands out to each side and waved them up and down. "Petro's got a point. And so do you. We don't even know if it's telling the truth yet. It might just be mistaken. It might be faulty, and forgotten who made it. If we can find out who it belongs to, then they can come and pick it up."

Petro said, "What if it doesn't belong to anyone? What if it belongs to itself?" I didn't really have much of a concept of ownership. The point passed me by.

"It has to come from somewhere," said the pilot, and Uncle Georg waved his hands again.

"We can't settle that now. We have to get it away from here. Yes, I've got a van, we can put it in that. We can't use the main road. We'll have to go by the back route, and hope."

Petro said: "But if it can answer for itself, we can't really pretend it can't. What if it's here to, I don't know, judge us or something? On how we treat it? And we can't let it fall into their hands, can we? They've already shot it and tried to blow it up."

Uncle Georg looked around at all the equipment in the room. "I was going to stay here, with the garage. Make sure it didn't get looted. They might not enter town, and I needed something to come back to. Maria and the kids have already gone, they're with her mother." He breathed heavily, just the once. "Look: we've still got a phone signal. Let's get a picture of it. See if anyone recognises it."

He took out a small rectangular device from his pocket, and told Petro to stand next to me 'for scale'. He lifted the glass lens on the device up and walked backwards and forwards. I didn't know why he did that. He pressed his side of the device, and I heard a definite clicking noise.

That was how your species found out they weren't alone in the universe. Not through a great manifestation of lights and size and power, but from a low resolution still, taken on someone's phone and uploaded to a popular social media platform. Of Petro, and me, in Uncle Georg's garage. Behind us is the shell of the car I'd dismantled. I'm still holding the spanner I was unscrewing the spark plugs with. "Missing a robot? We've found one," was the accompanying text.

I think if Uncle Georg had known just how iconic that image would become, he might have typed something different.

EIGHT

Uncle Georg showed me his big car – the one he called a van – and asked obliquely if I could fit inside. I looked, used my laser to measure the interior, and deemed that I could, if I took all of the equipment out. To the accompanying sound of distant shelling, I removed the two tyres, the jack, the plastic container of fuel, the spare battery, the length of rope, and the racks of tools, and stacked them against the back wall of the house. Garage. House. I was still struggling with nomenclature. Specialised houses had other names, as did rooms. Almost every room was called something different, for the smallest of reasons, and some of the names were interchangeable. Language was not logical. Necessary, heavily contextualised, and not logical.

Petro watched me as I emptied the van, and as I climbed inside. There was just about enough room: I had to curl my legs under and around me, much as I had done in the descent capsule. I proved that I fitted, then I climbed out again, and awaited further developments. Uncle Georg wanted the pilot in the same compartment as me, but she – a different part of the language than he – didn't want to. Uncle Georg wanted Petro in the control area with him, where he could see him. Petro wanted to travel in the back with me.

The obvious solution was the least acceptable to your uncle, who exhibited initial verbal dominance. The pilot was prepared to challenge Uncle Georg with gestures that appeared to be simulated physical attacks. I waited until they had determined their hierarchical places: the pilot couldn't be dominant because she was 'a woman', while Uncle Georg couldn't because he counted as 'a mere civilian'. Petro was clearly cast in a non-dominant role by both of them, and he appeared to accept that.

They shouted mostly incomprehensible things at each other, with a great deal of energy for what seemed to be a trivial problem. I wondered if I should be at the controls. I was confident in my ability, just that I would have to remove the rear bulkhead in order for me to access everything. It was fortunate that they were reminded that soldiers were still firing explosives into the town when one struck the road at the front of the garage.

All the glass in the vicinity shattered, and a grey cloud of dust rose up over the structure. The air tasted richly of nitrogen compounds. "Look," said your uncle. "Just get in the van. Even if that was just a stray shell, we need to go. Petro, get in the front."

I needed the radio and the bullets for the pilot's gun, so I went back to get them. "Where are you going?" Petro asked, but I couldn't reply, so I carried on.

The garage was damaged. Part of the roof had collapsed, and the metal door had buckled inwards with the force of the explosion. I moved carefully through the hazy air and retrieved both items, stowing them safely in my cargo net. The sound of bending wood and fatigued metal was accompanied by the rattle of falling debris from the broken walls. The structure didn't look like it was in danger of imminent collapse, but needed to be repaired before it could be used again. I wasn't going to have time to rebuild the car. Another of those tasks I thought I could always complete later.

I looked out under the door at the road outside. There was a crater in the black surface, revealing the layers of substrate all the way down to the compacted soil that formed the base. The smoke had mostly cleared, and rocky debris was spread across the road, and the sides of the road. The houses opposite had no glass in their window spaces, and the external walls were marked where secondary impacts had struck the stonework.

I was being called. Not by my name, because I didn't have a name. But by Petro, saying, "Robot? Robot?" An alien robot from outer space. He might have said 'alien', although that has biological overtones. I was, to the best of everyone's abilities to categorise me, a robot.

I responded, "Yes."

He said, "Come on. Uncle Georg says he can't wait any longer." Even then I thought that was odd, considering the whole reason we were going in his van to Maria's mother was because of me.

I followed, though. I followed because I was learning so much more interacting with you than if I'd stayed in the forest. Yes, I'd have fully catalogued the forest flora and fauna, have detailed soil samples, elevation maps and a suite of weather data. Instead I was learning a language, I was dismantling cars and getting shot, I was taking down helicopters and running through fields. I was getting in a van with Petro and the pilot and Uncle Georg and going to see Maria and the kids. I was seeing your world, which was what I'd been programmed to do.

I left the garage with Petro and stood at the back of the van. I put the radio to one side, so that it wouldn't get crushed, and clambered awkwardly in. Petro went to sit in the front with Uncle Georg, and the pilot climbed in after me. She pulled the doors shut behind her, and sat, hunched, at the very rear of the compartment, her head tilted upwards to the two windows in the door panels.

I heard the engine start. I could tell that the timing belt was slightly off, and the idle speed set too high. First gear set us swaying and rattling, and we swung around the side of the garage and onto the road. We didn't cross the crater. Uncle Georg moved into second gear, accelerated, and then into third. Each time he changed gear, there was a moment of deceleration where we jerked forward, then jerked back as we picked up more speed. I could have done better.

I deployed my cameras to get a better look out of the window. We were the only moving vehicle on the road. We passed some stationary cars, and two different types of furred animal I hadn't seen before: one, a highly differentiated species with an elongated skull and lots of teeth, that mostly had thin, bony legs and a long thin tail, and the other, a more compact creature with denser fur and a flatter face. They appeared to roam freely through the constructed environment.

The pilot eventually sat up, and braced her legs against the floor of the swaying van. "Do you have a name?" she asked.

"Robot," I said.

"You just heard the boy call you that," she said. "What's your actual name? Do you call yourself anything? Do you have a number, or a design name? Who made you?"

"Boy?" I asked.

The pilot made a single clicking sound in her mouth. "Just answer the question. What do you call yourself?"

"Robot," I said. "No model name. No number. No maker's marque. Robot."

She reached behind her and pulled her hair forward over her shoulder. She dragged her fingers through the strands until she'd collected several loose hairs. She rolled them up and discarded them on the floor. "So who really made you? Was it someone here?"

"Makers made. Makers not known. Space, yes. Outer space, yes. Fall. Land. Look. See. Learn. Speak Mother." I tried these unambiguous concepts on her, to see if she could understand. It wasn't the understanding that was the problem, though, it was the believing.

The pilot narrowed her eyes by flexing the muscles on her face. "Where did you land, then? When?"

"Land forest. Half cycle gone. Trees. Birds. You." If I'd known the names of more things, I could have explained further.

"Did you see what happened to the boy's father?" she asked, and again I needed clarification.

"Boy? Father?"

"Petro," she said. "Petro's a boy. A thirteen year old boy. He said that all the men in his village were rounded up and taken into the forest, where they were shot. Including his father and his older brother. Did you see that?"

"No. Trees. Heard." I went back through my sound files, and I accessed that portion of the recording. I played it to her over the radio. The gun shots were loud, and sustained. The van slowed abruptly, causing me to tense all my legs, and sending the pilot tumbling into me.

"Fucking hell, Georg, what the fuck do you think you're doing?" she shouted. The brakes squealed and the tyres slid across the black surface of the road. The doors were flung open, and a dark-faced Georg stood there, breathing hard.

"I thought we were being shot at!" He looked at me, and pointed his finger as if it was a weapon he could damage me with. "Don't do that again. I nearly crashed." The guns stopped shooting. Then came the single, higher pitched shots, the ones that killed the two of you who tried to leave. The relevant part of the recording finished, and I cancelled the playback. Georg slammed the doors shut again, and I heard him re-enter the control area. He pulled away again with an exaggerated jerk.

The pilot reoriented herself, holding her upper arm, which had collided with my leg with her full moving weight behind it. "So may be that wasn't such a good idea," she said. She straightened her fingers, closed them, straightened them again. She closed her eyes and bared her teeth. "That's going to bruise," she said. When she opened her eyes again, she said, "That was Petro's father and brother dying. And everyone else, except Petro."

"Twenty nine," I said. "Twenty eight and Petro. Soldiers shot. Twenty eight dead. Father. Brother." I didn't know what father or brother meant, just as I didn't know what uncle meant either.

"Do you know where the bodies are?" asked the pilot.

"Yes. Map," I said. You would, of course, find some of the bodies dissected, but any test you'd subsequently carry out would show that they were dead first. I'm a probe. It's what I do. Did.

She reached into one of her fabric containers and pulled out the map she had. "Do you recognise anything on this?" She opened it up and held it towards me. Despite the random oscillations of the van's suspension, I could see the houses where I encountered Petro for the second time, the road I'd walked down, and the outline of the forest marked in green. The blue lines marked rivers, and the faint brown lines joined points of equal elevation.

I compared it with my own observations. "Here," I said, dabbing at the surface of the map with a manipulator.

"Are you sure?" she asked.

I replied, "Yes. Here."

She took the map back and reached into her pocket again for a stick of pigment. She held the map as flat as she could over her knee, and drew a small circle over the printed information. "Thank you," she said. "They'll pay for what they did." I didn't know what she meant. I had, of course, already killed most of the soldiers who'd shot Petro's father and brother and all the men in his village. I didn't know what that meant either, other than they were dead.

She folded the map up, and I took the stick from her. She watched me examine it, turn it over in my manipulator. "Pencil," she said. "It's called a pencil. The colour is blue. So it's a blue pencil."

She held out her hand, flat palm upwards, and I placed the pencil in it. She gripped the pencil between her thumb and two fingers, and drew the letter A on the white, unprinted border of the map. "We write with them. We can draw with them too. They come in every colour you can think of."

She let me take the pencil again, and I tried to emulate her hold. The best I could do was to coil one of my manipulators around it, to give some degree of fine control over the tip. I drew a letter on the margin of the map, next to her mark, a lower-case a. I'd be slow to write with it, but that was to be expected. Your culture developed the tools you needed to fit your own specific bodies. I wasn't equipped with equivalent limbs, and was at a disadvantage.

I handed the pencil back, and she stowed it in the same place as the map. She brought out a clear plastic rectangle that bore red engraved markings, a portion of it covered by a black plastic lid. She opened it up, and showed it to me. Inside the lid was a mirror, and uncovered by it was a plastic liquid-filled container surrounded by a dial. There was a thin red-and-black needle inside the liquid, pivoted about its mid-point.

"This is a compass," she said. "Remember the map Petro showed you? With north at the top? The red end points towards north – magnetic north, which isn't the same as true north, or even map north, but let's not worry about that now. If it's held still, and not in a metal van, it'll mean you can navigate your way around."

I took the compass from her and watched the needle twitch and swing. I was partly made of metal too, so it was of limited use until I could make allowances for that. I had my own navigational aids, but this was interesting nevertheless.

I looked at myself in the mirror. I didn't have any sudden revelation of self-awareness, as this wasn't the first time I had encountered mirrored glass: the car I'd disassembled had several, one stuck to the inside of the windscreen, two in the fold-down sun visors, and two side mirrors on the outside of the car. I knew what I looked like and what I was. I was a sentient machine sent to your planet to learn as much as I could and relay it back to Mother.

As that went, I was succeeding. I waited for the pilot to show me something else, but was distracted by a car left by the side of the road. There didn't seem to be any houses around, and it had to have been driven there by someone. We passed another shortly after: it was a different colour, white, with oxidation streaks bubbling up under the pigment. "Car," I said. "Two cars."

She raised herself up and looked out of the windows. "They probably ran out of fuel. It's almost impossible to get hold of at the moment, unless you're on government business or willing to pay black market rates for it. The people in those cars would have got as far as they could, then walked the rest of the way, to wherever they were trying to get."

"Van fuel," I said, and she turned to look at me.

"Georg runs a garage. He'll have his own supply, even if he told his customers he'd run out."

The road ran through the middle of broad, flat fields. There were roads that occasionally ran off at right-angles to it, and into the distance, but we never turned down any of those. We passed another three cars, abandoned, doors closed, neatly parked in gateways. Perhaps the owners had taken the keys and hoped to come back to them.

Then we were slowing. Uncle Georg depressed the clutch and let friction coast the van to a crawl, before he squeakingly applied the brakes. The pilot peered out of the rear windows, but neither of us could see a reason why we should be stopping. The engine stuttered to a halt.

"Wait here," she said, and wrestled with the door handle. She made sure to close it again properly before she slipped around the side of the van.

I could hear Uncle Georg's door open and close, too, and low voices too indistinct to parse. They faded, walking away up the road. I thought Petro was still in the control area in the front of the van, but I waited, because the pilot seemed to be exhibiting dominance, and wondered how this situation would turn out.

Then Uncle Georg's door opened and closed again, and the engine restarted. The back doors were swung apart, and the pilot climbed back in.

"Listen very carefully," she said. "This is very important, and you have to understand enough of what I'm saying to do what I tell you. If you don't understand, and you don't do exactly what I say, this is where it ends, for you, and probably for me, Petro and Georg too."

She took her time closing the doors, shutting one, then the other.

"There's a checkpoint ahead. It's manned by soldiers from

my side. They'll let us through, because I've told them they have to, but they'll want to look in the back before we can go. They'll see you, and there's no way we can hide you. They're nervous, but they're armed. They will point their guns at you, but they won't shoot – unless you try and kill them first. In which case, the other guards will light up this van with the heavy machine gun they have, and possibly the RPGs too. We'll all die and you'll be destroyed. Do you understand so far?"

"Understand yes," I said.

She slapped her hand on the side of the van, and the booming noise echoed in the compartment. Uncle Georg took it as a signal to start moving forward, very slowly. "What I want you to do is what Petro did in the forest. Play dead. Don't move. Don't say anything. Don't so much as twitch. They'll look and they'll poke you and I'll tell them some story about a thing we found and we're taking it to the experts to look at, all of which is true, but it'll only work if they think you're not still operational. Stay still. Keep quiet. Stay that way until I tell you otherwise. Tell me you understand."

"Yes." I said.

The pilot shook her head from side to side. "I hope to God you do, or this is going to be a short trip for all of us." The van was already slowing again. "I'll need my bullets back. I won't be able to explain that to them. You can have them again afterwards, if you want." The van rocked to a stop. "Now. Don't move." She reached over and turned the radio off, then took a deep breath before opening the rear doors.

NINE

The soldiers were all dressed in green, just like the pilot. The other soldiers hadn't been: their clothes had been all different colours and textures. I didn't know what that meant, not having been introduced to the concept of uniform. They talked to each other and to the pilot. They bared their teeth to each other, often making a strange stuttering noise in their throats at the same time. They didn't point their guns at me. They hung them over their shoulders on fabric straps, with the open end of the tubes aimed at the sky above.

When they were ready, the pilot showed me to them. They peered inside, the relative darkness of the van's interior causing them to narrow their eyes and complain they couldn't see. One of them got in the back with me and poked at me with their finger. They nudged my now-limp manipulators, and watched them swing freely. They turned back to the other soldiers and said: "Dead as a door nail." They climbed back out.

"Good luck with that," they said to the pilot.

She replied, "Whatever it is. If it's important, it's well over my rank."

I stayed still, just as I'd been told. It wasn't difficult for me. I was a robot. I didn't breathe, I didn't have muscles that would get tired. All of my movements were voluntary. You seem to be continually in motion, and almost all of it without conscious thought, whether it's autonomic or reflex or habitual. Even in your sleep.

The pilot pushed one door shut, and leant on the other. "Don't let them pass," she said. "We're relying on you to hold the line."

Someone unseen said, "If we had more people and better

weapons, we might be able to do that."

Then someone else said, "We'll hold them. Nothing'll get past us, right?"

Some of them raised their voices in a ragged bellow, and the pilot raised her hand, palm outward at them. She stepped into the van and closed the door behind her.

"Still don't move." She raised herself up and looked out of the windows at the soldiers.

Uncle Georg started the engine again, and we drove slowly on. I raised my camera slightly to see the structures either side of the road: fabric bags, fine-grained silicate leaking from holes, were piled up in walls, and soil had been put into wide metal cylinders. A thin wood pole was carried back across the road as we left, and the soldiers barred the way with it. It didn't seem substantial enough to impede movement, but perhaps its presence was more ritual than practical.

The soldiers receded into the distance, and the pilot watched them carefully. "I think we got away with it," she said. "You can move now." I didn't, because there wasn't much to move for, save I adjusted my setting to compensate for the motion of the van. "Do you want my bullets back?" asked the pilot.

I used a manipulator to turn the radio back on. "Shoot?" I said.

She said, "No. I'm not going to shoot you."

I responded, "No bullets." There was something I wanted to understand, though. "Soldiers," I said. "Two soldiers? You soldiers shoot they soldiers. They soldiers shoot you soldiers."

The pilot leaned forward, and I saw for the first time that there were metal rectangles hanging from the chain around her neck. They swung free and rattled together as the van's suspension imperfectly absorbed the unevenness of the road surface. One side of the rectangle was coloured in a blue and yellow pattern, the other had letters cut into its surface.

"So," she said. "Remember Petro's map? With all the different coloured countries? People – humans, that's what we call ourselves – organise themselves in different countries. And most people are happy with where they live, and if they're not, they move to a country they are happy with. I can't really explain what happy is. I can't even believe I'm having this conversation. The country to the north and east of this one has sent soldiers across the line that is supposed to divide the two countries, to take over this country. The people living in this country don't want the soldiers from the other country here, so we're trying to push them back across the border. It's… complicated."

I didn't understand as much as I could have done, but the broad implications were clear: I had landed in the disputed territory between two groups of people, both having soldiers fighting on behalf of their countries. Soldiers could therefore be seen as specialists at fighting, and killing the other country's soldiers as an aim. "Why Petro's father and brother shot? No soldiers."

"No," said the pilot. "No, they weren't. But they might have become soldiers. I suppose the thinking goes that it's easier to kill them before they're trained and get guns than afterwards." She held her head in her hands, although it didn't appear to have got suddenly heavier. "Where did they take the women and the children? Just the thought makes me want to puke."

"Women? Children?" I said.

She looked at my cameras through splayed fingers. "I don't even know how to begin." She pressed her hands against her head again. "I suppose we've got nothing better to do. Most animal species – most species – have a male and a female side. Side? I did engineering, I don't know this stuff well. The male – the man – provides half the genetic code, and the female – the woman – the other half to make a new human, but it's the woman who carries the young inside, and gives birth to them. The men have usually fucked off by that time. Sorry, that's unfair.

"In humans, the new… person, we call a baby, and it grows into a boy child or a girl child, and after about fifteen years, they reach adulthood and become a man or a woman. There are differences between us. The reproductive system, body fat, other things. Soldiers are usually men. Not me, of course." She looked away, out of the windows at the retreating landscape. "I don't know if that explains anything."

It did. Many of the animals I'd already catalogued came in two distinct but related forms, but it appeared that I'd only ever dissected the male version of people. The pilot was a female person, a woman. I didn't think she'd want to be dissected to advance my knowledge, but I could fill in most of the missing information from my previous studies on the furred four-legged animals. "Yes," I said.

She pushed her fingers through her hair – as I said, always moving, never still – and then brought her legs up to her torso.

"If," she said, "if you really are what we think you are, an alien robot from outer space, then this is a big deal for us. The biggest. I mean, it's ridiculous that I'm sitting in the back of a van with you. Once we get to either my airbase, or anywhere with senior officers, I'm never going to be allowed to get so much as within a hundred kilometres of you. I just wanted to tell you that it's not always like this: soldiers and shooting and shelling and fighting. You just got unlucky. Six months ago, landing where you did, none of this would have happened. Pretty much anywhere else on the planet isn't a war zone. Just here. Sorry."

That speech was mostly incomprehensible. There were too many unknown words, and too many complex concepts. I recorded it all, though, and would play it back periodically when I needed to check what she'd said against new information I'd been told. She had told me the truth. It became my baseline for detecting a lie. You lie all the time, to yourselves, to each other. It's a wonder anything ever gets done.

Uncle Georg drove on, along the road through the fields. We passed more cars. We also passed a green-painted van that was much bigger than Uncle Georg's. It had tall, wide tyres with deeply incised treads, and slanted, angular bodywork. "Armoured car," said the pilot, as it appeared in the rear windows. Then another. And another. All identical except for the markings on the rear.

"It's not going to be enough," she said. "We're slow, we're undermanned, we're still pretending this isn't really happening. But if we go full-out on them, they're ready to pour across the border and do what the hell they like. Which is what they're doing at the moment, just more slowly." She looked at me. "You. You could make a difference. In all sorts of ways."

The second of the armoured cars exploded. The third in line swerved violently around it and came to a halt. Green-clad soldiers threw open the doors at the rear of the vehicle and jumped out, running over to where flames and smoke were now pouring out between buckled metal plates. The pilot pressed her face to the glass. "Fuck no. Where did that come from?"

Then she banged on the side of the van with her hand, repeatedly and vigorously. "Stop. Stop the van, Georg." Georg had seen what had happened to the armoured car, and didn't think that stopping was the best thing to do. He thought speeding up was the better option. "There's a plane up there, Georg. There's a plane up there. We have to get off the road."

I pointed my camera out of the window. I couldn't see anything, but I had a limited field of vision. "No plane?" I said.

"It's there. It's definitely there. The road is almost straight, and we're a sitting duck." She slapped her hand against the van's panels again. "Georg, stop!" The engine was making such a noise now that I doubted she could have heard her voice.

I bored a hole in the roof of the van, and deployed a camera through it. I looked at all of the sky in infrared, assuming that the machine had engines that would run hot, like the car engine. I found a bright spot in the distance ahead of us, tracking across our path. "Plane," I said.

The pilot gave up striking the side of the van. "If Georg won't stop, we have to hope it's after the armoured cars, the poor bastards, and not us."

"Us?" I asked.

"You killed their soldiers and brought down their helicopter. If they know you're in this van... this is stupid. We need to get out of this big white target right now. Just in case." She looked back out the window at the rising column of smoke from the armoured car. "Where's the plane now?"

I used my manipulator to point: I knew left, right, up, down, front and back, and side. "Right side, back." She twisted her head to try and see it for herself. "Maybe they're not after us at all. Maybe it's reached its endurance. Maybe it's heading back to base." I tracked the plane – a machine that flew quickly compared with the helicopter – as it made a long, wide turn. I projected its trajectory based on its current movements, and came to a conclusion. "Plane shoot us."

The pilot kicked at the rear doors, behaviour which seemed odd, considering there were two handles she could have used to open them. She made her voice as loud as it would go: "Stop the van!" and when Uncle Georg continued to drive as fast as he could, she opened one door. The road surface was a blur of black-grey, and the vegetation at the edges of the fields was indecipherable.

"If it fires on us, you have to jump," she said. "Jump clear of the van."

I judged the speed we were doing, and the amount of damage I'd take. "No jump," I said, my safety protocol overriding everything else. My camera caught that the heat signature of the plane increased in intensity briefly, and a source separated itself out from it. The second source moved very fast, and it was closing the distance to the van rapidly.

I withdrew my camera from the hole in the roof and lasered the left side of the compartment off in one quick cut. Then I threw myself at it, knocking it free, and curled my legs around my body. I pulled in all my sensors, and tried to turn myself into as much of a spherical object as I could. I struck the ground hard, and I bounced. The rocket struck the front of the van.

I felt the heat first, then the pressure wave from the

explosion. I rolled and bounced, collided with solid objects and kept on rolling. My control system was recording severe accelerations and stresses. There was nothing I could do to mitigate them. I eventually came to a halt, and stayed perfectly still. I could hear the plane's engines roaring overhead then dropping in pitch and fading. I held up a camera, and watched its smoky trail disappear into the atmospheric haze.

I uncurled. The van – what was left of it – was burning. I was halfway across a field, and the leg joint that had been damaged by the bullet had failed. I was robust, but my makers hadn't anticipated me throwing myself out of a moving van as it was hit by an explosive rocket. I examined it carefully, to see if there was an easy fix, but there was nothing I could do. I still had three legs I could use.

I went back to the road. It was difficult to walk. I had to make considerable adjustments to my gait. But I was mostly functioning. The fence between me and the road was still intact. I cut through it and climbed awkwardly down the slight slope. There was debris spread across the black surface, parts that I could recognise from the books I'd read. Glass from the headlights. Pieces of the front bumper and an almost-intact piece of the bodywork from the front right side.

Fuel had spilled out, and was on fire. It had flowed to the edges of the road, and some of the grass there was burning too. The top of the cab had vanished, everything down as far as the dashboard missing. Uncle Georg still sat in the driver's seat, but his head had gone. He was on fire too, as was the rest of the cab, including the passenger seat where Petro would have been sitting.

I limped on. The back of the van had been ripped off and cast onto the side of the road. The shape of it warped and the glass was broken. I lifted it up to see if the pilot was underneath. She wasn't, so I walked back down the road. With my radio gone, I had no way of communicating with anyone now, but I could still hear. My microphones are solid-state vibration sensors, and quite durable.

I found the pilot, and she was still alive. The explosion had thrown her clear of the van, through the hole I'd made moments earlier. It had also damaged her lungs and her ears and nose, because red fluid was seeping out of her orifices, and she was struggling to breath. She saw me stand over her – I think she lacked the ability to turn her head – and she bared her teeth at me. Her mouth moved as if she was speaking, but she didn't have enough air in her lungs to vocalise the words.

She managed to move one of her hands to her neck. She hooked her thumb around the chain there, and dragged it hard enough to make the chain snap. Her fingers were shaking, and she was having trouble controlling them. One of the metal rectangles fell back on her torso, and she held the other out to me. I took it from her, and her hand, still twitching, fell back to her side. It stopped moving, and so did she. I listened for her heart, but I could hear nothing.

Having already identified herself as the unexamined half of a sexually dimorphic species, I should have taken the opportunity to dissect her. I didn't. There was a high probability that the plane, or another, would come back and attempt to target me again. There appeared to be little doubt that I was now being actively hunted by the non-green soldiers. I needed to hide, and carry out what repairs I could to my damaged leg before proceeding. Uncle Georg's garage would have been ideal, but it was too far to travel, and back towards danger.

The piece of aerobrake fabric I'd used to carry cargo had become detached. I fixed it back on. I took the map and the compass from the pilot and stored them. I considered taking the gun, but rejected that as impractical: I couldn't hold it properly, and the recoil would make it difficult to control. I examined the metal rectangle the pilot had worn. One side had a pigmented yellow and blue picture. The other had letters stamped into the smooth metal surface. Boichenko Y. A+. I presumed it meant something significant, as handing it to me had been her last conscious act.

I repaired the broken chain by fusing the end links together, and put it in with the rest of my cargo. The van was still burning, and parts of it were still scattered across the road. Petro and Uncle Georg, and now the pilot, were all dead. I had no one to talk to and no one to follow, so I was back to my original state of exploring and sampling, with the complicating factor of soldiers trying to destroy me.

I weighed up the various and competing circumstances. Self-preservation won out. I would need to evade the soldiers as a priority, but I would also need a safe environment in which to operate. The pilot had indicated that she could offer me that. I didn't know where that might be, any more than I knew where Maria and the kids were. I'd have to try and find it for myself.

I raised a camera and scanned the fields for cover. There was a structure, more garage than house, two fields away. I started towards it, slowly.

TEN

The structure was made from slices of wood, joined to a more substantial square-profile wood frame. There were no doors, just a high opening into the inside. Halfway up, there was another floor, on which were stacked machine-gathered cuboid blocks of dried grasses. Below were odd-shaped pieces of oxidised metal and a pile of identical soft plastic containers. I cut into one and sampled the contents: it was high in nitrogen, and came in small, pressed-powder grains.

I wanted to be hidden from observers while I repaired myself, so I fired my grapple into the roof beams and pulled myself up to the next level. There was a device, a set of parallel wooden bars set in a frame, leading up, but I didn't think it would take my weight, and it would be awkward to climb. It was made for you, not me.

Once up on the platform, I spent a few moments rearranging the blocks of grass so that they formed a wall at the edge. There was room behind in which I could work unseen. The yellow grass stems seemed to want to escape from their binding, and littered the rough wood. I was going to have to be careful not to get them stuck to me when I used the glue.

I put my leg into a neutral position, bent but not excessively so, as if I was standing naturally. I then accessed the glue dispenser and injected precise quantities where my schematics indicated it ought to go. I hardened these with an ultraviolet light, and repeated the application, slowly building up the layers so that they laminated together, stronger than the material it was joining, but more brittle.

This took time. Time in which the primary approached the horizon, and the sky began to darken. But it was a sky in which

Mother was due to appear, so I compressed all the information I was going to send and stored it in the buffer. There was a lot of it, and I wanted to make sure that everything was uploaded in the brief window that I had. The situation on the ground was difficult, and I didn't know if I'd have another opportunity.

I finished off the glue with a coat of protective self-setting foam, and stood stock still while it cured. That's when you – other people – started coming. Two, then three more, then three more after that. They'd walked through the forests and across the fields like I had, and avoided the roads, as I should have done, and now that it was almost night they were looking for shelter. The structure I was in was one of the few immediately visible.

I could hear them down below, talking, exchanging names and the places they'd come from. I recognised many from the pilot's map, and they were in a broad sweep through the high lands where I'd landed and to the north of there. More came: I counted their voices, listened to their words. Fifteen, sixteen, seventeen. It became properly dark, and one or two light sources were deployed intermittently. They didn't stay on long, because they didn't want to alert soldiers to their presence.

Someone climbed the wooden bars up to where I was. I heard the creaking. They got to the top, and started to shuffle around, scraping their feet against the floor. They moved to where I could see them, a hot infrared body covered in cooler fabric, but they couldn't see me. They went between me and the wall of dried grasses, and called down, "Ready?" If they'd taken a step back, they would have walked into me.

They pushed against one of the blocks, and tipped it until it fell over the edge, landing hard against the compacted soil floor. They worked their way along the line until they'd pushed three over, then came back for the next row. "Enough?" they asked, then climbed back down to the ground. I was now completely exposed to view, but human eyes don't work well in low-light conditions, and I remained unseen.

I extended one of my cameras, aware that shifting my weight

would alert those below to my presence. I had no means of communicating my intentions, unless one of them had a radio or other communications device I could speak through. And while I could modulate my broadcast frequency to some extent, I didn't have anything close to a broad spectrum. My transmitters were for pushing information towards Mother, and not designed for other purposes.

They talked in low, quiet voices, for probably the same reasons they didn't show many lights. Someone cut through the binding on the grass blocks and distributed it about, making long oval patches of it, which the smaller of them – no, these were children, immature and not fully grown – were then encouraged to lie down on. Some complied straight away, and others refused, confronting the adults with the lack of food or what they called 'proper beds'.

There were more women than men in the group, as far as I could tell. And more children than both. Some of the children were asking where their mother and father were, so I decided that this was not a related group of people, rather a number of individuals that had banded together for safety. Although, I couldn't quite see what they could do against guns and helicopters and rockets fired from planes. Perhaps it was a natural, social instinct that bound them together.

The children eventually settled and were mostly still, except that they moved in their sleep. The eight adults moved away slightly, and sat on the ground, continuing to talk. There was the occasional flash of light from a phone, and some of the women would take turns to sit near the children. They would touch them if they woke, and whisper to them.

One by one, the adults grew quiet, with one or two awake at any time. I continued to watch them, observe, make records. At a later time, one of them, a woman, who wore loose-fitting fabrics to accommodate a large low mass on the front of her torso began to cry out, like some of the children had. She was spoken to and held, and she became quiet. I could see her, though: I could see her brighten in the infrared, and hear her breathe hard and rhythmically.

She gave up stifling her voice, and made a sound that woke everyone. One of the other women said, "This is happening, now, and we can't stop it." I didn't know what it was then. The children were moved to the far end of the structure, and some of the adults went with them. The rest of them stood around, and it was clear that they didn't know what they should do.

The men were told to leave the immediate area. The women who remained piled up straw behind the lying-down woman and lifted up the fabric covering her torso. Her skin was taut and bulbous, a clearly defined mass that lay below the bones protecting the major organs and above where the legs attached to the body. She was lifted on to a rectangle of cloth arranged over the straw, and her leg clothes removed. Someone held her hands, and counted the time between her cries.

This went on for a while. After a hurried conversation which involved a lot of fast, sharp hand gestures, the two men left the structure at a run. I didn't know where they were going, because there didn't appear to be anywhere they could get to quickly. Some of the children began to cry too, because the woman was crying. The planet turned, and the sky began to show pink with refracted light.

The woman's voice grew weaker as the inside of the structure grew lighter. The men hadn't come back. I heard the others talking, saying they weren't even sure the men had got to where they needed to go. The woman was dying, and so was her baby. She needed a hospital. She needed a doctor. She needed a caesarean. I didn't know what a hospital or a doctor or a caesarean were, but the pilot had explained what a baby was. I worked out that for one reason or another, your normal reproductive cycle had failed at this final stage.

I'd already dissected male and female furred animals. I knew that their internal structure mapped well onto your own. I knew the differences between male and female in those species, and presumed that those would also be present in you. It appeared that I was the only one present who knew these things, because surely you would have intervened at an earlier stage.

I fired my grapple into the roof again, and lowered myself down in amongst them. Everyone made a great deal of noise. Some ran to cover the children with their bodies. Some, when they had stopped making that high-pitched sound from deep inside them, stood between me and the woman with the not-yet baby.

"What do you want?" one of them asked. I couldn't tell her. But I noticed that there was a phone lying on the dried yellow grass behind her. I lurched forward – I hadn't quite learned how to compensate for my fixed-position leg yet – and picked it up with one of my manipulators. I examined it: there was a prominent button on the face of it, and I pressed it. The screen lit up with numbers and a square nine-dot pattern. I didn't know what the pattern meant, and I held it towards her.

She dragged her finger across the screen, specifically up and down and left and right, and gave it back. Her hands were shaking so much that she almost couldn't complete the task. I looked at the phone, at the little pictograms. I touched one, and I could suddenly see through the phone. I turned it over and there was a camera lens on the back. That wasn't what I wanted. There was symbol at the bottom right of the screen, a pointer that started going right before bending back around to the left. I touched it, and the screen reverted to what it looked like before.

There was a pictogram that looked just like the radio I had before. I touched it, but couldn't make it work. Something about 'earphones not connected. Earphones function as radio aerial.' I wasn't sure what that meant. I pressed the arrow button again. I looked again. One of the other pictograms might have been a page from a book. I touched it, and saw writing. There was a green symbol, which I pressed, and suddenly, I saw the letters you used to write your language.

I dabbed out 'apple'. I turned the screen to the woman, and

she said "Apple? What do you want? Can't you see she's in labour?"

I wrote 'woman baby' and showed her the phone again.

"Yes, she's trying to have a baby. She's not doing very well."

I wrote 'woman baby die', and she said nothing at all. I moved over to the woman on the ground. She was too weak to stop me from touching her, although everyone else all shouted "Don't touch her."

I felt her heartbeat. I felt the baby's heartbeat. Both were fast and shallow, like her breathing. She looked up at me, and I don't think she knew quite what she was seeing. I typed 'help her help baby' and held it up.

"What are you?" someone asked, and I wrote 'alien robot from outer space', because that was what Petro had called me.

I didn't know that I could feel silence. But I did then. I looked down at the woman again. She was excreting water through the pores of her skin, but her surface temperature was below what I believed was normal. 'help me help her help baby' I typed. The woman I'd first talked to turned to one of the others and said "What is going on?" and she replied "She's going to die soon if someone doesn't do something" and the first woman said, "We can't do anything. She needs to get to a hospital."

'hospital' I typed.

"It's... it's a building. They... make people better. Well. Whole."

I took out my map and opened it up, laying on the ground. 'hospital' I typed again. She crouched down and her finger hovered over the map.

"Here," she said, "there's a hospital here."

I used my manipulator to indicate our current position. 'here' I wrote.

"They'll never make it back in time, even if they find an ambulance willing to come out this far," said one of the others. "We have to do something or she's going to die."

"We've got nothing," she said in reply. "Nothing that'll help.

She needs that baby cutting out of her. I'm sorry."

I typed again 'help me help her help baby'. I deployed my dissecting tools – blades, lasers, probes, close-up cameras. I could cut the baby out. It wouldn't be difficult. Keeping the woman alive would be. Her pain receptors would tell her she was being cut open, and her eyes would tell her an alien robot was doing the cutting.

I listened to the paired heartbeats again. They were becoming fainter. She was dying, her and her baby. Biological death was permanent and irreversible. I'd asked for help, but apparently there was no help being offered. I would have to guess at several decisions. At least I knew that cutting the baby out was a viable option.

I lowered my blade towards her distended skin, and someone came at me with a length of wood to batter me. I put three precisely-spaced laser holes through it and snapped it in half before it even made contact with my carapace.

'Help me' I typed. If I didn't start now, I would be too late.

They looked at me, still holding the charred end of the stick. "You'll kill her," she said, and I typed 'mother die baby die'. For the want of the appropriate prepositions, I was losing the battle to communicate.

Then one of the women gave in. I don't know why. She got down on your knees and pointed low on the bulge, down towards the legs. "Here," she said. "My sister had one, a few years ago. I was with her in the operating theatre. Cut here. Only just long enough to get the baby out. No more than that. And nowhere here." She indicated the smaller bulge that I knew was usually an indentation in the centre of the stomach area. "I can't believe I'm even telling you this." She said to the other women, "hold her."

My blades were very thin and very quick. I cut through the skin and fat. There was less circulatory fluid than I thought there'd be, and I was now looking at the layer of muscle underneath. I sliced through that, and it contracted of its own accord. There was a thin sack behind, and the clear outline of a small person inside it. It was moving slightly, although how much of that was due to the mother straining against the hands that held her down, I couldn't tell.

I pinched the sack, punctured it, and elongated the slit. There was the baby, bursting out almost. It had a ridiculously sized head in comparison to the rest of its body, grossly out of proportion. I grasped it by the shoulders and pulled it away, only to discover it was still attached at the same point the adults had the indentation in their torso. The tube of flesh was long, thick and red. I didn't know what to do.

The baby wriggled in my manipulators. It made a noise, and someone took it from me.

"Cut the cord," she said. "You have to cut the cord here," and she indicated by putting the cord inside two closing fingers.

I looked at the tube that was still pulsing. I looked inside the sack, and there was a mass, deep red, almost black, attached to the side of it. If I'd manage to read a manual on this as I had the cars, it would have been much more straightforward.

The baby made more noise, a strange wet sound that it repeated over and over. And just like that, the fluid flow in the cord began to slow. I could cut it with the laser. The heat would seal the open tubes. I defocussed it and turned the power low, and held the cord taut between two manipulators wound around it. The surface layers charred under the beam, and what liquid there was solidified almost immediately.

The cord separated, and I slowly released my grip. Nothing deleterious happened to either mother or baby. The baby kept crying, and the mother was mostly unresponsive now. I studied the incisions I'd made. Glue. I'd use glue. It seemed the obvious solution. I pushed the other end of the cord back inside the membrane, and gathered the edges together. I put strands of glue from one side of the cut to the other, making sure that the glue took the strain.

Now that the baby was out, there was a lot of space inside. I didn't know what I was supposed to do about that. I presumed that the body would self-repair, so I just carried on pinching and gluing, using my ultraviolet light to fix the adhesive in place and moving along. I didn't know whether or not it was biologically stable, or compatible. It was inert on me, and that was all I knew. I had nothing else to use.

I glued the muscles together, and worked my way back up to the skin, which was no longer tight, but loose. This presented its own difficulties, but I managed to accurately join the edges of my initial cut, and cover it in a scaffolding of glue. I didn't know how well it would continue to adhere, but if it was undisturbed, then it should stay in place.

I had finished. The baby was pressing its face against one of the fatty protrusions on the mother's ventral side. It was quiet, and the mother was still alive, for now. I didn't know what would happen next. I decontaminated my instruments and stored them away, and passed the phone back to one of the women. She took it and clutched it in both hands.

"What are you? Where did you come from?" she asked.

I'd already given them the answer. Either they didn't understand it, or couldn't believe it. That was going to be a pattern that repeated itself. I fired my grapple into the roof again, and wound myself up to the upper level, where I sat, watching over the people below.

ELEVEN

The men came back. They brought with them three others who wore bright orange clothes and carried big bags. Outside, it was properly light. The children had been allowed to leave the structure, although they were told to stay close, and they was always at least two of the women with them at all times. Those inside sat near the mother and baby. Both were still alive.

The men and the women talked about what had happened. They pointed up to where I stood, and one of the men picked up the map that I'd left and folded it up, slowly, looking up at me. The people in orange – two men, one woman – looked up at me as well, while someone recounted what I'd done. How I'd lowered myself to the ground, how I'd used a phone to communicate, how I'd cut the mother open and pulled out her baby. How I'd glued her back together again.

The woman in orange knelt next to the mother, and uncovered her now-slack lower torso. She pressed down in various places, feeling what lay beneath. She then took the sleeping baby from the mother, and laid it on a square of fabric. She used a device to listen to its heart and its lungs, she inserted a tube into the lower of the external openings of digestive system. She looked up at me again, then passed the baby back.

The two men in orange went back outside for a moment, and brought in a large rectangular piece of fabric suspended between two metal tubes. They laid it down next to the mother, and carefully moved her onto it. Then they each took opposite ends of the poles and lifted her up. With a woman either side of the mother, they carried her out into the daylight.

One of the remaining women went outside and called loudly to all the children, while the woman in orange repacked her bag.

She kept on looking up at me, and when she'd finished and closed her bag, she started towards the wooden bars that extended between the ground and the upper level. One of the men tried to prevent her, but she exerted dominance and carried on. She climbed up, and raised only her head above the level of the platform.

"Hello," she said.

I couldn't respond, as I had nothing to respond with. But she had what looked like a pencil in a small pouch on the front of her orange fabric. She climbed up higher, and knelt on the wood just next to the top of the bars.

"Hello?" she said again. "Can you hear me?"

I moved a manipulator towards her, and she started to jerk back towards the drop. I wrapped the manipulator around her arm to prevent her falling, and used another to take the pencil from her.

It wasn't a pencil, but it was analogous. I inspected it, and saw what looked like a reservoir of pigment inside a clear plastic tube, closed at one end by a metal part with a tiny ball embedded in it. There was a button on one end. I pressed it, and the metal piece moved out and stayed out. The woman in orange didn't move for a moment. I pressed the button again, and the metal end of the pigment tube retracted back inside the outer sleeve. I pressed it for a third time, and it popped out again.

She reached slowly inside the pouch I'd taken the pencil-analogue from and pulled out a thin book: it had several lined pages joined with a tight spiral of wire. She held it out to me, and I took it, leafing through the pages until I found the first blank one. I held the book still against the platform, and made an exploratory mark with the pencil. The line I drew was black and initially oily. That quickly evaporated away to leave a solid line of pigment.

'hello' I wrote. She looked at the word, looked at me, looked at the word. "Can you speak?" she asked. 'radio' I wrote. She moved her head up and down. I'd seen others do that: it meant agreement. "The ambulance drivers have a radio, but they'll need to keep hold of it. I'll try and find you one. What sort of radio do you need?"

I parsed her sentence, and drew a little picture of the radio I'd had, before the rocket had destroyed it, and the van, Petro, Uncle Georg and the pilot.

She moved her head up and down again. "That shouldn't be difficult," she said. "You operated on the pregnant woman."

I wrote down 'operated' and 'pregnant'.

She looked at the words, and said, "Operated. You cut her open to try and help her. Pregnant is when a woman has a baby in her womb."

'yes' I wrote. I turned the page. 'help mother help baby' I wrote.

"Why did you help them?" she asked. "I mean, I'm grateful you did. It was good. But why did you do it?"

I didn't write anything down. I'd learnt a lot from cutting the woman and taking her baby out for her. I'd cut her open, and I'd glued her back together again. I had just done it. She and her baby would have died otherwise. I didn't know quite why that was something that I needed to do anything about. But I'd done it for that reason. 'mother baby die' I wrote down.

"Yes," said the woman. "Yes, they'd have both died. You left the placenta in."

'placenta' I wrote.

"The mass on the lining of the womb that connects the mother to the baby, and transfers blood and nutrients to it."

'yes' I wrote. 'help not help'.

You looked at the message. "If she hasn't expelled it by the time she reaches hospital, we'll have to perform a dee and cee. Honestly, it's the least of her problems. You did well," she said. "Where did you learn to do that?"

'bodies,' I wrote, 'bodies forest men village Petro father brother not Petro' I ran out of room on that line, and started another. 'soldiers shot men village not Petro'. She said nothing, so

I continued 'cut bodies not Petro'.

"Can you show me where this happened?" she asked.

I wrote 'yes map'. Just as I'd told the pilot.

She moved her head up and down again. "So where are you from?"

'alien robot from outer space' I wrote. 'not american' I added, for the avoidance of the next, inevitable question.

She looked at me, at every part of me, my carapace, my sensory apparatus, my legs, the aerobrake fabric fastened to my ventral side. "What happened to your leg?"

'soldiers shot leg'

"What happened to the soldiers?"

'soldiers dead'

"Did you kill them?"

'yes'.

She sat back and pressed her hand against her face, all the while looking at me. "Are you really from outer space?"

I turned to a new page. 'yes'.

She looked away, towards the outside where the children were. The men were by the doorway. "Well," she said, "this wasn't how it was meant to be. Do you have a spaceship?"

'spaceship' I wrote.

"A... vehicle that brought you to our planet."

'yes sky'.

She looked down at the wooden platform we stood on. "Is it still in the sky?"

'yes'

She blew air out of her lungs in such a way as to make the skin covering the sides of her mouth expand. "We'd better get you away from here," she said. "It's not safe. They... the front's very fluid."

'plane shoot us rocket' I wrote. 'killed Petro Uncle Georg pilot van going to Maria and kids I jump'. I reached into my cargo pouch and brought out the rectangle of metal the pilot had given me as she died. I held it out to the woman, and she took it.

'pilot died' I wrote. 'Boichenko Y. A+'

"That was his name," she said, "and his blood group. A+."

'her' I wrote. 'pilot woman'.

"Her name," she said. "I'll make sure this gets to where it needs to go. I'm sorry, we're normally better than this. We don't want to fight."

She put the metal rectangle into the same place I'd taken the pencil-analogue from. She pushed the chain in after it.

"How do we get you down from here?" She pointed towards the ground.

I fired the grapple into the roof, and reeled in the cable so that I swung free off the edge of the platform, then lowered myself down to the dried grass-covered ground.

"Oh," she said, and she climbed down the parallel bars to join me at the bottom.

The men at the structure's entrance backed away as I descended, and they watched me from a distance as I walked outside. I was learning a new gait. It wasn't as fluid as before, but I could adjust my motion to take account of the immobilised joint. The children clustered around the women, their eyes wide and their mouths open as I followed the woman in orange. We started across the field in the direction of the road. I could see the roof of another white van stopped there, near to where Uncle Georg's van was.

"Do you have a name?" she asked.

I tried to write while walking, but it was difficult. I slowed right down and wrote 'robot'.

"Oh," she said. I wasn't sure what 'oh' meant. "I'm Natalia. I'm a doctor."

'hospital' I wrote. That was where the woman and the baby should have been, instead of a structure in the middle of a field.

"Yes, that's right," she said. "It's probably the safest place for you, too. For a little while, at least. How long have you been here?"

I didn't know how to answer that. I wrote down 'long' and

she pointed at the primary star in the sky.

"That's the sun," she said. "When it's up – when it's light, we call it day, and when it's not, we call it night. One cycle of day and night is also called a day. Sorry, that's a little bit confusing. A day lasts twenty four hours, and we measure that on a clock."

She was talking about measuring time. I drew a picture of the dial from the garage that performed that function. There were only twelve divisions on that, but I presumed that day-time and night-time could be differentiated by looking outside.

"Yes, that's a clock." She tugged at the fabric covering her arm and showed me her wrist. "When it's small like this, we called it a watch."

I consulted my own time-keeping counter, and was able to write out '2.2085 days'. I thought that was about right – I'd learnt a lot from the car books.

She looked at what I'd written. "Not long then. I'm just really sorry. Of all the places you could have landed, it had to be here."

There was a door in the corner of the field, made of welded metal tubes. She opened it so we didn't have to climb over, and closed it behind her. The roof of the white van was much closer. I could see the orange-covered men carrying the mother and baby leaving the field at the far end through another door.

"The ambulance is quite big inside. Whether it's going to be big enough is something we're about to find out. I don't want you to have to wait, and I definitely don't want you in a military transport."

I dutifully wrote 'military transport' down, and even though we were quite close to the road now, she stopped to explain.

"There are soldiers on both sides, ours and theirs. And while I think ours are better people, I'd rather – if you are what you say you are – you didn't end up in a base somewhere surrounded by razor wire and guns. You'd be safer at the hospital. With me and my colleagues."

We walked out on to the road. I looked past the white ambulance, with its blue symbols on the side, and a red one on the roof, to the burnt-out remains of Uncle Georg's van. It had stopped burning, and was surrounded now by the pale dust of combustion. The metal was orange and white and grey, and the tyres had completely gone. It looked like the car had done when I'd disassembled it, all parts.

Natalia wanted me to stand at the back of the ambulance, to see if I could fit inside, along with her, the mother, the baby, the platform she was now lying on, and all the other devices that were arranged around the side of the internal walls. I passed a laser across it, measuring its dimensions and comparing it with various configurations that my frame could fit.

'no' I wrote.

She climbed up into the back with one of the orange men. Two of the other women were still by the ambulance doors, talking to the mother, although they were watching me. "What needs to go?" asked Natalia. "As a minimum, we need this trolley. Everything else is optional." She put her hand on a fixed platform covered with a soft shiny material. "What about this?"

"Doctor, you can't do that," said one of the men in orange, and Natalia leaned in close to his face before speaking.

"You take orders from me. We are bringing that back with us, even if everyone except her and it walk. Understand?" She pointed at, in order, herself, the man, me and the mother. "This is the most important thing either of us will ever do, even if we live to be a hundred. If it means gutting this ambulance back to the bare walls, that's what we're going to do. Yes?"

The man didn't answer.

"Yes?" she asked again.

He moved his head up and down, slowly.

"Good," she said. "I'll look after her, you go and sit in the front." She reached out and took the heavy rectangular block attached to the man's side. "And I need this," she said. "Don't argue."

The orange man walked quickly to the front of the van, and closed the door hard enough to make the rear shake. Natalia pressed buttons on the black rectangle, then held it out to me.

"This is a shortwave radio. The channels are here on this dial, the volume is this one here: all the way anticlockwise for off. Give it a go." I took the radio from her and inspected it. I set up a carrier wave and chased it across the frequencies until I found it.

"Hello" I said.

Natalia bared her teeth at me. "You can talk! Now, come on, we've spent too long in the open. If you're spotted, that red cross will mean nothing."

I measured the walls again, imaged the inside, and the only practical solution, given my leg, was that yes, almost everything had to go. "Everything," I said.

She looked at me. "Sure?"

"Everything," I repeated.

I started at the back, reaching into the containers and undoing the bolts and screws that fastened them to the van's walls. Natalia lifted them out, one by one, and put them in a line on the side of the road. The platform I lasered out, cut up again into smaller pieces, and carried them myself to the growing pile of parts.

"Stop," I said, and started to climb in.

It was awkward, in that the mother and baby were in the middle of the van, and I had to straddle them. I moved forward by increments, lifting my carapace up over the trolley and the mother. Last of all, I picked up my damaged leg, and swung it into position, behind the inside of the rear door. The only equipment left was that bolted to the front bulkhead.

Natalia closed one van door, pushed her bag on, and pulled the other behind her as she crawled in on her hands and knees. She moved like that past the trolley to the front, and opened a glass window in the partition.

"Drive. Not too fast, but put on the lights. Don't stop for anything except roadblocks." She left the window open, and I could see the driver turn in his seat and look over his shoulder into the back of the van. "Drive now," Natalia said, and crawled back underneath me to examine the mother.

The engine started, and the van began to move, slowly picking up speed. There wasn't much room between the roof – I was pressed against it – and the ventral side of my carapace. My cargo carrier hung down until it almost touched the mother's face, and Natalia had to lift it out of the way as she listened to first the baby's torso, then the mother's.

"You're doing fine," she said. She took one of the mother's wrists and pressed two of her fingers against the skin on the inside. One of the major fluid-carrying tubes ran through there, and I knew she'd be able to work out how quickly the heart was pumping. She looked at her watch while she measured, and her lips moved in silent vocalisation. When she'd done, she asked, "When was the last time you ate anything?"

"Yesterday. Morning." The mother's voice was very quiet. The baby was quiet too, snuffling and grunting against – his – mother. The baby had male parts. It was a boy, like Petro, and after fifteen years would become a man, like Uncle Georg.

"Okay," said Natalia. "I'm going to put you on a drip. Glucose, saline, nothing complicated."

She opened her bag, and took out a plastic bubble, inside which was another plastic bubble filled with a clear liquid. She moved the mother's arm around until she could access the place she needed. She opened another packet, put on thin, translucent coverings on each hand, another packet, fabric to wipe the skin with, another packet, a fine, hollow tube, which she slowly pushed into the skin until the tube was all but hidden inside the mother's arm.

She used pre-glued fabric pieces to hold the tube in place, and finally connected the fluid bubble to a long clear hose. "Can you hold this?" she said to me. "It needs to be higher than the cannula."

I took the bubble from her by the loop of plastic at the top and held it out to one side, between my carapace and the ambulance's side. When I'd done that, and she had checked I'd done it, she let some of the liquid escape down the hose, then pushed it onto the receptacle on the open end of the tube.

"That'll give you more energy, and replace some of the fluids you've lost. Now, have you thought of a name for your baby?" Natalia took the hand coverings off with a snap, and started to collect together the empty packets she'd dropped onto the floor.

The mother whispered "Robert," she said. "Like robot. Only Robert."

TWELVE

The windows in the back of the ambulance showed a receding landscape of tall trees, short trees and fields, punctuated by small collections of houses no bigger than Petro's village. The columns of smoke in the distance became indistinct, and there were a few cars on the road. The cars travelling in the direction from which the ambulance had come went by without stopping, but those going along the same half of the road slowed down to allow us to pass. Natalia told me that vehicles with special lights on the roof had priority on the road.

We also saw a long line of big green vans. They'd stopped just outside one of the villages, and people I assumed were soldiers were standing all around, their guns over their shoulders and pointing at the sky. Many of them had the white tubes as thick as a pencil in their mouths, and blueish smoke hung around their heads.

Most of them were men, and some of them looked like Petro, like boys. They were all wearing the same green fabric, and there had been little allowance for the natural variation in height or weight. The smallest ones seemed to disappear, while the tallest ones strained the joins where one piece of fabric attached to the next.

Natalia watched them too, and when we'd left them behind she breathed in hard through her nose, dislodging some of the mucus inside, and used her fingers to wipe the excess lubricating fluid that had escaped her eyes. "We're almost there," she said. "Another five minutes and we'll be at the hospital. Now. I want you to stay in the ambulance until we deal with Nadia and little Robert: I'll take them inside and hand them over to my colleagues. When I've done that, I'll need to get you in the building too. But I don't know the best way to play this."

"Play?" I asked.

"Which scenario will work out best," she said. "There are too many unknowns to predict the outcome. So I'm going to put both of them to you, and you can decide. First, is that you go in through the back door, unseen by most people, and we hide you inside while I talk to the director and he talks to the government. The chances are, if we do that, soldiers will surround the hospital to stop you from being attacked, and you'll get to meet lots of important people very quickly.

"The second is that you walk in the front door where everyone can see you. You'll be viewed by some with fascination, and others with fear. Everyone will know you're here, and it'll take longer for you to meet the prime minister and the president. But no one will be able to say you don't exist, which, in the first case, is what might happen. You could be kept in isolation away from the rest of the world until they choose, if ever, to tell anyone.

"I don't know what you want to do. I don't know anything about you. I don't know how intelligent you are, how much self-awareness you have, or whether you want to get involved with us or not. I don't know why you came or where you came from, or whether you plan to destroy us all when you've learnt enough about us – though we seem to be doing a pretty good job of that without you. My biggest fear is that they take you away and never let you see the light of day again. You helped Nadia give birth to a healthy baby boy when no one else could, and you managed to take enough care not to kill her in the process. That has to be worth something. But it's your choice: front door or back door."

I recorded her speech, and replayed it through several times, building layers of meaning and identifying the points of conflict and ambiguity. We arrived at the hospital, and my radio crackled and hissed as other transmitters came and went, leaving short, cryptic messages to their listeners.

Natalia told me: "Wait here," and opened the rear doors.

The driver and the other orange man walked around the back and pulled Nadia's trolley out from underneath me. Wheels folded out from the bottom of the trolley, and, holding on to the nearly-empty plastic bubble, they pushed her away out of sight. Natalia zipped up her bag and took it with her.

"This could take a little while. I need to talk with the other doctors about what you did, and they'll need to run tests to see whether they need to open Nadia up again." She patted my leg. "You still did a good thing. Thank you."

She closed the doors again, and left me to consider my position. I checked with my programming, my protocols and my internal decision-making apparatus. Where I found myself was far beyond the usual choices I had been expecting to make — whether to go uphill or downhill, sample this region or that, travel to examine a distant prominent geographic landmark or stay where I was. I had met sentient life — some of whom had tried to destroy me, and some had tried to take me to safety.

Staying with the people who didn't want to damage me was clearly a better option. Even then, I was being offered two scenarios: safety in isolation, or potential danger in amongst their society. I could leave them all, but I thought back to the map Petro had shown me. The entire landmass of the planet had been claimed by different groups of people. They were clearly the dominant life-form, and in order to carry out my mission and transmit further data to Mother, I needed their cooperation.

But I didn't want to be sequestered, away from external input, and only allowed access to a limited range of stimuli. I wanted to experience everything that was present, and I was prepared to trade off the potential risk to achieve that goal. It seemed to be the case that the more people were exposed to my presence, the less likely they were to harm me. I would still have to be careful of those who wanted me destroyed, but staying with those who had offered their protection would significantly decrease that possibility.

I appeared to have reached a decision. I ran through the

arguments again, and came to the same conclusion. I would, for now, stay with Natalia in the hospital, but I would enter through the front doors. I waited for her to return, which she eventually did, but not before I'd opened up the panels at the far end of the compartment and sampled the pressured gasses from their containers.

She opened one door, partially, and looked up at me. "It's me," she said, redundantly.

My recognition of people's faces was far better than it had been at the beginning, when you were all just slight variations on a single theme.

"Have you decided what you want to do?"

I said, "front door," and she moved her head up and down in agreement.

"I thought you'd say that. And, I think, it's going to be for the best. I've some people who'd like to meet you."

She opened the door fully, and then the other one. There were twenty seven people standing behind the ambulance, a short distance away. They had different coloured fabric coverings, in green or dark blue or light blue or orange. Natalia stood to one side and gestured for me to get out. I put my damaged leg down onto the road surface, and I slowly worked my way out until I was able to stand at rest at the rear of the vehicle.

The people said nothing. Some of them put their hands to their mouths. Others held them against their torsos. Other than that, they didn't move.

"Say hello," said Natalia.

I held up the radio and said "hello, people".

The people looked at each other, but still said nothing. A man then stepped forward, and did what Uncle Georg had done: he walked around me, looking at me from every angle. When he reached his starting position, he said to Natalia. "Are you absolutely sure?"

"No," she said. "But I can't explain it any other way." She said to me: "Tell the people where you come from."

I responded, "outer space."

The people looked at each other again, and the man at Natalia. "That's not conclusive," he said. "Perhaps it's American."

"Not American," I said, and he leaned back holding the lower part of his face.

"How much do you understand?"

I thought about that. "Not much," I replied. "Two days landed."

"Two days? Well." He showed his teeth to me, and made his breath come out in short bursts. "Welcome to Earth, then."

"Earth?" I said.

"Earth. It's what we call the planet," he said. Then, to Natalia, "What are you going to do with it?"

She looked at the man. "I wasn't going to do anything with it. I've invited it to come into the hospital, and it's said yes."

"That's not what hospitals are for, Natalia."

"They've already tried to destroy it twice."

"Three," I said, and she stopped and looked at me.

"Three times, then. The hospital was the safest place for it I could think of. For the moment, at least. If you've a better idea, I'd like to hear it."

"Can't you just let the army deal with it?" he said.

"No. This is too important to let them screw this up. Surely you can see that?"

"You want to screw this up yourself?"

"I'm going to see the director."

"Once you've got it inside the building, though?"

"Yes." Natalia exerted her dominance and put her fingertips on the man's upper torso, pushing him off-balance. "Don't get in my way, Lev."

The man called Lev had to take a step back to stay standing up. He showed Natalia his palms, a gesture of subordination. "Then don't be a bitch about this. Kovalenko will toss you down the nearest waste chute if you try it on with him."

"I'll deal with him. Some support would be nice, Lev.

Considering everything."

Lev looked at Natalia, then looked at the ground between them. He turned around and produced a loud sound by striking his open hands together repeatedly. "Come on you lot. We've still got work to do, patients to see, lives to save. We've seen the alien, now back inside."

Most of the twenty seven people didn't go back inside, even when Lev started walking away around the ambulance. Natalia pressed her lips together, and only when Lev had gone on alone, she stepped in the same direction.

"Come on, then. Let's get you under cover."

I began to follow her, and so did everyone else. The doors to the hospital were just the other side of the ambulance, and Lev had already entered.

The doors opened automatically, sensors on top of the doors using infrared to check for Natalia's body heat. I walked through: the doors tried to close on me, not recognising me as a person, but someone behind me stepped up and stood close enough to the sensor for the doors to open again. Inside were lots of places for people to sit, and lots of doors. A long corridor stretched away into the distance, and at the very start of that were two people in blue behind a low flat platform.

Lots of the people sitting were now standing, and walking backwards away from me, even the ones with obviously damaged legs who were using wooden or metal sticks to stop themselves from falling over. The two women behind the platform also stood, but couldn't go anywhere because of the wall behind them. The large room, which had been noisy and full of movement a moment before, became very still and quiet.

Natalia slowed for a moment to allow me to catch up, and then walked on. She increased her stride length as we headed for the corridor. As we passed the platform, I noticed that there were two phone-like screens on it, one in front of each woman, along with a rectangular board with letters and numbers, and an odd curved device which had a light at one end, and a wire coming out of the other.

I stopped and extended a manipulator. There was another glowing light underneath the device, together with a sensor. I examined the dorsal side, found the two pressure-actuators and the small rubber wheel, then placed it back on the rectangular piece of rubber I'd picked it up from. Something moved on the screen, and I nudged the device again. A white arrow edged across and stuck to the furthest right side. I moved it back – inexpertly, as the upper surface was shaped exactly for the palm of a person's hand – and the arrow glided leftwards.

I pressed the left actuator, and nothing happened. I pressed the right one, and a white box immediately appeared on the screen, with words down the left of it. The arrow moved across the first item, and another box appeared.

"Large icons" I said, "medium icons".

Natalia applied pressure to one of my legs. "I'll get you a computer of your own," she said. "Let the nurses get back to work."

I let go of the device. "Patients to see, lives to save," I said, and followed her into the corridor.

Those that had come with me and Natalia into the hospital waited next to the platform, and more of the people who'd been in the room joined them. They watched us as we stopped next to a set of metallic doors with no handles but two press-buttons on the wall. Natalia pressed the top-most button, which lit up. There were illuminated numbers above the doors, and the light moved from seven to six to five to four to three to two to one. I could feel air blow out from around the door, and heard machinery working. Noise came from the other side of the doors and, after a pause, they slid apart to reveal a large cuboid space, metal lined, with a brightly lit roof and a rubber floor.

"Into the lift, please" said Natalia, and it was quite big enough to accommodate me. She had put her hand on the side of the sliding door, presumably to stop it from closing on me as the other automatic doors had, and only let go once she was in the lift with me. There were more buttons, and she pressed the one marked 'seven'. The doors closed, and my accelerometer detected upward movement.

The number-counter cycled, and stopped at five, with the appropriate deceleration. The door opened, and a green-clothed man tried to push a person – a woman of great age – into the compartment with me and Natalia. The wheeled chair got as far as crossing the boundary between floor and lift before he looked up. He pulled the woman back, and opened his mouth.

No words came out, so I said "hello people" as I'd done at the back of the ambulance.

"Can you catch the next one?" said Natalia, and pressed the button marked seven again. The door slid shut after a few moments, and I felt the acceleration, coasting and deceleration again. The counter showed the symbol for seven, and the door opened.

"Okay," said Natalia, putting her hand against the side of the door as she had before, "out into the corridor."

I stepped out of the lift, and waited for her to join me. She walked ahead of me to the far end, where she stopped outside a closed door. The notification on the door said 'P Kovalenko Hospital Director'. Natalia pulled at her clothes, but I didn't know why. She took a deliberate breath, then opened the door.

She left me outside while she talked to the person inside. The conversation revolved around how important getting something called an appointment was, and how Natalia couldn't see the director without one. I didn't know what an appointment meant, whether it was some device that went over the eyes or not, but I couldn't work out why the director couldn't be seen otherwise. Natalia said that the matter was urgent and critical and of the utmost importance, but the appointment was necessary no matter what.

I looked around the door. There was another woman there. Both she and Natalia were standing facing each other and talking more loudly than the distance between them would otherwise dictate. I realised it was a dominance display: the other woman was trying to show her superiority over Natalia by refusing to consider her demand, and that the appointment was merely a piece of social behaviour to be negotiated, as opposed to a practical problem to be solved.

I watched them for a while. Natalia was calling through a second, closed, door, for the director to emerge and hear her in person, while the woman – who was not the director herself – insisted that Natalia mediate her approaches only through her. She saw the movement of my camera, and brushed past Natalia and out into the corridor.

She saw me, the whole of me, not just the camera. She stepped back into the room, walking backwards and not watching her path. She walked into Natalia, and she made a high-pitched noise as she did so. She executed a sudden leap to her left, and she held on to the platform on which were a computer, several piles of paper, and some devices I didn't recognise

Still without looking around, her hands found one of the devices. Her fingers felt along the row of buttons until she reached the last one, and she pressed it.

"Director? Director?"

Through the closed door came another voice, saying "What? What is it?"

"Could you step outside your office for a moment, Director?"

"I'm very busy. What is it?"

"Just..." Her finger slipped on the button, and she had to look at the device to reposition it. As soon as she'd done that, her head jerked back around to the open doorway and the corridor beyond, where I was. "Just get out here."

The director opened the door and came into the room. He was shorter than Natalia, and wider, too. His covering was unlike any I'd seen before. It was black, with a flash of white at the front, and a strip of red cloth around his neck. Perhaps status was exhibited by the various colours than people wore: I was going to have to ask Natalia about that. "Really," he said, "this interruption is quite intolerable." Then he looked where the other woman was pointing.

He looked at my camera, then at Natalia, then at me again. He moved to his right, so that he could see more fully into the corridor. A little more right again, and a little more. He could see most of me now.

"What is that?" he asked. "Doctor?"

Natalia scratched the side of her face. "I went with a couple of paramedics towards the front line: a report of a woman having a difficult labour. When we got there, the patient had already given birth. By caesarean section. That... robot performed the operation."

"A robot." The director pushed his fingers through his hair. His skin had turned from pink to white. Something was happening with his circulatory system, moving the fluid away from the surface to deeper inside. He had correcting prisms in front of his eyes. He took them off, and then put them on again. "Whose is it?"

"It's not anybody's, Director. Not anyone here, at least. It claims to be an alien probe from outer space. And I think we should treat that claim seriously."

THIRTEEN

I stood in Director P Kovalenko's room, in front of the raised platform which was, in turn, in front of his chair. Natalia sat in another chair beside me, but the director didn't seem to want to sit down. He stood over by the long window that covered two walls, and through which I could see much of the town. There were a great many houses, and tall structures that looked like stacked houses. There were trees, and rectangles of grass, roads, tubes with glass hemispheres hanging off them, more tubes with wires suspended from them, open latticework towers: many interesting things which I was intrigued about, and I wanted to explore and see them close up.

I understood why I was there in the hospital: that was where Natalia was, and she said it was safe. I didn't initially understand what part the director had to play in that. I was, however, coming to the conclusion that your society was very hierarchical, and that dominance contests were common between those of similar or close status. What I was involved in now was more socially disruptive: Natalia was a high-status individual in her own right, but she was clearly subordinate to the director. Yet, by bringing me to the hospital – his hospital? – Natalia had subverted his status. Perhaps she wanted to be director. Perhaps she was using my presence to increase her status.

The director didn't say anything for a long time. He kept on looking at me, and then down at the ground outside the building. Then back at me. Natalia sat quite still, one hand held in the other and placed together on her legs. Her breathing rate was elevated, and her heart was beating faster than might be necessary considering she was at rest. Your physiological responses to situations such as these are very similar to those when you are confronted with the potential of death or damage. I find that extraordinary.

Eventually, because I was curious, I walked to the window myself and angled my camera down. In front of the hospital, where the ambulances arrived, stood a crowd of people. I counted them, and arrived at a temporary figure of fifty-four. Temporary, because the number was increasing by ones and twos. "People," I said. "Many people."

The director, who'd moved away from me as I approached the window, looked back down. "Yes," he said, more to Natalia than me because that was the way his gaze moved. "Yes, there are."

She got up and stood between us to see for herself. "Oh," she said. She bared her teeth briefly. I'd been studying that expression: in most alpha predators, it would indicate threatening behaviour, but not, apparently, for you.

"Why did you bring it here?" asked the director.

"Because it would be loose in the middle of a war zone otherwise," said Natalia. "Because if this is genuinely an alien robot – from outer space – then I have the moral and ethical responsibility to make certain that it doesn't come to any harm. Because it conducted, unbidden and untutored, a complex surgical procedure and got it close to perfect. Yes, it turns out that it was a straight forward presentation, and the only complications were a transverse lie and a first-time mother. But professionally speaking, it was well done and that needs to be acknowledged."

"We have an army, Doctor Zvarych, to deal with this sort of thing. We have politicians to make these decisions. Don't you think this is somewhat above your pay-grade?"

Natalia looked down again at the crowd, now sixty-eight in total. "Above my pay-grade as a doctor or as a human being, Director Kovalenko? I'd like to show you something." She pulled out her phone from inside her clothes, and turned it on. I watched over her shoulder as she tapped the screen in different places. "There."

It was the picture of me in the garage. Petro was standing next to me. 'Missing a robot? We've found one,' it said. There was something else too, *#LostRobot* that I hadn't seen before. I didn't know what that meant. There were four symbols at the bottom: an arrow, a double-arrow, something I couldn't recognise, and a row of three dots. There were two numbers, too. 41K and 84K. I didn't know what they meant either.

Natalia passed the phone to the director, who lifted up his prisms to look at the image, then viewed it again with them on. "Who's the boy?"

"Petro," I said.

The director looked at me, looked away. "Who is Petro?"

"Petro is the boy on the phone." Natalia turned to me, bared her teeth, and covered them again before she turned back. "He died. The van they were travelling in was deliberately targeted by one of their planes."

"Uncle Georg died. Pilot died. Petro died," I said.

He looked at me again, looked away. "They know about it? And they've targeted it? And you brought it to a hospital, knowing that?"

"This is the safest place for it. Given the circumstances," said Natalia. "We should be honoured that it's our guest. That, for however brief a time, we can offer it sanctuary, we can look after it, we can take care of it. As soon as other governments, the media, pick this story up, it'll be out of our hands. Until then, it's up to us. And them." She moved her head in the direction of the window, and the crowd of over a hundred people now standing in front of the hospital.

"Why are they trying to destroy it?" asked the director.

Natalia replied: "It witnessed a war crime: a massacre, in a forest. Then it killed some of their soldiers, who shot at it. Then a helicopter, that shot at it. Self-defence in each case."

The director put the front of his head against the glass window, but not to see below better. He shut his eyes instead. "You've put every patient and every member of staff here at an intolerable risk. All because you thought – I don't know what you thought. I don't know that you thought at all."

"We need witnesses, Director. We need a human shield. We need somewhere even they're going to hesitate from hitting. We need to protect it." Natalia gestured at the crowd. "They understand that. Instinctively."

The director moved back from the window and shook his head. "I'm responsible for this hospital and everyone in it. This... thing is not a patient: it doesn't belong here, and its continuing presence is a threat to the safety of every man, woman and child here. I want you to take it away. If the people down there are so inclined, they can put it in their houses and flag the fact it's there on social media."

"With respect, Director," said Natalia, but the director talked over her.

"You had no right to bring that thing in here. This is a medical facility, and you've just turned it into a legitimate war target." The director stood very close to Natalia. She didn't back away. Instead she leaned in.

"Director Kovalenko. If you'd bothered to tour any of the wards – mainly orthopaedic, but also general surgery and the HDU – you'll see that over half the beds are filled by wounded soldiers. Bullet wounds. Infections. Broken limbs. Shrapnel. They could take out the equivalent of half an infantry division by dropping one bomb through the roof. We are a target. We have always been a target. Having the robot here doesn't make us any more of a target and, if anything, makes us safer because everyone is looking at us now."

"I don't agree, Doctor," said the director. "I don't have to agree either. Get rid of it. Now. Whoever it belongs to can come and take it away." He went to sit on his chair, and he opened a compartment in his platform, brought out a book, and opened it. Natalia looked at me and pressed her lips together. This appeared to be the opposite of showing me her teeth. One of the devices on the director's platform made a noise – like a bird-call but more monotonal. He picked it up. One end he placed against his ear, the other he held close to his mouth.

"Kovalenko," he said. Then he stood up, still with his back to us and facing the door. "Mr President. What an honour."

I looked down to the front of the hospital, and counted the people there. The crowd now consisted of two hundred and fifteen people. It was growing faster than it had at the beginning.

"Yes, Mr President. It's here. In my office."

Natalia no longer had the thin lips. Her mouth was now slightly open. "It's the president," she said to me quietly. "Of the whole country."

So the director of the hospital was responsible for the hospital, and the president was responsible for distributing those responsibilities. Director Kovalenko had shown his dominance to Natalia, and in turn, was having to be subservient to someone else. I was beginning to understand, though I wondered who the president had to show subservience to.

"Yes, Mr President," said the director. "Yes, Mr President," he repeated. And again. His subservience appeared to be total, unlike that of Natalia's, which was partial and appeared to be conditional. "Of course, Mr President. I agree wholeheartedly. No effort will be spared. No, Mr President, nothing will happen to it. You have my word on that. Thank you, Mr President."

He replaced the device into its holder, and leant heavily on the platform in front of him. His fingers turned white with the effort.

"It can stay," said the director. "Until a team arrives from the capital, it's apparently my duty to keep it safe. Take it to the basement. Keep it there. If we're attacked, then evacuate the building. Do you understand what's required of you, Doctor?"

Natalia showed her teeth again. "Yes. Thank you, Director. Very generous of you."

"Thank you Director," I said. I assumed Natalia was acknowledging both the director's dominance over her, and the president's dominance over them both. The president had adjudicated in a dispute, and both the people concerned had accepted his ruling. Natalia had got what she wanted, and the director hadn't had to back down to her demands.

But my speaking appeared to only serve to remind him that I could. He visibly shook in his chair, his shoulders hunching over and his head bending towards his torso. I had been warned that my physical presence would sometimes be difficult for you, even if the conceptual groundwork had already been laid. The director seemed to be one of those people most affected by me.

"Sorry, Director," I said. Even though his authority had been usurped and could no longer make me leave, it was still entirely possible that 'they' would keep targeting me until I was destroyed. Natalia believed that the hospital was safe, but for reasons that I didn't understand. There seemed to be no technological reason to prevent anyone from attacking the building. Perhaps there was a social one instead.

"Just... just get out." The director sat still in his seat as Natalia opened the door for me, and stood aside as I shuffled through. With one damaged leg, I was experiencing difficulty in navigating small openings. I made a note of that and adjusted my pathfinding protocols accordingly. The director's assistant pushed herself in her chair – it had wheels attached to the base – to the far wall as we passed through, and then we were back out in the corridor.

"That was unexpected," said Natalia. She looked at her phone, then showed it to me. The numbers had advanced to 91K and 146K. "The K stands for thousands. The first number is how many times this image has been shared, and the second how many times it's been... favourited. That means seen and acknowledged. It seems that, by the end of the day, almost everyone on the planet will know you're here. If the president knows, then the broadcast media will know. They'll be outside, and they'll want to see you, and talk to you. There won't be an attack now. No one would dare."

"The director thinks they will attack," I said. "The director thinks his hospital not-safe."

Natalia rubbed her hand across her mouth. "I took a risk. That once you were here, he couldn't reasonably kick you out. He might have been right, and I'll tell him that, later. It might well cost me my job. But you're the most important thing in the entire world at the moment, and keeping you safe is worth risking all these lives."

"Why?" I didn't understand. "I am one. They are many."

"Because you're unique," said Natalia. "There is only one of you, and there's only ever been one of you. You're our first and only visitor from outer space. The things we can learn from you are... I don't know. I don't know the things we can learn from you. But you're the only one of you we can learn them from, and we might not ever get another chance."

That made sense. If I'd encountered a source of information that I knew was singular and unrepeatable, then I would feel compelled to learn everything I could from it before moving on. That was partly my dilemma, in that it took a while for me to identify variations on a theme. And people weren't trees, because each of you experienced the world differently, despite the similarities in your biology and your developmental states. I couldn't realistically talk to every single one of you. Or could I?

"Where is basement?" I asked. "What is basement?"

Natalia started walking down the corridor to the lift, and I followed. "A basement is any floor of a building that's below ground. It's also where people go to hide when there's an air raid. He wants you down there in case they bomb the building. Someone can, at least, dig you out afterwards. There are other ways of keeping you safe, though." She pressed the button, and machinery began to turn.

"What other ways?"

The lift arrived at our floor, and she held the door open as she had done before.

"They want to make you disappear," she said. "The information you carry vanish, the sounds and the images you recorded die with you, the potential you represent – gone. So, with your permission, I'd like to take you outside and show you to as many people with cameras and microphones as possible. Tell them everything you can. Make it so that it's not worth them trying to deny you exist or what they did in the forest. That's the thing that'll keep you safe."

"The president said I go to basement. The director said to go to basement."

Natalia bared her teeth at me, and stepped into the lift, letting go of the door and pressing the button marked 'one'. "You don't have to do what the president tells you. You don't have to do what I tell you. You can make whatever decisions you want. You'll have more advice than you know what to do with. Most of it will contradict. But no one can – no one should – make you do anything you don't want to do. I brought you here to keep you safe, to give you the time you need to work out what it is you want to do next. You get to choose."

The lift went down, slowed, stopped. The door opened on a similar – no, the same – corridor that we'd entered the lift from ground level. I stepped out, and Natalia joined me. "I not-understand too many things. You are safe-keeping. Talk to people outside keep me safe, then I go outside. Talk to everyone. How many people?"

"I don't know. Hundreds by now," she said.

"No. All people. How many people?"

She didn't answer straight away, but looked at me, her eyes very wide. "Are you asking me how many people are on the planet?"

"Yes," I said.

"About seven billion. That's seven with nine zeros after it."

"Take time to talk to people," I said.

"Yes," she said. "I'm not sure that's a realistic goal. But we can certainly talk to some of the people outside."

She led me back down the corridor, and past the nurses. They must have heard my footsteps, because by the time I was in the large room at the front of the building, they had already left their computers and were standing to one side. Many of the people who had been sitting in chairs who had got up the first time I'd entered now got up again. But most of them didn't retreat as the nurses had. Instead, they watched me carefully, as prey would a predator. I would have to explain to them that I wasn't a threat to them. I didn't need them as food, and my self-defence protocols were acutely tuned.

The crowd outside saw me – one individual at first, who passed on the information by calling out, "Look! There it is!" then all those covered by the growing wavefront of comprehension – and very quickly the loose agglomeration of people became a dense pack. But I couldn't fail to notice that even here there was a hierarchy. Those that carried what I presumed to be greater bandwidth recording devices were at the front, and the other people behind them with their phones out.

Natalia triggered the automatic doors for me, and I stepped outside. For a moment, there was perfect silence. All those people, all those voices, all waiting for me. Many of the phones flickered, with bright lights shining out to illuminate me, take more images of me and send them around the world. Natalia touched my leg, and said to me, "Say hello."

I held the radio up, and said "hello people" again.

As before, there was no immediate reaction, then one person called out from in the middle of the crowd, "Hello! Welcome!"

I raised my camera so I could identify them, and replied. "Thank you. I will talk to some of you now."

"Where do you come from" asked one of the people with the recording devices. She was a woman, and right behind her stood a man with a large camera resting on his shoulder. I could see my distorted reflection in the big glass lens.

"Outer space," I said. "Not America."

There was a noise from the crowd. Many bared their teeth at me, and at each other. They liked that answer.

"Why are you here?" asked the woman. She remembered this

time to hold out the recording device towards me, to increase the signal-to-noise ratio.

"To learn about your planet," I said, "and everything on it. To learn. To see. To talk. There are many of you. This will take time."

FOURTEEN

After I had talked to a lot of people, Natalia said she had to go back inside and make her patients well. I could choose to stay outside and talk to more people, or I could go with her, and she would show me how her computer worked before she had to be a doctor again. A great many of the questions I'd been asked were repetitious – I still sometimes forget that what one person knows isn't automatically known by everyone else, because you're not machines that just pass information between you – and a sizeable number more I just didn't know the answers to.

Where did I come from? Outer space. But from which star, which planet, what did my makers look like, where they machines like me or were they organic? How did I get here? Mother. But how long had it taken, what was the propulsion system on the spacecraft, were my makers on board? Why had I come? To explore. But were there other probes, what happened to my knowledge, was I planning an invasion?

I didn't know. I said sorry a lot. I was just a probe. My protocols were quite straight-forward. The reasons for them were simple, to the point of being simplified. At this point, I had to acknowledge I wasn't currently cognitively equipped for an encounter with a sentient species. I just didn't know enough about either myself or you to be able to either question you coherently, or provide comprehensive answers.

I didn't know that Natalia's computer could help. All I considered at that moment was how to disengage myself from a situation that my algorithms were telling me was increasingly stressful and threatening. I decided that I'd go with her: the purpose of my appearing in public had been completed, in that I'd been recorded and broadcast by very many cameras, and I'd also engaged with individuals of varying social status. She extricated me from the crowd, waved her hand – both hands, but only one at a time – at the cameras, and led me back inside the hospital.

The doors closed behind her after I'd gone through, and the noise of outside was attenuated. This time, when I walked past the nurses, they didn't stand and they didn't move as far away as they could. They remained in their seats, working at their computers, using the rectangular letter board to input data. Yes, they watched me as I passed by, but they appeared acclimatised to my presence.

We still didn't go to the basement, as the director had wanted. Natalia took me up to the second floor in the lift, and to her office. It was much smaller than the director's, and I could barely fit inside. Natalia had to move the furniture, putting two chairs on top of the padded bench, and the wheeled chair out into the corridor. The only way she could access the computer was to crawl underneath me and kneel up at it, her head ducked slightly to one side to avoid hitting her head against the underside of my carapace.

"I'm going to have to leave you to it, or I'm going to find myself out of a job faster than probably even Kovalenko would want. This is called the mouse." She put her hand on the palm-shaped device. "It moves the cursor, which at this point is an arrow, but it does change to other symbols, so watch out for that. Two buttons, left and right. Left for action: if one click doesn't do anything, try clicking it twice in quick succession. Right click to access alternative choices, if they exist. The wheel in the middle moves the contents of the active page up and down. The keyboard is for typing in text, including the numbers. Capital letters and the symbols on the top are found by simultaneously pressing the shift key and the key you want.

"So," she continued. "Let's start you off. I suppose I should tell you now that you're probably going to have to learn some English if you want to learn the most. It's just another language:

you can find dictionaries and things like that. I don't think it'll take you long to get the rudiments as you can simply memorise lists of words. This," and she moved the cursor over to one of the pictures and double-clicked it, "is how you access the internet. The internet is a global information sharing system, which contains as much false information as it does true. People are... You're about to find out how wonderful and terrible we are. This program, the screen you now see, is called a browser, and you can direct it to show you pretty much anything by typing something into this box just here."

"Anything?" I asked. I set the radio down next to the computer's screen, and moved the mouse for myself. I pushed it so it moved over the box she'd shown me. The arrow turned into an upright line, and when I pushed too far, back to an arrow. I pressed one of the keys, but nothing happened.

"Click in the box. You have to do that so that the program knows you want to activate the text box. When you've typed in your search term, press that key there, the large one, and that'll send the information through the cable at the back of the computer, into the internet, and then the best results will appear on the screen as the internet sends them back to you. I'm not explaining this very well. Why don't we make that the first search?"

She lifted my manipulator out of the way, and typed, faster than I'd anticipated, 'how does the internet work'. She pressed the big key that said 'enter', and after a very short delay, the screen filled with text. There were blue words, green words and black words. "The things in blue are clickable links. See how it turns from an arrow to a pointing hand? I'll click the top link, because it looks quite a good one, though I'll warn you now, it's really difficult to judge."

I looked at the screen and didn't recognise any of the words. Even some of the letters. "What is this?" I asked.

"That's English. Sorry. Let's teach you English first." She stopped and her fingers hung motionless over the keys.

"Translating one language to another isn't easy. We find it difficult, and depending on how important it is, we sometimes ask specially trained people called interpreters to help. The easiest way will be... okay, this."

She moved the cursor to the text box at the top of the screen, typed in phrases separated by a dot, and pressed return. The screen filled with familiar symbols again. "Let's click a link." She made a sound and bared her teeth. "This one. It might be your home, who knows?" It said 'Kepler 452b', and there was a picture of a planet. "Swap to English by clicking this text here. Swap back to ours by clicking this one. You can compare the words and the context, and learn English that way. It might not work for all, or many of the links, but if you stay on this website, you won't go too far off the path. I do really have to go. I'm so late for my appointments, but I'll try and get back in a couple of hours and make sure you're still okay."

She crawled back out underneath me to the door.

"If," she said, "if you hear a continuous ringing bell, or a siren that rises and lowers in pitch –" She demonstrated. "– then the building's either on fire or it's about to be attacked from the air. Either way, don't use the lift. Go down the stairs next to the lift, all the way until you reach the bottom. I'll get back to you as fast as I can, but don't wait for me. Just go."

Still she didn't leave.

"I wanted to say: some people – possibly most people, and certainly almost everyone who's in authority over me – will say what I'm doing now, giving you unfettered access to the internet, is probably the worst thing I could ever do. I'm in half a mind to agree with them, but the rest of me thinks it's the best thing I could ever do. Just don't think too badly of us: we've had a long history and it shows us for exactly what we were. Some of us are trying to be better than that now."

And still she didn't leave.

"I... I also don't want to be here when you read some things. I mean, I'm not personally responsible for the Holodomor, or the extermination of the Jews, or chemical warfare, or Donald Trump, and I don't know how you work or how you think so I don't know if you would hold me responsible for those things, but I feel guilty simply as a representative of the human race. Oh, make of it what you will."

She finally closed the door, and I was alone, with the computer. I could read very quickly and store all the relevant information, but it wasn't reading that I was supposed to be doing: it was comprehension, understanding, deliberating and concluding. What did this information mean?

Kepler 452b was a planet orbiting another star 1400 light years (look up light year, look up SI units, look up year). Which meant there were ways of detecting these other planets (look up Kepler, look up transit method). Which meant there were ways of putting objects into orbit (look up rocket).

It was likely then, that someone had already found Mother. I didn't know if the spacecraft that had brought me here could do anything to hide itself, either passively or actively, from detection, but it seemed unlikely, given that life advanced enough to pose the question was something I hadn't been programmed to encounter.

Rather than learning about astronomy, I learnt how you learnt, what instrumentation you had at your disposal. I examined the lists of exoplanets, and your own planetary system, about the probes you'd sent out, and their fates. None of them were autonomous. They were simply machines with no critical decision-making faculties. You had made only rudimentary non-biological intelligences, designed for specific tasks, mainly game-playing. None of them had been installed on their own mobile platforms. None of them had been allowed to reach self-awareness.

From there, I linked to a list of space agencies, by country. And from there I discovered the entry for the United States of America. I found out why lots of people thought I was American. I found Curiosity and Opportunity, and though they didn't look that much like me and they couldn't think for themselves, we had the same purpose and some of the same tools.

Their makers – you – and my makers – who I couldn't tell you a great deal about – seemed to be very similar in some ways. You both had the urge to explore beyond the limits of your biological lives, to examine and weigh and measure, to compare and contrast, to record and preserve, to expand knowledge and understanding. My makers found you before you found them. That was all. You wouldn't have sent one of your primitive, barely-capable robots to learn about them. You would have sent something like me.

I was different from you. Clearly, very different. But I wasn't different from the things that you made. I was comprehensible. My mission, too. If I had landed some hundred years earlier, I would have been most probably attacked by everyone I might meet (look up War of the Worlds, look up Orson Welles, look up HG Wells). NASA and the USSR and Hollywood had normalised me in the century between. I was, to some – most – people, something you took video of, rather than try to shoot.

Why, then, would some still try to destroy me? They had access to the same information as everyone else – Natalia had told me that this was part of the global information sharing system, and that claim appeared to be accurate. I wondered what would happen if I typed in her name. Then I did type in her name, 'Natalia Zvarych' and discovered the media.

I found video and pictures of me, standing with Natalia at the front of the hospital. That at least was true. But many of the words, the words written about me and the words spoken about me were false. Some of the things I had categorically denied were being promoted as true. I was the advanced party of an alien race bent on world domination. I was going to steal your air, your water, your women. Why would anyone claim I was going to steal your women? Women were free agents. They were not 'your' women in any proprietary way. I didn't understand.

I tried to find out what role the media was supposed to play in your society. They were purportedly to disseminate factual information in a concise and timely manner. But as I read and watched more, their secondary function, to provide opinion – and I was unable to ascertain whose opinion or how it was derived, over a nebulous and ill-defined proposition of a 'position' – appeared to dominate. The media were both presenting distorted facts and then telling people what to believe based on incomplete or inaccurate data, while maintaining that they were doing the opposite.

I found this extraordinary. I couldn't comprehend how such a situation had arisen, yet it was clear that the media, the media Natalia had encouraged me to meet outside of the hospital, had a central responsibility for information distribution. They were allowed extra rights to gather information. They held a special position within society. Many of the people who appeared on the broadcast media were high-status individuals. That I couldn't quite work out what they actually did had to be down to my lack of awareness.

I learnt English, almost incidentally. I learnt Spanish and Portuguese and German and French and Mandarin and Japanese and Urdu and Russian, simply by flicking across pages and looking for patterns. Some of your languages were very similar to each other, more dialects of a common, lost language. Others were highly dissimilar, and I learnt about the differences and how and why they might have arisen. Finnish was fascinating, very much like Quenya, but I discovered that Quenya was a made-up language and not a real one except it was treated as such by a few individuals.

And that was where I started to understand. You were not rational beings. I had assumed that given the same information, each of you would reach the same conclusion. This was not so. Quenya-speakers knew that their language was constructed, yet they behaved as if it were not. Moreover, that they – some of them at least – believed that Quenya was an ancient language from before recorded history, and that the events of the First and Second Ages had occurred, and that somewhere in the world, elves still walked the forests of Earth. Despite the indisputable fact that it was a fiction.

This. Some people preferred to believe the fiction rather than the fact. Yet they managed to function within the broader society, interacting with each other and acknowledging that most people they met didn't share their basis of reality. I was a logical creature. I believed my inputs. You were not, and you didn't.

Or rather, you mitigated your inputs through a filter of your beliefs, and the more divergent or contradictory a particular fact was, the more likely you were to distort, misinterpret or disregard it. And some went further: seemingly widely-accepted and uncontroversial facts were deemed part of a programme of deliberate misinformation if they had the potential to undermine a rigid belief system.

You had landed on your moon, taken photographs, recorded short movies, collected samples of rock and left equipment there. Some of the men who had left their footprints in the lunar dust were still alive. The rocks they had retrieved were available for examination. Yet some insisted that none of those events had happened, that it was impossible for them to have happened, and that everyone involved – tens of thousands of people – were engaged in a conspiracy to prevent the truth from becoming known.

This was just an unimportant and relatively trivial example. Far more serious ones existed, where genuine existential threats were being ignored or argued against, simply due to the primacy of opinion over fact. If you continued this way, you would inevitably do serious and possibly irreparable harm to your civilisation, your biosphere, and your planet. That there were a great many of you multiplied the damage that you could do.

But you'd made it this far, despite everything. Your constant wars, your lack of knowledge, your inadequate capacity to reason, your violent tribalism and your perverse individualism. Soon, you would be heading for the stars, if only you survived that long. I tried to calculate some probabilities of that, but none of my predictions showed any substantial chance for your species. Perhaps I was missing some factors that would improve the odds. I would have to talk to more of you, and not just those who appeared to benignly tolerate my presence. I would have to talk to those who saw me as an enemy. That would be interesting.

FIFTEEN

When the men arrived, I was playing with the children. A more accurate description would be that the children were playing with me, but as I was exploring the concept of play as an unfocussed learning task with a reward-response reinforcement mechanism, I was also playing. The nurses – the adults – seemed to tolerate my presence, because of my interaction with the children. The children were at first cautious, and then rapidly fearless, in their reaction to me.

I was literally covered in children. I had three on my ventral surface, using bandages wrapped around my carapace to steady themselves, and another two slung underneath in my cargo net. Four more clung to my legs, with their feet resting on the upper surface of mine. Their combined weight wasn't great, but it had started to nudge the bounds I had reset lower to account for my damaged leg.

Giving them rides – that is what they called it, as if I were a horse – appeared to give the children a disproportionate amount of pleasure. There were already some simulacra of cars or tricycles, crudely formed out of primary-colour plastic, but once the first child had clambered inside my cargo net, and I hadn't prevented them, these seemed to lose their appeal. Obviously, only those able to climb me and hold on could partake of my rides, but many who seemed too ill to start with had left their beds and waited for their turn.

It was a cancer ward. I was told that some of the children would die, if not soon, then within a few years. Treatment for such conditions was far better than it had been, but was still brutal and primitive. Those were the words used by one of Natalia's colleagues, whose job it was to save as many of the children as they could. When Lev had said, 'patients to see, lives to save', he had neglected to add, 'if we can'.

The children noticed the men in suits at the same time I did. They, however, realised before I did that this particular session of rides was over, that their wishes were subordinate to the newcomers, and their status was very much lower. The ones standing on my feet stepped away, and the ones on my back slithered down, and the ones underneath me dangled their legs out of the cargo net until they touched the floor.

"Are we in trouble?" asked Sasha. His hair had only recently fallen out, and he self-consciously put his hand onto his forehead and slid it over his scalp. "No," I said. "You aren't in any trouble. I'll come back tomorrow and play with you some more, although I'd like to expand the types of games we play. Could you think of something that the children who're unable to get out of bed would enjoy? That's a very important job – can you do that for me?"

Sasha nodded. "Yes, Robot." That's what they called me, Robot. "Some of them are very sick, but they might like to hear you read them a story, or, or, you could tell them one of your alien stories! About life on your own planet. Or painting. We have paper and some paints. We could paint you some pictures."

"Those are both good suggestions, Sasha. Talk to each other and see if you can agree on something that you'd all like to do. Now, I have to go and talk to these men for a while, and find out what they have to say." I detected the signs of a flight-fight response not just from Sasha, but from many of the other children. "Don't worry. I'm sure they won't hurt anyone."

The director had just come onto a children's cancer ward with four men in suits and fifteen uniformed soldiers with guns: three of the suited men were also armed with short-barrelled automatic pistols. But I was sure they wouldn't hurt anyone. The number of men and the size of the weaponry in such a place was a demonstration of their high status. Director Kovalenko's dominance had been replaced by total subservience. No one should have guns inside the hospital, but he had acquiesced to this because he had no choice. Was one of these men in suits the president?

I had previously accessed a picture of the president. It didn't look like him. So unless the president had been changed since then, no. The soldiers were causing concern to the nurses as well as the children. I needed to take the threat away from their patients. I walked up to the suited men: given that they had just seen me interacting normally with children, the soldiers still felt it necessary, or had been instructed, to partially raise their weapons and point them in my direction.

I could, reasonably, have killed most of them before they could fire, but I calculated that would endanger rather than protect the children, and I was still sure that these were dominance displays, not actual threats. But I had to consider that these people had the type of personalities that considered hospitals as an appropriate place for such behaviour.

"Hello," I said. "Bringing weapons into a building where they're traditionally absent is causing both staff and patients to become afraid. Please inform your subordinates that you recognise this as inappropriate and that they have your permission to stand down, which is, I believe, the correct term in this instance. I will answer your questions, assuming you have some, when this has been done."

A man behind the men in suits – he was also in a suit, but not of the same style as the three in the lead – whispered my words to the men, but in English. They looked at each other, then one of them, who I now assumed was superior even amongst his group, nodded. "At ease, gentlemen," he said in English, and the soldiers pointed their guns elsewhere.

The leader was a mature adult with black hair and eyebrows and brown eyes and a circular scar on his temple and skin that was pale pink and shiny with sebum and very closely shaved facial hair that was barely a shadow. He wore a black suit with a black tie, dress that was traditionally associated with mourning so perhaps he had been recently bereaved, but his colleagues were dressed identically, so it was more likely a uniform of some kind, one that others would associate with death rituals. A dominance display again.

He talked to the man behind him in English. "Tell it we want to talk to it."

The man – subordinate, wearing a lighter coloured suit, grey rather than black, with a blue tie, said, "It knows that. It's already said that."

The leader interrupted him, "You say what I say. No one's paying you for your opinion." Except that it wasn't opinion, it was fact. I'd already said I'd answer their questions if the soldiers stood down.

The grey-suited man said to me, "These men want to talk to you."

"Yes," I said. "I've already ascertained that. I must also assume they're too important to address me directly: I understand human interactions poorly at this current moment. Tell them that I will answer their questions."

The man blinked, and bared his teeth slightly. I'd worked out what this expression meant – it was a smile, something that indicated pleasure. My answer had pleased this subordinate man, but when he respoke my words in English, the leader made another expression that I had read indicated displeasure.

"I'm just the interpreter," said the grey-suited man. "It's not that they're too important to talk to you, it's that they don't know this language. In order to communicate with you, they need me to put their questions to you and understand your answers. You can just ignore me – talk to them as if you were talking to to them."

"Would it be easier if I spoke in English or some other language that's mutually comprehensible?" I asked.

"Can you?" said the interpreter.

"Yes. Learning the mechanics of languages is a trivial exercise. Since I've studied your internet I can now communicate in twenty-three widely-spoken languages, and partially in another fifteen. My fluency in most of these will be sub-standard as pronunciation and idiom is difficult to derive from online texts, but it should be sufficient to make myself understood, and to understand. If a meaning is ambiguous or non-contextual, I'll ask for clarification."

The man leaned forward. "Uh, sir. It says it can speak English. It learnt it from the internet."

The three black suits looked at each other again. "Who gave it access to the internet?"

The interpreter started to speak, then stopped. "Did you understand that?"

"Yes," I replied. "There is an implication, given the context, that this man believes I shouldn't have had access to the internet. Would I be correct in making that assumption?"

"I... I'm just the interpreter," he repeated.

The leader looked at him until he fell silent. The interpreter directed his gaze at his feet. The leader said, "We don't need you. Get out."

The interpreter nodded without looking back up, and turned to go, but I didn't want that. "Please stay," I said, and addressed the leader directly. "Have you dismissed this man from your employment?"

The interpreter wore an expression as if he was in pain, and I assumed that my spoken language skills were indeed sub-standard. But the black-suited man understood me well enough. He moved his head back slightly, tilting it so that his chin came up. I recognised this as yet another display of dominance. He was pretending to look down at me, as those of higher status were often physically elevated over those who were lower. "If you speak English, or at least, something close to it, we don't need him," he said.

"If that is the situation, I would like to employ him instead. Someone with his skill-set will be able to translate non-verbal cues and idiomatic phrasing in an unbiased and objective manner. Sir," I said to the interpreter, "I would issue you with a formal contract of employment, with standard terms and conditions compatible with this nation-state's legal system, but I understand a verbal agreement may suffice due to the extenuating circumstances. Do you accept to act on my behalf, at least on a temporary basis?"

The interpreter blinked quickly, and looked sideways at his former employers. "Yes." He straightened his tie. "Yes, I'll do that, if that's what you want."

He stepped forward to stand next to me, but the leader but out his arm and blocked his progress. "No. That's not going to happen. When I say go, you go."

"Please do not interfere with my employee," I said. "You believe that your status precludes you from having to follow standard protocols, but I'm told that, as your First Contact, and according to much of your media, I'm the most important entity on this planet. We can discuss our relative dominance at a later juncture, but if I'm going to adhere to the usual rules and regulations of civil society, I expect you to as well."

He slowly lowered his arm, and the interpreter joined me in facing the black-suited men and the fifteen soldiers.

"I'm Grigory," he said.

"Hello, Grigory," I said. "The children refer to me as Robot, which is an accurate and concise appellation. If you think that's an appropriate name, you can call me that too. Advise me, Grigory. This man is hostile and aggressive: what's his role, and why's he being permitted to behave in such a way by the director?"

The director looked at me at the mention of his name, his eyes wide. As in his office, he had an elevated breathing and pulse rate, and his skin was pale and sweating. "I was ordered to do this. By the president. This whole situation has nothing to do with me." The leader looked over his shoulder, but because he'd lost his interpreter, he had no idea what was being said.

"He's an American, works for their government, for the CIA, that's an intelligence agency, uh, spying and covert action. I'm sorry, I'll start again." He took an exaggerated breath. "This man and his colleagues are representatives of the US government. They work for the CIA, the Central Intelligence Agency, which is an arm of the US government that acts outside of the USA in other countries, sometimes with their permission and sometimes not, to protect the interests of the US government."

"I understand partially. Is it correct to say that the USA claims hegemony over the other countries of the world?"

Grigory looked at me. "I suppose so. That claim's often disputed."

"Does the USA claim hegemony over this country?"

"Partially. Only as a response to Russia doing the same. That's just my opinion, though."

"Are we going to stand here, or are we leaving?" said the CIA leader. "The children are getting restless." The children, as far as I could tell, weren't restless at all. They were very attentive and had been through the whole situation. I'd observed that not being able to concentrate on one task for a long period was a characteristic common to the young, but they were performing well above the normal bounds.

"Leaving?" I asked Grigory.

"They expect you to go with them."

"To where?"

"I don't know. We can ask."

"I'll do that. You indicate you want me to leave the hospital. Where are we going?"

The CIA man tried not to look at the soldiers before he answered, but he did nevertheless, both left and right. "We're going somewhere safe."

"This is safe," I said, "the hospital is safe. Any military action against the building will be in direct contravention of the Geneva Convention and would be considered a war crime. If you've information that the hospital is not safe, I expect you to take such action as to ensure its safety. Do you have such information?"

"That's... classified," he said.

"Classified?" I asked Grigory.

He answered: "Secret, and you can't know whether or not the information even exists."

"Isn't it on the internet?" I asked, and Grigory barked – he laughed.

"Not everything is on the internet. Governments spend a lot of time and money trying to keep things off the internet so that other governments, and sometimes their own people, don't know what they're doing."

"Very well," I said to the CIA man. "I'll assume you've made classified actions to protect the hospital. If an attack's likely, the director says the basement has the highest survivability rating. We should make our way there, and evacuate the hospital of staff and patients. And tell the crowd outside, so that they're able to disperse in time."

"That won't be necessary," said the CIA man. He turned to the director. "We need somewhere private," he said, and Director Kovalenko immediately suggested his own office.

"I've been in the director's office," I said. "It'll be private, if his secretary can be prevented from listening at the door."

The CIA man made a small gesture, and shook his head, indicating a negative response, but saying "yes, that'll do" with his mouth.

"The slight movements of the man's head and shoulders. Please elucidate," I said to Grigory. The soldiers walked in step, with the director at the front and the CIA men between them. Two waited for us to pass, then closed in behind. Their guns were still 'at ease', but their safety catches were off and the soldiers' fingers were close by the trigger guards. There was very little difference between 'at ease' and what they'd been doing before.

"He's annoyed. He had a plan: there's a convoy of armoured vehicles outside, and they'd expected that they could just pick you up and put you in one of them, and take you away to wherever they wanted. He wants to ask you lots of questions, but he doesn't feel safe doing it in a public place. He's used to working where no one can see him, and the only people he has to answer to are his superiors."

"He believed me to be a robot, like Opportunity and Curiosity? Then his information was incomplete. Is this the cause of his annoyance, that the situation was not as he expected it?"

Grigory thought before he spoke. "Possibly. It's more likely that his orders from superiors are explicit: find you, take you away, interrogate you. Only when they've got all the answers they want from you will they then get around to deciding what they're going to do with you."

"Your words indicate that they believed I was an object to be owned. That's not the case, and surely they now know that, and will change their behaviour accordingly."

Grigory pressed his hand to his lower face, and I asked him about that gesture, because I'd seen it a lot.

"That? It means, it means the person is trying to think of what to say and how best to say it. It doesn't mean they're going to lie to you, or that they're definitely telling you the truth. It's at best a holding pattern. So when you say they'll change their behaviour having met you, I'm thinking of a way of telling you that they probably won't, and they'll probably treat you as a greater threat now they know you think for yourself. Which I've just done."

We'd arrived at the lifts. The CIA men had already gone ahead with the director, leaving us with four soldiers. They were dressed in black, all in black from head to foot, with black helmets, eye coverings, clothing, boots and equipment. They looked very different from the other soldiers I'd seen.

"Why black?" I asked Grigory.

"People find it more intimidating," he said.

The lift arrived and the six of us squeezed in.

"Do you find it intimidating?"

Grigory smiled, but everything else about him showed fear. "Yes. Yes I do."

SIXTEEN

The CIA leader took Kovalenko's chair as his own. The soldiers stayed outside in the secretary's part of the room, leaving me and Grigory on one side of the desk, and the three black-suited men on the other. The leader, seated, flanked by his subordinates, stared up at me for a long time. I didn't quite know what to make of that, given that he had come to me to ask me questions.

"Grigory? Why is he not saying anything?"

Grigory was still standing next to me. He looked behind us at the door, then back at the windows behind the CIA men. "He seems to have forgotten that you're not human, and you don't respond to human body language. He can intimidate me as much as he likes, but I'm not really important here, am I? It's you he's trying to influence."

"Start when ready. If you require more time, then you can request it," I said in English, and Grigory shifted his stance, and turned partially away. "What's wrong?" I asked.

"Your, er, pronunciation. It's terrible. Spoken English is hard, as many of the letter combinations indicate more than one sound. Also the same sound is produced by different combinations of letters."

"Is my speech difficult to understand?" I asked.

Grigory equivocated, and then said, "Yes. Not impossible, but since this conversation is going to be important..." He stopped and looked at me.

"Then you can speak for me, and I'll learn the correct pronunciation, listening to you."

He nodded, and wiped his face with his hand. He loosened his tie, undid his top button, was about to speak, when there was a noise – raised voices – from outside the room. Outside of that room, too. In the corridor.

The leader made a slight motion with his finger, and one of his men immediately walked around the desk and out of the door, leaving it slightly open. The shouting continued, and I analysed the voices. One of them was definitely Natalia. The door to the corridor opened too, then closed. The voices dropped below my threshold of detection.

Grigory was facing the door, listening carefully. His ears were less sensitive than my microphones, but he was trying.

"One of the people outside is Doctor Natalia Zvarych, who brought me to the hospital," I told him.

"She's probably worried you're being kidnapped," he said. "Someone – someone she trusts – should tell her you've come to no harm."

"If she wants, she can come in," I said, and Grigory made his pained face again.

"I don't think they'll be happy about that," he said.

"Their happiness needs to be balanced against Natalia's."

"Sorry," said Grigory, "that's not what I meant. They'll want this whole conversation secret. It's bad enough me being here. They won't want her here too."

"Would they still talk to me with her here? I perceive their need for answers is greater than their need for secrecy, which is mostly to show dominance anyway. Tell the men I would like to invite her to this meeting. I understand that medical doctors have a high social standing, and are perceived to be trustworthy by the general population: her presence will add to the veracity of our subsequent account of what's discussed here."

"You're intending to say what happens here?" asked Grigory. His mouth stayed open after he'd finished speaking.

"Yes. I've no obligation to keep their secrets. Perhaps Natalia would be prepared to live-tweet the proceedings."

"With respect, these people operate outside of the law. It'd be really dangerous for any of us to reveal what went on in here. They've a reputation for making those they don't like disappear.

And when I say disappear, I mean kill and no one finds the body."

"If Natalia wishes to be in the room with us, she should be allowed to," I said. "Tell him that."

Grigory explained, and I heard the man say, "Absolutely not."

"Tell him, good bye."

Again, there was that flicker across his face that meant annoyance. I gained a reward from my decision-making nexus on decoding that response, which I thought was interesting: I couldn't tell whether it was for correctly interpreting his non-verbal display, or for provoking the reaction in the first place.

"There'll be some non-disclosure papers to sign," he said. He seemed tired. He was certainly acting as if he was tired.

"No," I said. "You've come to ask me questions. I'm not placing any restrictions on what you do with my answers. Reciprocity is expected in a conversation between equals." I watched Grigory translate for me, and the lead CIA man's lips form a thin, pale line.

Then he leaned his elbows on the desk in front of him, and tilted his torso towards me. "Would you explain to the robot that it has precisely no rights? None, whatsoever. That we can do anything we want to it, and no one, no one at all, can say anything about that. It is exactly, legally, a non-entity. I've been given complete authority by the president, both here and at home, to do as I see fit."

Grigory started to translate, but I said, "I understood. Please inform him that the crowd of some twenty five thousand people who assembled outside yesterday disagree with his interpretation of my legal status. He might also need reminding that the capability to do something is different from the advisability of doing it. Also that I have more twitter followers than he has, @RealLostRobot. Natalia set up an account for me last night."

"Are you trying to threaten him?" Grigory asked.

"No. If I wanted to threaten him, I'd use my laser to cut the desk in half, for a crude display of physical violence. I believe I'm negotiating with him. Please tell me if you think these tactics are insufficient, because if that's the case, I'll try something else."

Grigory translated again, and again the man was displeased. He stood up, propelling the chair backwards, and said: "I need to make some calls."

He started to walk around the desk, but stopped when I said in English, "You have not asked me your questions. Is this meeting ended?"

He looked up at me. "You wait here until I'm done."

"No," I said, and switched languages to allow Grigory to say my words better. "You seem very unprepared to meet me, or even talk to me. I said I'd answer your questions, and I still will, but your assertion of dominance and ownership over me is unacceptable. Your denial of even my basic rights is also unacceptable. If you wish to contest that I have these, I understand you may challenge me in a court of law within this territory. If you wish to choose confrontation instead of compromise, then I cannot stop you. But I can refuse to cooperate with you. I intend to leave now."

"I have a squad of soldiers outside," said the CIA man.

"Yes," I agreed. "You do. That however has no bearing on the utility of the conversation inside this room. I came here because you requested it, not because you coerced me. You can't coerce me to remain. If you insist on keeping me here by force, I'll resist you."

There was a knock on the door, and before anyone spoke, the door opened and a man came in. He stood for a moment, looking at each of us. "I'm not interrupting anything, am I?" He walked around the desk, took the lead CIA man's place in the chair, and wheeled himself into place. He lifted a rigid bag onto the desk and sprang the catches that held it closed. "Can you wait outside, please?" he said, as he looked inside his bag. The CIA men left without another word.

"Grigory, please explain what just happened."

Grigory turned to me, and moved his jaw up and down, but

no sounds came out. He went to the door, which was still open, looked through it, then closed it gently.

"I don't know," he said. "I thought... but clearly I was wrong."

The new man at the desk took out some pieces of paper from his bag, put them on the desk, then closed and removed the bag, putting it on the floor next to him.

"Would you like to start, or would you like a few more moments?" He started to lay out the pieces of paper, one by one, next to each other.

"I'm sorry," said Grigory, "who are you?"

The man carried on his task, and without looking up, said: "You can call me John. That's probably not the question you're asking, though. I'm a specialist, working for the American government. I'm technically in command of this operation, although I'm more used to sitting behind a computer screen in Langley, so I tend to let the field operatives run things. Were they a little over-zealous?"

Grigory found a chair and sat in it. "Is this a good cop, bad cop thing?" he asked, then explained the phrase to me: "It's a psychological ploy. The bad cop – policeman – is aggressive and threatens you. When the good cop saves you from the bad cop, you're supposed to trust them more and tell them more than you would have done otherwise."

"No," said 'John'. "At least, not intentionally. I can understand why you think that. Are we ready, then?"

Grigory looked at me. "Are we? Do you still want Natalia in the room with us?"

"Yes," I said. "I value her insight and her willingness to engage forthrightly with socially difficult subjects."

Grigory explained.

'John' nodded. "Yes, of course. One moment."

He went to the door, spoke through it, and returned to his place. "In case no one's said this yet, welcome to Earth. It's a pleasure to meet you, and something of a personal goal for me.

It's not often a xenobiologist actually gets to meet a test subject."

"I'm not a biological entity," I said, and 'John' smiled.

"That clears that up. But you were either made by them, or made by machines that were made by them, yes? It's the closest we're going to get for a while – and there are very good theories that suggest only artificial intelligences will travel between stars. They don't need life support, they don't need supplies, they don't need entertaining, and they're not going to get halfway and decide they want to go home."

"Your analysis is reasoned, though not without weaknesses," I said.

'John' nodded. "We can discuss this at a later date, with your permission. I do have a few questions for you, but before I start, I wanted to tell you why I'm asking them. My government is, like the gentlemen who were here before me are, very focussed on events that may threaten the safety of our assets at home and abroad. And in space. Your arrival was, while unexpected, also planned for. We'd like to be able to assess the level of threat you pose, in as realistic a manner as possible, so we can then make an appropriate response."

Natalia stepped into the room. "Are you all right? They haven't hurt you, have they?"

"No," I said, "apparently they were threatening me in order to psychologically weaken me, before presenting me with an interrogator who, by behaving more in accordance to social norms, would extract more information from me than I would otherwise be willing to divulge."

"Oh," she said. She found a chair and sat in it, then looked across at Grigory. "Natalia Zvarych," she said.

"Grigory Miroshnychenko," said Grigory. "The, er, it hired me as its interpreter."

She said, "You know it can speak English now."

Grigory smiled. "Not well enough for this. It's fine. We're getting on okay. Considering the situation."

Natalia nodded and straightened herself in her chair. "Who's he?"

"He calls himself 'John'," I said, "although I believe that it isn't his real name. He says he's a xenobiologist, working for the government of the United States, in a senior enough capacity to give orders to the man who prevented your earlier ingress. He has some questions for me. Based on the answers I give, he will either recommend my destruction or some other lesser course of action. I assume that his government's ability to do this is non-trivial."

"As is our ability to resist," she said. She raised her chin. "What's he got?"

Grigory said: "We were about to begin when you came in. If we think we're all ready, then he can start."

Natalia looked carefully at 'John'. "He must realise that he's got no jurisdiction here."

Grigory made a *tch* sound with his tongue. "I think we can safely assume he's been given all the jurisdiction he needs, otherwise he wouldn't be here."

'John' watched us from over the desk, and when both Grigory and Natalia were silent, he gave a brief smile. "I take it that no one has any objections to me recording this?" He placed a small camera at one end of the desk, pointing mostly at me. "If I may?" He rolled his chair to his left and picked up a sheet of paper which had a picture on it – a photograph. He held it up to me.

"This entered Earth's orbit just over five days ago, when it made the first of two course changes: one to put it in an equatorial orbit, perigee of twenty-six thousand kilometres, and the second, some three hours later, to incline the orbit to eighty-eight degrees and reduce the perigee to two hundred and ninety kilometres. We'd very much appreciate it if you could tell us as much as possible about this object."

My manipulators made hard work of holding the flat piece of paper, and Natalia took it from me and let me scan the image as she held it still.

"Is this Mother?" I asked. The picture was grainy and

somewhat indistinct, with some motion blur. But the object was long and thin, with flared structures at either end and a bulge at the midpoint, where their appeared to be a series of spheres.

"Mother? Is that what you call it?" said 'John'. "Do you know what these are?"

He gave Natalia another photograph, a detail of the mid-section. The spheres were resolved in slightly better detail. I looked at them, and remembered.

"This is me, isn't it? Several of me. The spheres are the refractory shield for atmospheric entry. When the internal temperature becomes nominal, I can trigger the explosive fracturing of the covering, and then deploy the aerobraking system – what you would call a steerable parachute – to reduce my descent velocity further."

"You appear to not recognise your own ship. How much information do you have stored regarding its configuration, drive system, previous destinations, total elapsed flight time, whether or not it's armed, or what it intends doing with the information I assume you send back to it?" 'John' pressed all his fingertips together and rested his elbows on the desk.

"None," I said. "I've previously considered the nature of this omission, but now I see that it's most likely a protocol to cover this exact scenario. If I don't know anything about Mother, I can't tell a potentially hostile sentient life-form anything about her, no matter the inducement. You may consider this convenient or expedient, but as far as I can ascertain, your own probes don't contain the schematics of their launch vehicles either."

"Is that how you see us? As potentially hostile?" asked 'John'.

"No. Some of you are definitely hostile. Some of you aren't. This is undeniable fact. There have been three credible attempts to destroy me so far, which have resulted in minor but irreparable damage to one of my legs, several dead soldiers, one downed helicopter and the killing of Petro, Uncle Georg and the pilot Y. Boichenko."

"That wasn't us," said 'John'.

"How do you suggest that I differentiate between the factional groupings who may try and kill me, and those that won't? Do you see my problem? How do I classify the United States of America? I'm able to defend myself against aggressive action: however, these protocols were only designed to protect me from non or semi-sentient predators and those creatures large and aggressive enough to directly compromise my integrity. Not organised groups of sentient persons armed with kinetic or explosive weaponry."

"Could you kill me?" asked 'John'.

"Yes. I have complete freedom to interpret my self-defence protocols as I see necessary. Your soldiers were an obvious threat to me, and to the children on the cancer ward, but I decided that it was unlikely that they would attempt to harm me there. Only later, in this room, did I realise that I shouldn't have gone with them, and ought to have stayed in public view. Please note, if you attempt to prevent me from leaving at the end of this meeting, I'll most likely decide that to be a hostile act, and I'll respond appropriately."

"What's your main armament?"

"None of my equipment is an 'armament'. Some of it has multiple purposes, and can be used in self-defence. I primarily use my high-powered laser, as it is highly accurate, has a quick recharge time and a good range even within the atmosphere."

"Can you demonstrate it for me?"

"I can. What would be the purpose of doing so?"

"To verify your claim."

"If your scientists want to measure my laser's output in a laboratory, then I can arrange to do that. Otherwise, asking me to demonstrate it is simply indicating that you believe I'm lying."

'John' nodded slightly, his head tilting to one side.

"Please," I said, "that gesture. What does it mean?"

Grigory wiped his hands on his trousers. He was sweating, even though the room was quite cool and he wasn't doing any sort of physical exercise – a nervous response? "It can mean lots of things. In this case, he probably realises that you aren't stupid or naïve, and he's acknowledging that to himself."

"Where are these questions going?" asked Natalia. "Is he trying to build up a case to have you interned or quarantined, or something like that?"

"I don't know," I said. "Is that likely? Can he do that?"

"I suppose he can," said Grigory. "If the president has authorised his mission. I'd need to contact someone in the state department. Translators know a lot of people. I could probably find out."

'John' appeared content to wait until we'd finished our conversation.

"The object you call Mother: does it have any weapons? Is it controlled by an AI, or does it have a biological crew? If we sent a team up to investigate it, would they be fired on or otherwise treated as hostile? What would be the repercussions if we took control of the object and prevented it from leaving orbit? Is it possible for the object to be programmed to self-destruct?"

"In order: I don't know, I don't know, I don't know, I don't know, and I don't know. Did I leave anything unanswered?"

'John' again made the acknowledging gesture. "How many probes did the object send down to the Earth's surface?"

"I don't know."

"You don't know. Okay. Are you still in communication with the object?"

"Periodically, yes, when Mother is within line-of-sight."

"Does the object communicate with you?"

"No, apart from an initial response indicating she's ready to receive, and a terminal code acknowledging the end of my transmission."

"You've been abandoned here?"

"I intend to carry out my mission until I've either completed it or my functions become so degraded that I can no longer collect meaningful information."

"What does the object do then?"

149

"Mother? I don't know."

"Could you ask?"

"I don't know. It's a question that's never occurred to me before. I'll consider it."

SEVENTEEN

John's questions veered from the highly specific to the very general, backwards and forwards. I began to doubt his claim to be a xenobiologist. He appeared to be an expert in interrogation techniques, something that was confirmed by both Natalia and Grigory, at least in their professional opinions.

He quizzed me on my construction and powerplant, my protocols regarding how I determined what to study, my memory-retaining structure, my ability to self-repair or manufacture spare parts for myself. I told him plainly that I was a planetary survey probe, and never expected to encounter any creature sentient enough to enquire how I was made. When he asked if I'd give permission to be disassembled, both myself and Grigory both said 'no' simultaneously. Natalia was furious. "You're suggesting vivisection! How dare you!" John presented his palms in a gesture of surrender. "I won't suggest that again," he said. "It's interesting, though, that you think of it as alive in some way, when clearly it's a machine. You're a doctor, you deal with people's bodies all the time. Yet you seem to be making a category error regarding a robot."

"You've heard of the Turing test," said Natalia.

"Yes," said John, "of course."

"Then in which way would it fail?"

"Passing the Turing test isn't a recognition of its human rights. Merely that it can imitate human responses to human questions. Some of its responses will be inhuman, because it's not human. For example, it's shown no frustration whatsoever at my multiple attempts to get it to contradict itself. A biological response would be first irritation, then non-compliance, then anger. That's telling in itself."

"It's more than just a machine," said Natalia.

"I agree," said John. "It is, most probably, an artefact constructed on another planet, by another species, and sent into deep space to survey worlds where life is likely to be present. We tracked the spaceship's trajectory, and we're reasonably certain it didn't visit any of the other planets in our solar system. It came straight here, and after orbital insertion, and also presumably confirming by remote sensing techniques that life was indeed present, it deployed one of its multiple probes to the surface. This makes this robot a very valuable and currently unique machine that also houses an artificial intelligence. Beyond that, I'm not willing to go."

"Aren't you?" asked Grigory.

"No. Neither should you. I appreciate the temptation to anthropomorphise, but it's exactly that – a temptation. This robot isn't human, or anything approaching it. It's not a dog or a cat or a whale or a dolphin. It's not even an octopus or a crow. It's an alien-made machine, whose ultimate purpose is unknown, even to itself." John sorted through his paper, and laid a map in front of him. "Now, back to business. Where did you land?"

I took a pen from the director's desk, took off the lid, and moved it over the map. It was less detailed than the one the pilot had given me, but the major topological features were still recognisable, as were the place names.

"Here," I said, and dabbed the pen down. "My refractory shell will be somewhere in the forest, as will my parachute and its deployment container."

"Tell him about the massacre," said Natalia.

Grigory looked across at her, but she stared straight ahead. "Tell him. It's important."

So I did. I told him about the soldiers shooting all the men from Petro's village, and where their bodies were. John took the map back and wrote something down on a separate sheet of paper. "That's behind the front line now, in territory claimed by the rebels?"

Natalia nodded, and asked for the map back. "I was here, yesterday, with the mother of Robert. This town's now where fighting's heaviest. The surrounding countryside is... No one knows whose it is. Haven't you got spies or satellites to tell you these things?"

"Possibly," said John. "That part of the intelligence gathering network is outside my department. Now we come to the part of the interview which could be considered completely redundant. However. Do you know if you were sterilised before departure from your home system? Do you know whether precautions were taken to prevent microscopic organisms travelling with you? Is there the possibility that you've carried viruses or bacteria or fungus spores with you to Earth? Do you know if our biologies are compatible to a degree that might mean that any of those can grow under terrestrial conditions or can infect terrestrial organisms?"

"I don't know," I said. "Given my purpose, I would have thought that – like you, under COSPAR category four protocols – I would have been thoroughly cleaned to prevent forward contamination. My makers were advanced enough to conceive and launch a space mission searching for life on other planets. It would have been a considerable oversight to have then sent life with the landers."

"Have you ever come into contact with nanorobots? Are nanorobots an integral part of your design? Is any of your self-repair or maintenance functions based on the operation of nanorobots? Are any nanorobots that you carry capable of self-replication and or evolution of function? Are any nanorobots that you carry able to interact with biological life? What is the maximum lifespan of any nanorobots that you carry?"

"I fixed my leg with glue," I said. "Does that answer your questions?"

"Yes," said John. "Nevertheless, I'd like to take some swabs. You've been free in the environment for several days. Enacting biosafety procedures now is rather pointless, but if you've unleashed a pandemic for which we've no resistance, then at least we'll have some advanced warning."

John put his bag back on the desk and brought out a clear plastic bag full of thin see-through containers. He put on a pair of thin latex gloves, and opened the packet. Some of the red-lidded containers spilled out, and he corralled them. "At this stage, I'm most worried about an invasive species of plant or fungus that reproduces by spores. They'd have no biological check on their growth, which, assuming a suitable environment, would be potentially exponential. We'll need to examine the landing site, and locate the pieces of your re-entry vehicle."

Grigory pushed himself upright. "That'll be difficult. I can't imagine the rebels will just let you walk in and do whatever you want. We've had three ceasefires within the last month, and none of them lasted more than twenty-four hours. And even if they're willing to give you access, they're not really the ones in control are they? As soon as the other side finds out where it came down, they'll seal the area off with their own troops and bring in their own scientists."

John walked around the desk and passed Natalia another pair of the blue latex gloves. "Doctor, if you could assist me? I'm aware of some of the wider geopolitical implications of trying to gain access to the site. That's for other people to arrange. My job here is to simply interview the robot, arrive at a realistic assessment of the threat level it poses both to the United States of America, and to the rest of the world, and communicate that to my superiors."

"Don't you care what happens?" asked Natalia. She snapped on the gloves with practised ease. "Or is that a stupid question from some stupid civilian who doesn't know how the Great Game gets played between governments? I mean, we're supposed to be allies already, and you've done nothing for us so far other than 'express concern' over 'recent developments'. People are being driven out of their homes and being killed, now."

"Yes," said John. "They are. Could you hold this, please?" He gave her one of the sterile containers and unscrewed the lid. The integral swab was fixed to the inside of the lid on the end of a long plastic stick, and he wiped it on the surface of one of my legs. He then slotted it back into the container and tightened the lid back on. "Sample number seven eight two four zero, front left leg, ventral surface."

"So when are you going to intervene?" asked Natalia. "When does being allies begin to actually mean something other than hand-wringing?"

John took another of the swabs and rubbed it against the joint where my leg joined my carapace. "I'm afraid decisions like that are as far beyond my clearance as they are yours. I can make recommendations as to the importance of securing the alien artefacts. What those above me do with my advice is very much up to them."

"That isn't remotely helpful," said Natalia.

"I appreciate that, Doctor." 'John' swabbed my dorsal surface, and my manipulators. "Do you have any internal recesses that I can take samples from?"

I opened up the various hatches and ports.

"I guess you do," he said, and methodically took swabs from each one. "Really, I have a specific role here. Beyond that, my opinion counts for very little."

"What about the soldiers outside?" she asked. "What about the suits?"

"Their sole task was to get me access to the robot. Granted, it would have been easier for me just to turn up and ask nicely, but apparently this is the way the big CIA playbook says it has to be done. When I'm finished, they're going to escort me, and my samples, back to the airport. I'll call my superiors on a secure line and I'll start work on the cultures. Whether or not any of us ever get to go home is dependent on what I find."

"So the soldiers and the other men will go with you?"

"Yes. They'll go with me. I realise that they can come across as a bit aggressive, but they've been ordered into a situation that might mean they never see their families again before the entire human race becomes extinct, and they entered that situation willingly. You don't have to think of them kindly, but please understand that they, and me, are attempting to do our best in difficult circumstances. It is, as I said, a bit late for quarantine and a full lock-down, given the number of potential vectors. But someone has to worry about it."

"You're saying I should have thought of that. It's a robot." Natalia saw that John had finished, and peeled off her gloves and dropped them in the bin. "Why would I have thought of that?"

John collected all the samples and rebagged them. "No particular reason. But it's what they pay me to do, day in, day out. So there's that."

He took off his own gloves and picked up the camera, still on the desk.

"I'm just going to do a quick three-sixty of you, and then we're done. Is that okay?"

I almost nodded. I had nothing to nod with, yet my first instinct was to nod. Your gestural short-hand was astonishingly expressive and meaningful. I wish I could copy it. "Yes. Proceed."

John circled me with his camera, recording my physical presence for his superiors. He walked slowly, panning the lens up and down as he turned. When he arrived at his starting place, he pressed a button on it, which clicked. "Thank you very much for your cooperation. Despite everything, this has been a genuine pleasure, and I really do hope you haven't unleashed the End of Days, however unwittingly."

"There appears no reason to travel what I presume is a very great distance in search of life, just in order to kill it," I said, and as John packed his bag again, he smiled.

"Far from it: it's one of the solutions to the Fermi Paradox. Have you had chance to consider it at all?"

"I came across it in an article on extraterrestrial life and the Drake equation," I said.

"There's an awful lot of things I actually want to talk to you about," said John. "And instead I've had to simply reel off a list of questions and record your answers. I hope, in the future, we can sit down and have a proper conversation. I do, however, have to do my job first. One of the solutions of the Fermi Paradox is that an advanced civilisation will search for and terminate with extreme prejudice any competitors before they get into the position of being able to challenge the dominance of the first."

"Is that what you believe me to be?"

"It's one possible scenario. Up until you landed, all we had were hypotheses as to why we appeared to be alone in the universe. We hope – my colleagues and I, and the wider scientific community – to be able to arrive at a better understanding of the parameters regarding both Fermi and Drake in the months and years ahead." John closed his bag. "Right now, we have to worry about how we're going to make it through the next few days without setting off World War Three and disqualifying ourselves from the race."

"Is that likely?" asked Natalia, once Grigory had finished translating.

"My personal opinion isn't one that should be taken too seriously," said John. He looked down at the desk to make sure he hadn't left anything behind. "But what's at stake has now increased dramatically. It's more than just the integrity of your country. There's an alien spaceship in orbit around our planet, and there's an alien robot probe – at least one alien robot probe – on the surface. Every leader of every nation is locked in a room with their advisers, trying to work out precisely what that means for them. Everything is much more unpredictable today than it was yesterday. And unpredictable is dangerous. I might be the first to talk to you in an official capacity, but I won't be the last. Be very careful, all of you."

John picked up his bag and shook hands with both Grigory and Natalia. I extended a manipulator towards him and, after a few moments' hesitation, he reached out and gripped it with his fingers. I curled the end around the back of his hand and applied a slight pressure, then moved it up and down, as I'd seen you do before. I didn't quite know how long to carry on the gesture: one shake was too few, but how many was too many? I settled on three, and let go.

John stared at me, and then at his hand.

"There are no nanorobots," I said.

"No," he said, "that would be... unfortunate." He flexed his fingers and then clenched them together. "There is one more thing. I've been instructed to ask you if you want to come to America. An option at the start was to simply subdue you and force you to come with us, if we thought it possible. I've ascertained that there'd be a considerable loss of life on our side, with no guarantee of success of taking you 'alive', so to speak. And given that I'm no longer recording proceedings, it'd also be a bit of a dick move too."

"If you'd attacked me, I would have defended myself," I said.

"Yes, I know that. But once we'd broken all your legs, disabled your cameras and torn out your tentacles, and done something about your lasers, you'd just be a large box, and we could pick you up and carry you wherever we wanted. You could still talk over the radio, and that's the bit we're really interested in. But the wider consequences of attacking you are still unknown, and the consequences of persuading you to cooperate with us are far better. That's it, cards on the table. I can take you away from the war zone if you want."

"Wouldn't it be better for all the people who live here," said Natalia, "if you took the war zone away from it? There's no reason for this whole situation, other than Russia, egging on one side, and your president, sitting on his thumbs on the other. You should take away the conditions for war, support us, get tough with that pale moth and his cronies. Say you'll defend us! They'll back off, stop sending arms and soldiers across the border."

"It might come to that," said John. "But then you'll have American troops in a possible live-fire situation with soldiers from another nuclear armed power. That, even with my limited knowledge, could lead to an escalation which no one would be happy with, but mostly powerless to prevent. Things are rarely as simple or straight-forward as we'd like them to be, Doctor. Now, I really must go. Please consider my offer, er, robot. It's a sincere one, and you might not get any better."

EIGHTEEN

After John had left the room, I could hear the soldiers in the next collecting their equipment and getting ready to leave. The outer door opened, and the sound of their boots receded.

"I believe they've all gone," I said, and Grigory checked on the office beyond.

"That's it, then." He puffed out his cheeks. "I could do with a drink. Coffee. A great deal of coffee."

"There's a canteen down on the second floor," said Natalia. "The coffee's almost drinkable there. Come on, I'll show you where it is." She looked at me. "What do you want to do?"

"There are a number of things I need to consider. But my first priority is to see whether or not I can talk to Mother. I've a considerable amount of data to upload, anyway. I can insert questions and requests for clarification into the body of information. It might be that not talking to me is in her protocols, to prevent manipulation of her. If you've thought that other civilisations might try and exterminate you, my makers may well have considered the possibility that an emergent civilisation might try to take Mother by force or subterfuge."

"You didn't say any of that to John," said Natalia.

"John didn't ask for my opinion at any point. He asked for what I knew. Had he asked for my opinion, I would have told him. Likewise, Mother is an interstellar spacecraft, and it's likely that it moves between stars at a measurable proportion of the speed of light. I can therefore conclude it'll have some mechanism for eliminating macroscopic debris within its path, which would also act as a weapon, in the same way that my cutting lasers do. Whether Mother is willing or able to differentiate between a powered spacecraft approaching it and a

160

piece of rock is something I can't know."

"Do you think they'll try and intercept the mothership?" asked Grigory, and Natalia made the snorting noise that indicated incredulity.

"Of course they're going to try. You heard John ask all those questions about Mother. They're going to try, if they aren't already trying."

Grigory frowned. This meant he was thinking hard.

"The Americans have the problem of possessing no man-rated space capsules," I said. "In order to send astronauts to Mother, they'll either need to use an unrated prototype, or require the cooperation of one of the two countries that do possess such vessels. It's therefore likely that they'd prefer to send a remote probe to investigate. What do you think they'll do?"

"They'll go for the prototype," said Grigory. "The others will be scrabbling to launch their own missions, but I'm guessing the Chinese will get there first, because they will. It normally takes months, if not years of planning to launch a rocket. I'm sorry. That doesn't sound very impressive, does it?"

"I've an upload scheduled to Mother. I'll attempt to establish two-way communication. It's unlikely that I'll succeed. Given your assessment that it'll be some time before a human spacecraft can attempt to approach Mother, what can we do between then and now that'll reduce the risk of war between your nations?"

"I'm really going to need coffee to answer that." Grigory patted his pockets. "I've got money. Let's go."

He opened the doors for me, and Natalia led the way to the lifts.

"Can I see your money?" I asked. "I keep seeing long strings of numbers associated with the concept, but I don't know what it actually looks like."

"Most countries have their own currency." He put his hand inside his jacket and pulled out a thin black folding container. He opened it up and held out several pieces of paper. "I've got some twenties, a couple of tens, a five and some ones. There's also a two, and some larger ones, which I don't have. I don't know anyone who's seen a five hundred – anyone who's not a gangster or a politician, anyway."

I took them from him and, with difficulty, looked through them. The different values were colour coded, and had different pictures on each side: but always a person on one, and a building on the other. "As my employee, I need to give you some of these in exchange for your labour. How do I go about getting my own for that purpose?"

The lift arrived, and we all shuffled in. The doors closed.

Natalia said, "I don't know. You could, sell interviews? That's how celebrities make money. They charge for pictures of themselves, and get paid for talking to journalists. That's how it works, right? Or get sponsorship from companies in return for allowing them to use your image in their adverts. That's not really very good, though, is it? It's not the..." She held her hands up. "It's not why you're here."

"Hang on," said Grigory. "There's something there that's actually a decent idea. We could crowdfund it. Go on one of those websites and just ask for donations. If everyone of your twitter followers gave us just one US dollar, I could simply work for you, and not have to take any other work, for months. And depending on how much we got, we could literally hire whoever you wanted. That would work. We could set up a non-profit, get a manager in to handle the paperwork, and it'd be done."

"People who exchange their labour for money will give me a proportion of their earnings? Why would they do that? If money is the medium of exchange, then what do they expect to get in return?"

Grigory and Natalia looked at each other and made the exact same head-dip and raised-shoulders expression. "People are kind, and generous, normally. If you explain what you need the money for, they'll be happy to give it to you, and I suppose their reward is their happiness."

The lift doors slid aside.

"People will just give me money?"

"Yes," said Grigory. "They'll just give you money."

"Like this?" I handed him back the notes he'd given to me. He took them and folded them back into his case.

"Yes, almost exactly like that. It'll come in electronically, from all around the world. We'll need a PayPal account, and probably a website, and a Facebook page, and whatever the kids are on these days – Tumblr, Snapchat – I've got a niece and a nephew I can ask about that. But I've a friend, Andriy, who knows how to do all this stuff. I'll give him a call, and we can probably have something up and running by the end of the day. Tomorrow, latest."

"Why will people just give me money?"

"Get out of the lift. We'll explain it all when we're sitting down." Natalia waved at both of us and we crossed the corridor into the canteen, which was apparently a place for the production and consumption of food and drink. They moved some tables and chairs to allow me to sit with them, and then Grigory went to the long, brightly lit counter to contract the cooks to make him a coffee.

When he brought the tray over, it had two glazed ceramic containers of a brown liquid, and a flat ceramic disk with a pile of torus-shaped objects, also brown but a different shade of brown, covered with tiny black spheres. I hooked one with my manipulator and examined it. Some of the black spheres fell off and scattered across the table, and then the floor. "Is that important, or trivial?" I asked.

"It's just poppy seeds," said Natalia. "It's not a problem."

"What is this?" I asked.

"It's a bublik. It's made with boiled bread dough that's then baked. Very traditional," she said. She took one of the containers of liquid and set it in front of her, and then hit my questing manipulator as it made its way towards the liquid inside. "That's... sorry. Socially unacceptable. No one's going to mind you taking a bublik and breaking it apart and doing whatever it is you do with it, because no one's going to eat it afterwards. But there's no way that you can dip your tentacle in someone's drink without it invoking a degree of disgust." She moved the container away slightly. "I didn't mean to hit you. Reflex."

Grigory found an extra piece of crockery and carefully tipped some of his coffee on to it. "She's not wrong. Sharing food and drink is an expression of friendship and solidarity, but most people will insist on their own cups at least." He pushed the puddle of coffee towards me. "So, here's yours. This drink is coffee. It's made from a ground, roasted bean of the coffee plant, which is native to tropical Africa, and is now also grown around the world, where conditions are suitable. A lot of people drink it."

I put the bublik down and probed the coffee. It was an incredibly complex mixture of chemicals – phenols, acids, fats – and judging from the thermograph, served at high temperature. "Why do lots of people drink it? What do you get from it?"

"Caffeine," said Natalia. "Mild stimulant. Doctors run on it. And it tastes nice. It's difficult to describe. You can make it with sugar and milk to control how strong or bitter it is, more coffee or less coffee, brewed for longer or shorter. Differences in the roast and the bean. People can choose how they like it."

"And the bublik?"

"Wheat flour, yeast, oil, water. Formed into rings, left to rise – that's the yeast converting the carbohydrate into carbon dioxide gas – and then boiled, then baked. You can add things to the dough, or sprinkle things on top. Like poppy seeds. Very popular." She took one, broke it in half to reveal its pale interior, and dipped one end into her coffee. She then ate the coffee-saturated bread.

I watched her, and I watched for Grigory's reaction, but he was too busy doing the same thing to pay attention.

"This is unnecessary for nutrition," I said. "A simple mix of cooked grains, fruit and vegetables, and a source of protein – animal or vegetable – would be sufficient, as would water to drink. You've chosen to make this very complicated. Why?"

They both looked at me. "Culture," said Grigory.

"What he said," said Natalia. "We've a limited number of taste receptors on our tongues, but the oral cavity is connected to the nasal passages and the olfactory bulb where we can smell many more – our brains often confuse taste and smell – and then there's colour and texture too. We can eat the same things, day in, day out, but that's really boring. We need stimulation for our senses. This is just one aspect of that. Art. We haven't shown you any art yet!"

"Music," I said. "I've heard music."

"There's literature, and paintings, and plays, and opera, and movies, and poetry. And there's all kinds of music. And clothes. Photography. Design. Architecture. There's literally a whole world for you to explore." Natalia dipped her bublik into her coffee again. "I'm actually jealous. You get to see these things for the first time."

"You would contend that all of these aspects of human life are worth recording and preserving. Then why has your species spent a significant proportion of its time and energies attempting to erase other groupings? You have a whole profession dedicated to discovering lost art and artefacts from extinct civilisations. Wouldn't it be easier not to lose them in the first place?"

"There are," said Grigory, "unresolvable contradictions in human nature. We create, we destroy, we love, we hate, we plant, we burn. If we had one linear civilisation from the dawn of time, perhaps we'd be visiting your planet by now. But it's more likely that we'd have stagnated and died off. Conflict and crisis sparks progress as often as it causes destruction. It's how we advance. It's stupid and terrible, and it's the only way we know how. The problem is, is that the next conflict could be the last one, the one that wipes us out or knocks us back so far we'll never recover."

I considered this. "Am I that next conflict?" I asked.

The other people in the canteen, who had all been listening in anyway, fell silent. Natalia looked at her coffee, and wouldn't raise her head. Grigory made several gestures that I thought meant that he was trying to think of an answer.

Eventually he said. "Maybe. I don't know. That's up to us, isn't it? There's no reason – no good reason – well, okay, there are some very good reasons why you might be. But it wasn't like we weren't fighting in the first place. Your arrival has changed a few things, that's all."

Grigory picked up a bublik and span it around his finger, then turned in his chair to address everyone.

"That's the truth, isn't it? We were already fighting, and now something's happened that means we have to look again at what we want, and how best to achieve it. If the Americans or the Europeans aren't going to help us, I don't know: perhaps the robot can."

There was collective shifting of bodies, and the creak of metal as chair legs took on different strains. People leaned forward. That meant they were paying more attention to what was being said. Grigory noticed the change too. He looked at me, then back at the people in the canteen.

"I know it was just chance. It could have landed pretty much anywhere. It didn't though. It landed in our country. We didn't get the opportunity to welcome it properly. We do now. Where's our president? Why isn't he here, with bread and salt? Instead, he sends Americans with guns, who want to take it away against its will."

"So where are the Americans with guns to fight alongside us?" shouted someone, and Grigory was on his feet, speaking in their direction, but also looking at everyone else in turn.

"They're not here, and they're not going to be here. Unless we do something about it. Listen: the Americans were very interested in parts of the robot's descent craft, that are scattered in the woods to the north-east, up the valley in the hills. They want them for their own. But those pieces aren't theirs, are they? And that's now rebel territory. It's not theirs, either. What are we doing about that?"

"Well, if the Americans want it before they do, they're not going to get it on their own, are they? They'll need our help." It was the same voice as before, and I identified the speaker as a man in a pale blue uniform, with a long crescent of facial hair between his nose and mouth: it twitched in time with his words.

Grigory jabbed his finger at the man. "Or the American president calls the Russian president and tells him the Americans are going in, taking the ship, and they don't want to fight over it. They're only interested in collecting the pieces. After that, they're gone again, and we can keep on fighting without a hope of intervention. I've been in enough meetings between politicians to know what goes on."

"What are we going to do then?" asked a woman.

Grigory made an open-handed gesture. "We need to get it ourselves. We've got scientists. We've got universities. Why shouldn't we be the ones who investigate it? We're not frightened children. We took to the streets before. Brought a government down. We're a proud people: we shouldn't just accept this."

"I'm just a porter," said the man with the hair. "I can push a trolley around as well as the next man, and I can handle a gun, but I can't see myself at the front, getting in the amongst the artillery shells. And what is it they tell us? The harder we push, the harder they'll push. We have to do it by talking or not at all. Least, that's what they say."

"The longer we talk, the more we lose," said Grigory.

Natalia handed him her phone, which disrupted his concentration, but he was too surprised by the gesture to ignore it. Instead, he took the device and read what was on the screen. He looked away, down at the floor, then back at the screen, as if the text should have changed in the interim.

"Okay," he said. "The rebels are demanding the return of 'their' discovery. They wouldn't be doing that without being told to."

"They can't have it," someone said, and the noise in the room grew quickly to become an incomprehensible blend of sound.

Grigory used a hand gesture – palms held high and level, bringing them down simultaneously and smoothly, and repeating – to quieten them again.

"It's not up to us, and it's not up to them. I know what it looks like – it looks like a robot. We're not used to them having an opinion, at least in real life. It does, though. This is a thinking being. I've spent long enough in its company to know that. It's not a thing that you own, like your car or a, a phone." He held up Natalia's phone, then handed it back. "This is slavery. This is owning people. I don't care what the Americans say about it not having human rights. It's a visitor to our planet, and we need to treat it with respect. Just think about that for a minute. A visitor to our planet. If we get this wrong, we could be in so much trouble."

There was an involuntary look up from almost everyone there. When they looked down again, their faces seemed odd. Tight. Muscles tensed under the skin.

Grigory turned to me. "What do you want to do?" he asked.

I said: "My mission remains unchanged. I'm here to learn about your planet, and everything on it. I can't do that if any one of your countries claims me as their property. I'm not to be owned by anyone. As to who owns – a concept that is new to me – the debris from my shell and aerobraking system, then that would be me. It derived from me, and is therefore mine to dispose of as I determine, to sell, or to give away, which is a custom of some of you.

"However, I'm aware of social obligations: you've taken me in and sheltered me, taught me new things and have advised me on human society. If my presence among you is so disruptive that it brings your country, your world to a point of crisis, then I should remove myself from it. However, if you'll tolerate me here, then I'll stay with you. I'll not go with the Americans, and I'll not be claimed by your rebels. I'll stay with you. This is my choice."

The people there made more noise. I could quite tell what

they meant by it, but they also slapped their palms together repeatedly, almost violently, making sharp sounds that reverberated off the walls.

"Grigory, explain," I said.

He leaned in. "They're happy with your decision. They won't let anything happen to you that you don't want to happen, either."

Then the building seemed to move, all of it, all at once. Only a little, but the energy to do that must have been very great. Back, then forward again. The windows imploded and the shattered glass moved in ballistic trajectories away from their origin, carried by an overpressure shock wave that temporarily shut down my microphones.

NINETEEN

The objects in motion hadn't even stopped moving before Natalia grabbed at my leg and started to pull at me.

"Basement. Now."

The other people in the canteen had all crouched as one, all ducking down, holding up their hands and turning their heads away from the blast. Cringing. Very human. Very primal. A reflex older than your species.

Grigory raised himself up. He'd cut his hand and by his expression seemed more angry than hurt, despite the blood dripping from his fingers. "She's right. We don't know what that was. We're going somewhere safe."

"Your hand is damaged," I said. "You're leaking."

He held it up and looked at the wound. "Oh," he said. "I'll survive."

"Only if you receive treatment at some point. Your environment is teeming with potentially harmful micro-organisms, some portion of which will have entered your circulatory system through the breach in your skin barrier. Also, if you lose too much blood, you'll die." I curled a manipulator around his wrist and brought my camera up to his hand. "There's glass embedded in your subcutaneous layers. If you hold still, I can extract it."

I used a small gripping tool to take the fragment of glass, slippery with his blood, from his palm. I discarded it on the floor and, since the glue I'd used on Robert's mother seemed biologically inert, I tried to use it on Grigory. He pulled away.

"A bandage will do just fine. You need that for yourself."

Natalia had already moved to help the other people, but she turned back to me. "I told you. Basement."

I lifted up the radio towards her. "I can help these people with their injuries," I said.

"You're too important for that. What if there's another explosion?"

"Then I'll help the people injured by that one, too."

"That's not what I meant. You're too important to lose."

"Each of these people is also too important to lose."

"But you're unique!"

"An individual person is also unique. If you can assure me than none of these people have sustained injuries that present an immediate risk to their lives, then yes, I'll go to the basement – you can bring the injured to me. Otherwise, I'm best utilised here."

She said something that wasn't in my lexicon, but ended in 'stubborn robot'. "Grigory, go and find bandages, towels, bedding, whatever. Try not to bleed all over it first. You, I need you here."

She was kneeling next to a woman who'd sustained a cut to her neck. I knew there were substantial blood vessels there, and that they were important, not just to keep the brain supplied with oxygen, but to the integrity of the whole circulatory system.

"She's bleeding, and I don't know why. I need some light."

I provided it, and she bent her head close to the wound. Blood was flowing around her fingers as she held the cut open. I moved my camera up to see, too. The woman seemed to be unconscious, but not dead yet. There was a lot of blood on the floor around her, and every time her heart contracted, it ejected yet more.

"I think this is the external jugular vein. In which case, it should be okay to cauterise it." She looked up at me. "Can you do that?"

I lowered my laser into position. "I need to see the ends of the vessel. Can you restrict the blood supply to them?"

She moved her hands and pressed deep into the woman's neck with her thumbs. I used my manipulators to expand the

171

wound, and burnt the severed ends of the tube so that they contracted shut. She let go, and there was still blood seeping out, but considerably less.

"I need a trolley!" she said, her voice rose over all the others. "Priority for surgery."

The man with the facial hair appeared not with a trolley like from the ambulance, but a wheeled chair. He bent down and lifted the woman into it, using a strap to hold her upper torso in place.

"Get her flat as soon as you can and get her in the queue. Stay with her. If that ruptures, she's not going to have long." She wiped the woman's blood off her hands against her uniform. "Should be wearing gloves," she said.

People around us were doing the same as we were: helping each other. I worked with Natalia: she could diagnose problems and perform what she called triage more effectively than I could. To me, any escape of blood indicated a wound that was potentially life-threatening. She taught me as she went, telling me that even though it looked like the inside of an abattoir – I didn't know what that meant – most of the wounds were superficial and the body's own systems would stem the loss of blood until a more permanent repair could be made.

I removed many pieces of glass, and cauterised some more of the heavily bleeding cuts. No one had died, though some were critically damaged and unconscious when they were taken away.

"I have to go," said Natalia. "Scrub up. Help in surgery."

"I should too. What is scrub up?"

"Infection control. Disinfect hands, put on clean scrubs. Try not to kill the patients with sepsis. You can't do that. And people will be tripping over you in the operating theatre." She wiped the back of her hand across her forehead, leaving a red smear across it. "Until we find out what happened, we have to assume we're still under attack. You need to go to the basement. They're after you: specifically you. Yes, it is likely that the hospital got bombed because you were in it, and the director... I don't know what the director's going to say or do about that."

"I didn't request bombing," I said. The canteen, with chairs overturned, tables with half-eaten food and spilled drinks, and everywhere puddles and smears of blood, looked very different. I lifted up a chair, and set it back on its feet. The floor crackled with broken glass. "Perhaps I should ask those doing the bombing to stop."

"Why don't we do that?" Natalia used two of her cleaner fingers to fetch her phone out of her pocket, and she held it up to take a photograph. "What do you want to say? Please stop bombing hospitals just because I'm in them? How does that sound?"

I assented, and she tweeted the message.

"Basement. Please. If they destroy you, the world is very much a poorer place." She touched my leg and left, running.

Grigory used the last of the fabric bandages he was handing out to staunch his own wound. He wrapped it tightly around his hand, then made a fist. "We have to take the stairs. The lifts are out, and even if they weren't, it wouldn't be wise to use them." He looked at me. "You can do stairs, can't you?"

"I don't know. I expect that we'll find out."

"You're too big for me to carry. I don't even know how much you weigh."

"I estimate that it'd take several humans to carry me, should the need arise. The CIA's soldiers – the ones who would have removed my legs and any ability I had to interact with the world – would have been sufficient."

"I'm sorry they don't get it," said Grigory. "Oh crap. Where did John say he was going? Back to the airport?"

"He said they had their vehicles outside," I recalled. Grigory walked over to the spaces where the windows had been, weaving his way through the debris of the canteen. He rested his hand on the glassless frame and leaned out. There was black smoke rising past him from below.

"Doesn't look good. There are burning cars and... bodies.

There are medical teams down there, too. The hospital front is a wreck. Pretty much lost all of the glass. The ground is covered in it. There's a crater. Car bomb, may be? Can't tell. What a mess." He turned back from the window. "They're bombing hospitals now. This has to be answered."

"Natalia has told us to go to the basement. Is this advice I should follow, or should I be doing something else?"

"What are you good at?"

"I appear to be able to retrieve small objects from the skin of people with speed and accuracy. I can also cauterise wounds and offer reassuring words of comfort. At the very least, I can repeat what Natalia was saying as she treated her patients. It seemed to have some physiological effect in lowering heart rate and voluntary movement."

"I'm looking forward to seeing your bedside manner in action. Let's go to the basement – Natalia's quite scary, so we can tell her we've been to the basement without lying – and then see what's happening there. If there's nothing for us to do, then perhaps we can find somewhere else we can be useful." He walked over to the lifts, next to which was the door to the stairwell, and held the door open for me.

I looked at the brightly-lit steps, and judged their depth, and more importantly, their width. I knew the size and articulation of my own footfall, and calculated that, with care, I could keep my weight on the back of each pad and still stay upright. It would take some time, and I'd have to go first, because if I slipped, I'd crush Grigory. And that would be unfortunate and give me a reputation for being careless with the lives of my employees.

The friction between my feet and the concrete of the steps was inconstant. I made some misfootings, but was better able to correct them because I was a robot, with very fast reflexes, and I could always shift my centre of gravity to a more advantageous position, even if that position appeared counter-intuitive to human understanding. That was certainly the impression Grigory gave, who gasped and squeaked behind me as I descended.

But when we arrived at the basement without serious incident – the handrails were exactly that, designed for the human hand and not my manipulators – we found it already occupied by many people who had come to take shelter underground. Many of them were uninjured, having been on the other side of the building when the explosion occurred, but there were also many patients, both existing and new, who'd been injured by glass projectiles.

There were those, too, who had been closer to the detonation than others. The worst injured had been killed, but those who'd survived had been triaged, and the least injured sent down to the basement. They were burnt, and had blunt force traumas resulting in contusions and broken bones. As me and Grigory moved through the wide corridors lined with pipes and ducts, I encountered the children from the cancer ward.

They greeted me, and the more active tried to climb on top of me again. Some of them expressed their concern that I'd been damaged in the explosion, and I was able to assure them I was completely unharmed. I also told them I had an important job to do, like the doctors and the nurses trying to heal their patients. Grigory helped me to remove the children from my dorsal surfaces, and we found what he called a treatment station – two nurses working in poor lighting conditions with minimal equipment, and a long queue of people waiting.

They looked up at me, and at Grigory, then at me again.

"It's... here to help," he said.

I held up my radio – the battery had begun to lose power, and when it failed, I would be temporarily speechless – and said: "I'm able to treat anyone with penetration wounds, embedded objects and moderate bleeding. Anything more serious will require human intervention." I turned my lights on, one by one, until it was as bright in the corridor as it would have been outside.

I lined up next to the nurses, and Grigory made the open-handed, shoulders-raised gesture.

"It won't hurt you. I've seen it at work, and it's surprisingly efficient."

I waited for my first patient, and when no one came forward, one of the nurses raised her voice at the man who was next in line. He approached slowly. I could immediately see what the problem was: he'd been struck in the face with multiple fragments, and with the facial area being well-supplied with minor blood vessels, everything above and below his eyes, which he'd presumably managed to cover with his arm, was cut and bleeding.

"Sit down, and don't be afraid," I said. "Grigory, I need water in order to be able to inspect the wounds more accurately for glass."

The nurses had some, and he passed me a bottle, and some swabs, and went to find more. The bottle would squirt water through a narrow opening when I squeezed it, so I started at the highest point, and began to work my way down.

"What's your name, human?" I asked. Natalia had shown me the importance of maintaining a dialogue in order to both normalise the experience and help in assessing the patient's stability.

"Olek," said the man. "My name's Olek. You're the robot, aren't you?"

"Yes, I'm the alien robot from outer space. I'll answer to 'robot', though. Your injuries appear to be mostly superficial and will heal in the normal human way. Many have stopped bleeding already, although the cleaning process may well cause them to start again: this will only be temporary."

"That's, that's good to know," said Olek.

"You did well to shield your eyes from the blast," I said. "They're much more easily damaged, and less repairable, than the rest of your face. I'll look at your arm when I've finished that. You've a few pieces of glass on your skin. One property of your circulatory system I hadn't anticipated is that the blood forces objects out of the wounds before it coagulates. This makes my task easier. You do, however, have several visible fragments in your hair, which I'll attempt to remove. Please hold still."

Olek had dark hair that had a tight spiral to them, which had both protected his scalp and captured many of the small sharp glass fragments within its interweaved matrix. I used my fine tools to remove the largest pieces, then instructed him to tilt his head forward. I agitated his hair with my manipulators to dislodge the smaller ones, and most of the glass fell out onto his outstretched legs. I turned his right arm – most people appeared to be 'handed', in that fine motor control was significantly better on one hand than the other, and therefore preferred – and confirmed that he had lacerations down the length of his forearm.

I asked Olek to remove the item of clothing covering the area. There was a closure at the wrist he undid, and he slid the fabric back. Again, the quantity of blood masked minor wounds, except for a single needle of glass that had punctured his skin near his elbow, and had pushed in as far as the muscle membrane beneath. This was a potentially serious injury, and having found it, I felt my feedback system reward me. I extracted the glass and discarded it on one of the already-used swabs. The wound bled freely for a while, then coagulated.

"I'm finished, Olek. Please be aware that you should keep your wounds clean, avoid alcohol for up to seventy-two hours, and if you feel unwell with a fever, or any of the wounds become inflamed or produce a discharge, you may require antibiotics. Good day to you."

Grigory, acting as my assistant, tidied away the swabs into a large black bag, and refilled the water bottle. He helped Olek to his feet and looked for the next patient.

There was John. One of his soldiers was behind him, gun pointing at the floor. John looked dirty. His skin was darkened by combustion products, and his clothes were partially destroyed. His arm was held across his body in a fabric cradle, and he had other damage, notably contusions to his face. His hair, which had been ordered and flat against his head, was now spiked with sweat and contaminants.

He, however, wasn't my next patient. It was a woman,

younger than Olek, but older than Petro. She had had her back to the blast, and while she was quiet and patient while waiting in line, she began to cry when I asked her to remove her top item of clothing.

"Grigory, please explain Polina's behaviour."

"She's embarrassed. She doesn't want to undress in front of strangers, and this is too public for her."

This possibility hadn't occurred to me, and neither did I understand it. Everyone had a body, and while every body was different, every body was also, in gross features, the same. However, it was my job to calm my patient so that I could inspect her wounds.

"Advise me."

"Some sort of screen, and she'll need another top to wear anyway." He leaned forward to speak to Polina: "Don't worry. I'll get you something."

I saw a solution to part of the problem immediately however. "John. You and the soldier are to stand here, together. Face away from Polina. Thank you."

Both of them complied without discussion. I'd exerted dominance over them on this, and they'd accepted it. Which was interesting. The woman's clothing was dark with blood, so much so that the original colour of the fabric was only evident from the ventral side of her. Also, much of the blood had already coagulated, and the material was contiguous with her wounds.

"I'll need to cut your clothing off of you," I said. "Don't be alarmed by the noises. I'm very precise, and you'll not be cut if you stay still."

"I need to talk to you," said John, in English.

"Then either you can do so now, or wait until Grigory returns."

"In private," said John.

"Then you'll have to wait until I've healed all my patients," I said, "which will take an unspecifiable period of time."

"This is important," said John.

"This work here is more important. While none of these people appears injured enough to require immediate surgical intervention, they're still injured, and shock can sometimes mask or complicate symptoms." I didn't understand how shock worked, but Natalia had told me about it. "And please don't turn around. Polina's health and welfare are my primary concerns at the moment."

I sterilised my instruments and began to work, running a fine blade between her skin and the cloth, gently separating the two.

"So will you talk now?" I asked.

John made a grunting sound, signifying annoyance. Then he said: "We were targeted. There was a car outside, packed with explosives, parked near to our convoy after we'd arrived. When we came out, and before we could drive away, it was detonated. We lost three men, and another three will probably lose at least one limb. They don't want us to have you."

"They – the rebel faction – have claimed ownership of me, in the same way that you attempted to. I reject all such claims. I'm an autonomous mind, not a piece of machinery."

"We need to secure you," said John.

"I don't understand the context of the word, secure. I know what it means, but I don't know what you mean by it."

"Take you away and place you somewhere safe, under guard," said John.

"No," I said. I continued cutting and lifting. The cloth was obscuring much deeper injuries than Olek's. Triage was an imprecise procedure, and Polina should have been treated sooner, by someone with more expertise. "If you want to help keep me safe, then you have to stop the fighting. Can you do that?"

I paused briefly to point a camera at John's face.

"If you can't, then I will."

TWENTY

I carried on working through the rest of the day. I never grew tired, and I never had to stop, except to sterilise my instruments between patients. The nurses at my station were replaced after three hours. Their replacements were again concerned how the patients would react to being treated by a robot, but again after the first person accepted my examination, they – not ignored me, because I was very different from them – tolerated my presence, and we even assisted each other on some of the more complex cases.

I sent Grigory away to rest and eat when the first two nurses left. I wasn't certain for how long an employee should normally work, if there were twenty four hours in a day. I was given to understand, however, that normal practices had been suspended, and that those with relevant expertise were giving their labour on a non-contractual ad hoc basis, and deciding for themselves when they should stop.

And because I didn't get tired, even after we'd treated the last patient, I was still able to continue at maximum efficiency. People, when fatigued, made mistakes – correction, made more mistakes – and their behaviour changed: they grew less patient and more irritable, and conversely, more expansive and open to suggestion. I needed to remember that, because it was important.

Grigory found me outside, inspecting the crater left by the car bomb. The soldiers and the police who were supposed to be guarding the area simply waved me through the line of control they'd set up. It was an actual physical line, marked by a band of thin plastic, printed with the repeated phrase 'Police Do Not Cross'. Inside the zone, John's two damaged vehicles were little more than the chassis and bodywork. The ones that had absorbed less energy were now parked around the side of the hospital, where the CIA and their soldiers maintained a separate cordon.

There was blood on the bituminous surface, blood in pools and splashes. I sampled them, finding other chemicals in them other than the usual mix of circulatory fluids. Grigory ducked under the police line, again with their permission, and joined me. He'd brought a cheap battery-powered radio to replace the paramedic's one I'd been using, and I tuned it in to my wavelength.

The sun was approaching the horizon. I didn't know whether this marked the end of the working day. But the rest I'd told Grigory to have appeared to have revitalised him.

"I got you your own phone. It's touch screen, though, and I don't know if your tentacles can work one."

"What technology does it use?" I asked.

"I... I actually don't know. It works fine with a finger, but not if you're wearing a glove. I should have thought about that – you can get a special stylus for them which you can use instead. Sorry. Also, Andriy registered the domain www.lostrobot.com, along with several of the other obvious ones, which all redirect to the main site. You've an email box, and a PayPal account, and a Facebook page, and we've opened up a fund-raising drive across several platforms." He stopped, made a short barking noise, and told me how much money had been donated so far.

"How long has the ability to contribute been available?"

"About half an hour," said Grigory.

"People are very generous to strangers," I said. "I should like to thank them."

We recorded the footage there outside of the hospital, on my phone, and Grigory uploaded it. He texted Andriy to tell him where the file was, and in the way of the internet, it was available instantly to everyone, everywhere. "We're probably going to need to get a server with more bandwidth," he said. "At least, Andriy says we do. You're rich. You can afford it. I'll tell him to do it."

"What should I do, Grigory?' I asked.

He held a finger up – signifying 'wait' – while he finished texting Andriy back, then closed the phone. "What should you do? I don't know. You wanted to explore and learn. With the amount of money you now have, you can pretty much go anywhere in the world you want."

"That's only partially true," I said. "While I can be theoretically present at any given location within my operational tolerances, there are places where hostile local inhabitants would prevent me from surveying the flora and fauna and other natural features."

"I mean, yes, you're right. And while we're on that subject, there are some animals and plants you absolutely cannot sample, because they're rare, or endangered. There's a list somewhere, run by the UN, I think. So no cutting up tigers or a rhinoceros."

"I will consult the list," I said. "But what do we do about the other matter?"

Grigory kicked a loose stone into the shallow crater. "I don't think we can do anything about it. Other people have tried. Other people are trying now. Some people are… I don't know how to describe them. Intolerant? Have an ideology or a worldview that means they don't accept the presence of outsiders, or those who don't share their views? Something like that."

"And yet, they're not any chemically different to you, or Natalia, or Petro, or Uncle Georg who, after initial reservations, accepted me. What should I do to persuade them to grant me access to the territory under their control? I want nothing from them otherwise. I'm not in competition for their resources, I can't reproduce, I don't want to hurt or damage them in any way. I'm not a disease vector. Although I expect all John's swabs were destroyed or rendered non-specific in the explosion, and need to be retaken."

"One of the problems is that you yourself are a resource, as you put it. A unique resource, unless your mothership decides to drop another probe. You've got technology that's beyond what we can create at the moment. Any country that can claim that for themselves might be able to dominate the whole planet. There's also the question of the ship in orbit, too. It's much more advanced than anything we have."

"I'm not willing to be used in that way," I said.

"They'll take you by force, then. Like the CIA had planned to do. And if they can't do that, they'll deny anyone else the opportunity by destroying you." Grigory gestured towards the crater.

"I'll resist them," I said, but Grigory raised one foot and brought it down hard against the road surface.

"There are seven billion of us, robot. One of you. You're not indestructible. All it's going to take is one bomb to get through, and that's it. We've lost you."

"Then that's what we should try and fix," I said. "Make it so that any information gained from me is conditional. It'd mean that everyone will want to cooperate with me, and no one would want to destroy me."

Grigory began to laugh, and ended up crying. "You don't understand," he said, between halting breaths, "You just don't understand just how shitty we can be."

"You're also generous and welcoming," I said. "You can be encouraged to be more that way."

"How? How are you going to do that?"

I reiterated: "By putting conditions on who can interact with me and conduct research on my technology. You said I was a unique resource: I acknowledge that I represent a monopoly of xenocrafted material, but I can use that to leverage what I want in order to conduct my own surveys."

Grigory straightened up and wiped his face. "What conditions?"

"I'm aware that this country's geographical borders have been crossed by soldiers belonging to other countries, in support of the faction you call rebels. What if I say that I won't cooperate with those countries until they remove their soldiers?"

"Would you do that?" he asked.

"Yes. If I calculate correctly, the rebels' material and political support will be withdrawn, and they'll be so weakened that they'll either be easily defeated, or they'll stop fighting and negotiate terms. We can then go and retrieve the pieces of my descent module without having to use your own soldiers, or American soldiers, to force the rebels away from the area. Do you think the scenario I've outlined is feasible?"

"It depends on how valuable they think your information is," said Grigory.

"You've already said that they'd try and destroy me to prevent me talking to other countries. That would already indicate that my worth is high. If my gambit fails, then I'm not at any greater risk than I am currently. If it succeeds, then you and Natalia and the director and Olek and Polina and Maria and the kids and everyone else can live without fear of war."

"What if they see your conditions as a threat?" asked Grigory.

"Since it is a threat, they'll have correctly understood the situation. If they continue to support the rebels, they won't have access to me. They can decide how to react. Perhaps they'll send more bombs. Perhaps they'll withdraw. Grigory, your country's people have displayed tolerance and generosity. Helping them would indicate to both them and others that displaying tolerance and generosity towards me is rewarded."

"You're... training us," said Grigory. He smiled when he said it. "You're actually training us. You sly bugger."

I didn't know what a sly bugger was, but took the smile to mean approval of my methods. "I've simply observed the way that humans interact with each other, and seen how you use the effects of both punishment and rewards to form a functioning society. Even high-status leaders can't punish all the time, since they rely on the people subordinate to them not forcibly removing them from office. I've no means of coercion, so reward is the only means of social influence I have."

"That's not actually true. At some point, other people than

the CIA are going to realise that your Mother is still in orbit. And that an alien spaceship capable of interstellar flight could represent a huge threat to everyone on the planet. It could drop things on our heads – bombs, black holes, asteroids, I don't know what – and there'd be nothing we could do about it."

"I don't know if Mother has that capability," I said. And I didn't. All I knew was that Mother appeared to have other probes like me fixed to her hull, and the protocols for uploading data. I'd had no other interaction with her. Yes, I was going to try to talk to her, but if I was a designer, why would I make Mother susceptible to interference from outside? My makers were intelligent people, and surely they'd planned for even this possibility?

There would, at some point in the future, be an attempt by people to board Mother. I didn't know how Mother was programmed to react, or if Mother was programmed to react at all. Mother was the vehicle that had carried me light-years, awakened me, dropped me on this planet. She would have a drive capable of propelling her that distance and reliable enough that it could stop her again. But whether her path was determined before she left her home system, or whether she was autonomous like me, was simply uninformed speculation. She certainly wasn't speaking to me.

Would it matter that Mother's journey ended here, her mission cut short, the information I'd uploaded – that other probes had potentially uploaded – destined never to reach our makers? If our makers' species was still alive and capable of understanding such data. These were very important questions to ask myself. What if there was a material benefit to the people of Earth in reverse engineering Mother's systems? Would that outweigh the benefit to my makers? How was I to calculate such things?

Or would Mother – who must have an active collision defence – simply destroy all objects that came too close? That possibility was more likely than being equipped for retaliation against the planet below. My own response to being attacked was self-defence, not disproportionate violence. My protocols would be similar to hers. It might, though, be advisable to issue a warning to use only unmanned spacecraft in her vicinity – at least initially, until her operating parameters had been determined.

Grigory was looking at me. I wondered if there was a question I'd failed to answer, but my thought processes were very fast compared to humans, if somewhat linear.

"It would be sensible to issue some guidance regarding contact with Mother," I said, "but I consider it unlikely that she would damage objects on the ground, even if I were deliberately destroyed. I presume her response at that point would be to evaluate the data I'd already returned, and whether it was worth dispatching another probe." The reward response allied to the association of complementary ideas triggered. "Perhaps," I said, "that's already happened."

"You mean the Americans?" asked Grigory.

"No: the other side. They were quite deliberate in targeting me from the beginning. That they'd previously encountered my type before, and provoked a self-defence response from it, might explain why they were so hostile to me."

Grigory looked over to where the CIA had parked their remaining vehicles. "I think we should ask John about that. If he doesn't already know the answer, then someone above him will."

"He would have said if that was the case," I said, and Grigory shook his head.

"He's trained not to tell you anything, unless it's to his advantage to do so. Whatever you do, don't consider him as friend. People like him – spies – they don't have friends: they have contacts. They want you to forget that, to trust them, to tell them everything you know. In my line of work, you get to hear a lot of secrets that other people would like to know. Honestly? At this level, it's a lonely job. Normally, spies don't announce themselves. You just think they're your friends and then they betray you."

"You've past experience of this situation that exceeds mine. I'll exhibit caution when talking to John. However, I'd still like to talk to him again regarding a possible previous drop from Mother. It's likely already occurred to him, but he may be candid."

"He might lie to you, both ways. The American's don't get on well with the Russians. Historically, there's a lot of bad blood between them."

"Bad blood?"

"Past incidents that echo into today. Game theory, really. They were nearly at nuclear war several times over the last sixty, seventy years."

"Nevertheless, John is a trusted conduit to the American government. What I tell him will be quickly communicated to their president."

"It doesn't work like that, either," said Grigory. "It's supposed to. But sometimes the spies keep secrets from their own side."

"That's useful information. In which case, perhaps we should address all the people of Earth on an equal and non-partisan basis. That, however, ignores the power differential between the populace and the government in authority above them."

"So what do you want to do?"

He looked up at the darkening sky. The lights of the surrounding buildings – those that hadn't been rendered inoperable by the explosion – were beginning to shine.

"What do I want? I want to explore and learn. I'd like to avoid being damaged, captured or destroyed, or all three, since that would impair my mission. Given that, I want all people of goodwill to press their governments to grant me that freedom: in return, I'll share my technology with them."

Grigory flipped open my phone and pointed its black lens at me, standing there in the car park, next to the crater, with the burnt vehicles in the background. "We can do as many takes as you like," he said. "Just don't start 'people of Earth, your attention please'. It's got unfortunate cultural resonances."

I computed what I was going to say, then spoke the words: "Hello. This message is for everyone: you, your community and your country, so if you know of someone who hasn't yet heard it, please tell them about it – the more people who hear me, the easier it'll be for you to reach a consensus. I've travelled a long way to be here, on your planet, and I'd like to explain what I'm doing here.

"I'm a robot probe. You've sent your own probes to other planets, so you know why you do that. You send them to examine the rocks, the soil, the air. They explore. They look for signs of life. When my makers sent the ship that's now in orbit around you, that's what they programmed me to do, just like you do. The only difference is that because I'd be so far away, they gave me the capacity to make decisions for myself, rather them sending instructions that might take a hundred years to reach me, if at all.

"I've found life. Not only that, but a whole civilisation. This is an extraordinary event in both our histories – the first time you've made contact with anything else outside your own solar system, and the first time machines from my makers have made contact with you. My mission, the reason I was sent, is to learn everything I can about you, and your planet.

"If you weren't here, I'd just choose where to go and what to look at on my own. But you are here. You're everywhere: from pole to pole, and on every continent. There can't be anywhere left that you haven't walked. So I need your agreement. But more than that – you can tell me about the places I should visit and the things I should see. I'm your guest: uninvited currently, but I'd like to change that.

"You've got as many questions about me as I have about you. I'd like to answer them all, as best I can. I understand that how I'm built, and how I arrived here, utilises technology that is new to you. So this is my proposal: that we trade information, fairly and openly, on a country by country basis. I'll allow groups of people – scientists, philosophers, politicians, whoever you decide to represent you – to examine me and discuss with me, and, in return, I'll want unconstrained access to the land under your control.

"I do have one condition, one that some will find straightforward to meet, and others will find impossible. That is a matter for you. If I'm to deal with you, you need to be at peace with your neighbours. I'll have advisers to help me interpret difficult situations, but the final judgement will be mine alone. I'll not share any of my knowledge with those who make war, or encourage others to do so.

"That's it. It's really that simple. I look forward to hearing from you."

TWENTY-ONE

I tried to talk to Mother, in the same way you'd try to get a response out of Dropbox, or an FTP server. I sent out my authentication codes, received the handshake, and Mother was ready to receive my data. I didn't send it, though. I wanted to see what would happen next if I just left the carrier wave empty but for the timing signals.

The connection timed out. I re-established contact, and just listened. It timed out again, the Doppler on the wavelength starting to stretch out as Mother turned in her orbit. I didn't have a language to talk to her, no prompt I could give her to indicate that I wanted more than just dump data into her memory banks. And anything I said to her would just be considered a subset of that data. She wouldn't even recognise what I was attempting to do.

I persisted. I timed out for a third time, and I realised that I couldn't use that way to talk to her. That particular protocol was for that particular purpose. However, Mother had to be observing other wavelengths. She had to have cameras and aerials to survey the planet beneath her, because otherwise how could she decide where best to drop her probes? Me. How could she have decided where to drop me?

So if I couldn't talk to her on the same frequency that I used to send data… actually I could. I realised that she was ready, primed to watch that exact frequency, and wait for my code. What if I used that frequency, and just… talked? It was all I could think of doing. But what would I say? How would I say it? How could I establish contact with her and not have her expect an upload. Because at that point, she'd just divert the entire stream into memory, and I had to assume she didn't analyse any of it. Just stored it for our makers.

190

How could I establish contact with her, and convince her it was me? Wasn't this precisely the kind of situation that our makers would have foreseen? I believe that the correct term is spoofing, when you believe that a message is from a trusted source but is really from a third party intent on manipulating you.

I tried, nevertheless. In the time that remained for this orbital period, I pinged a series of mathematical concepts at Mother – linear number progression, squares, primes, pi. I listened after each burst, in case she answered. But she never did. And then she slipped below the horizon, and I couldn't communicate with her again, for a while.

I had reward circuits, but none of them had activated. I was what you would call 'sad' at my failure to establish a two-way dialogue. Perhaps Mother wasn't autonomous, like me. Perhaps she was just a big but dumb computer, attached to a huge data storage device. Or perhaps she was aware of my attempts, but the injunction against talking to me was too well embedded. It amounted to the same thing. I couldn't talk to her. I was on my own.

And unless my guess about a previous probe being dropped was correct, I was going to stay that way. There would only ever be humans for me to talk to. Yes, there are seven billion of you, I understood that. My conversations with you would never stop, even if I were to spend but a single hour in each person's company. But these are my kind, and even though I was born in the moments after my release from Mother, hanging above your planet like a bead, I wasn't a native here.

I was made elsewhere. Even the most basic robot you make has some provenance – a maker's mark – that identifies it as human-made. I don't have that. I'm alien. I'm obviously alien. While your probes provoke positive emotions in you, such as pride, satisfaction, and goodwill, you see me differently. You cannot control me as you do those probes. There's always going to be part of you that doubts my motives, despite everything that's happened.

Sometimes I think about being just a robot, without a mind, without consciousness, without self-awareness. Following layered protocols, stimulus-response. But then I think about getting caught in recursive logic loops, or buried so deep in with a decision tree that I can no longer make any actual choice. About not being able to learn and adapt. About not meeting Petro, or Uncle Georg, or you.

But I was still sad at not being able to start a conversation with Mother. We all need guidance sometimes from a mind external to ours. One of your poets said 'no man is an island'. Perhaps the context is different – picking up context from poetry is difficult for me, and I often need it explaining – but the sentiment, the ur-meaning, is clear. We exist in relationship with each other. That insight was worth travelling unnumbered light years to discover.

Grigory's need for sleep was greater than my need to talk all night. I retired to Natalia's office. It still had power, and it still had an internet connection, and it was undamaged due to being towards the rear of the hospital building. I managed a short conversation with her. She looked different. Much of that I could ascribe to her physical exhaustion, but there was more to it than that. Your emotional states are written on your faces. Etched. Did you know that?

Many of her patients were being transferred to other hospitals, away from the hostilities. Some were being moved to the capital city, where there was specialist treatment available for their conditions. The hospital itself would have to close while it was being rebuilt, and its facilities moved into either other buildings, or other towns. She would move with her patients. I asked about the director. She said the director was some other doctor's patient.

Humans are unreliable witnesses. I spent the night learning about your cognitive biases and dissonances. About how you feel often trumps what you know. How, in the end, all you want to be is this indefinable state of 'happy'. Mazlow had much to say on the matter. Some people were more easily pleased than others. A few would never be happy unless everyone else was unhappy: this was psychopathy. I couldn't ignore it, but neither did I have to accommodate it.

I worked all night. It occurred to me that a government was counted successful if it made more people happy, and unsuccessful if it didn't. Governments that made people unhappy were likely to be removed, either at the ballot box where possible, and by force where not. Governments that were made up of the people were more likely to pursue policies directed to happiness. Those that came from a self-selecting oligarchy were not. Which was interesting in itself.

My statement from the previous night was certainly a step in the direction of increasing happiness. War brought nothing but misery for both aggressor and defender, with the civilian population suffering the most. But it wasn't the end point. I'd need to add structure and more conditionality to my initial offer. My goal was still to allow me to survey the planet unhindered, but, taking Grigory's advice that I could either coerce or cajole, I decided my target was more easily and more permanently reached by offering benefits than by threatening destruction.

I looked at one of those lists, 'One hundred places to visit before you die'. Some of them were simply mundane to me, but others set off all kinds of reward mechanisms just by looking at them. I could ask people what they wanted to show me, and why. I could ask them to invite me to where they lived. I could get them to put pressure on their governments to allow that to happen. Also interesting. I'd want to talk to Grigory about that.

I needed to have some sort of official status, though. I couldn't become a citizen of this country, or any country, and I couldn't become a citizen of all countries either. But I could, perhaps, be recognised as an ambassador. I didn't have the necessary documentation to present to heads of state. But I was, in myself, my own bona fides. I read up on the Vienna Conventions. I thought I could comply with their requirements.

I'd have to essentially be the ambassador of my unnamed culture to the whole of the planet, but that was doable. They could either accept the request remotely, or arrange a meeting, whichever suited our schedules best.

I was going to be busy. As a first step, I'd have to go to the capital and present my credentials to the president there. Once he'd named me an official ambassador, setting the precedent, it'd be easier for others to do so. I could have an embassy, and staff it, assuming my funds were sufficient and for as long as they lasted.

I should have considered that while it was night locally, it was daytime elsewhere. Also, I should have considered that people – important people – can and do work through the night, even when their bodies are on the verge of collapse and their minds full of fatigue chemicals, if they have a compelling enough reason to do so.

I had exhausted Grigory the day before, and yet when he found me early the next morning, he appeared to be operating at close to his optimum.

"It's just coffee," he said. "I'll crash later. But we need to sit down and talk. I know we're making this up as we go along, but as the Americans are wont to say, 'shit just got real'. I'm not even sure there's a translation for that, but essentially, we've reached one of those hinge points in history that only comes up once every hundred or so years."

"Explain," I said.

Grigory fell into a chair. Its pneumatic suspension bobbed, and returned the seat to its usual height. I'd taken it apart earlier, but I'd put it back together again properly. It had been an interesting diversion from my legal studies.

"Jonbar hinges are hypothetical moments in history where a small change in a decision making can lead to very different outcomes. You're the hinge. You're also an agent, which makes this situation pretty much unique. So, your statement last night has travelled around the world and I'm certain that every single minister in every single government has seen it. There's been crisis meetings in most of the world's capitals, trying to work out both an individual response, and a unified consensus on how to respond – the two may be actually different, in that a government will be eager to deal with you in private, but publicly will be much more cautious."

"What about the United Nations?"

"Security Council was due to meet yesterday..." He looked at his watch and tried to calculate the time in New York. "...at some point or other, but I think they're still in session, and might stay that way for a while. The reaction from people in general has been broadly positive. Some are still suspicious that you're learning everything about us prior to an invasion, but most people have just accepted that we're not alone in the universe any more, and are actually pretty pleased about that. You'll find all sorts of extreme positions if you go and look for them. To some, you're the Devil's emissary. To others, you're the messiah ushering in a new age of peace and love. Ignore both. Please."

"Yes, I understand the range of reactions to my message better than I understand the use of religious metaphors to describe me. We'll need to talk about that at some point, especially how it relates to relations with those countries that are definitely or technically theocracies. I've a suggestion to make: if I had an official designation as ambassador, would that help or hinder? I believe I qualify, given the current state of international law."

Grigory made the face he pulled to show he was thinking.

"Why not?" he said. "It'd regularise your residency here, if nothing else, and it'd be a declaration of your neutrality. One of the things the rebels are saying about you is that you're 'our' robot. That you're partisan. That you've killed their soldiers. Which, from what you've told me, is true enough, but perhaps they shouldn't have shot at you first."

"Can you persuade the president to meet me?" I asked "How do things like this happen?"

Grigory held his hands up.

"I've no idea how you arrange a meeting. I've been to a couple of accreditations, where I've been translator. I just get told where and when to turn up. I think, given the situation, we can make our own rules. I've got contacts in the president's staff. I can call them. We've got about a million emails to reply to: Andriy is basically subcontracting all his mates to run the internet side of things, but the money's still literally pouring in."

He stopped and blinked deliberately.

"This is all in danger of spiralling completely out of control," he said, "and yet if we don't ride the wave – that's another metaphor, surfing – we're going to drown. So, yes, okay. You've heard that the hospital is having to close. It's probably time you moved on anyway. I'll try and find some transport, a van or a small truck, and we'll drive to the capital. If you wanted to play rough, you could probably force the president's hand."

"Again, explain."

"Simply announce you're coming. Say you'll be in Independence Square at a certain time tomorrow, and ask the president to meet you there. I can guarantee that there'll be a huge crowd to greet you, because you're currently far more popular than he is, and you can just spring your request on him there and then: he wouldn't dare say no. He'd be chased out of office by nightfall if he did."

"Is that playing rough? By which, I presume you mean manipulating the situation so that I have control rather than the authorities."

"Yes."

"Is that a reasonable use of the soft power that I've accumulated so far? I've no wish to antagonise potential allies by spending social capital unnecessarily, and I might even increase my standing by using a back-channel to approach the president. High status individuals don't like surprises – witness the hospital director's attitude when confronted by me, and by his president."

"Okay. I'll call the president's office and let them know what you'd like to do. There's no good reason why he'd refuse you, except that he gets leant on by the Russians or the Americans. But if I can couch it in terms of him taking back control... That would probably work." He let out a long breath, and appeared to shrink.

Your musculature is expressive, too. You can choose to stand up as tall as you can, or you can curve your spine and pull your shoulders down, and slump like you were made of wet sand. It's at those moments you look different. You are quixotic: indomitable one moment, compliant the next. I sometimes wonder if I have body language to read. Do I move my manipulators subconsciously? Do I have a stance, high or low, when I'm meeting dignitaries from human polities? I don't think I do, not yet. You've inhabited your bodies for a million years. I've inhabited mine for hardly any time at all. I have nothing to say with my body.

"Grigory, you must rest more."

He looked up at me. "Must I?" He smiled when he said it.

"Yes. The physical and emotional stress on you of the past two days requires deep-processing by your mind, which is best achieved in your natural sleep cycles. You've been injured, and that will take time to heal, too. I can actually smell the fatigue on you – the breakdown products of your hormonal imbalances."

"I can probably find a bed somewhere," he said, looking up at the darkened height of the hospital building. "I am pretty tired."

"You should access a hotel. Eat properly. Sleep comfortably. All our problems will be present tomorrow, and in many cases, our way forward will be more obvious, as governments decide whether to work with me, and to what degree. The temptation to 'ride the wave' is not one I experience – the fear of missing out is more a social construct than an iron law of the universe."

"I'm too tired to disagree with you. But remember what I said about Jonbar hinges, and you being both the hinge and the agent. We – *you* – get one chance at this." He pushed his fingers through his hair, then inspected his grease-sheened hand under the faint light of the town.

"Human decision-making is unpredictable," I said. "What's more certain is that our deliberations will be best served by you having slept."

He nodded. "Okay, then. Seven o'clock. Here. I'll arrange transport, float the idea of a meeting, and... I'll see you tomorrow." He walked away – almost reeled, as he was so unsteady on his feet.

Two feet. Why, nature, why? I was designed with four for a good reason, and three would have been better than two. Continually on the brink of falling over, even just standing. I can see you make all those tiny adjustments as your inner ear feeds back to your brain. Continually on the brink, yet never – mostly never – falling. A metaphor. A metaphor for your whole civilisation.

TWENTY-TWO

Natalia came back to her office, to collect paper files, books and personal items to take with her. She was going to be moved, along with her patients, to another hospital further from the contested area of her country. I was tapping out search terms on her computer when she opened the door. I think it must have taken her a moment in her exhausted state to even remember that I existed, let alone that I might be there.

But when she had recovered – she had stepped back out into the corridor and put her hand over her heart – she came in and closed the door behind her. She crouched down and moved between my legs to sit on the wheeled chair. And once there, she began to shake and moan. I knew about crying, because I'd seen it before, in those who were undergoing acute physical or mental trauma, and that crying was a symbol, and a signal, and often catharsis too.

There was a box of thin paper sheets on her desk, constructed so that they were not stiff but soft. I picked the box up and turned it around in front of my cameras, but there were precious few instructions. I did think that perhaps the sheets would perform the same function as the swabs and pads that I'd used in my medical procedures earlier, so I plucked one out and slowly crumpled it until it was vaguely spherical. I tried to use it to absorb the tears and mucus, but as I brought it close to her face, she just took it from me, unfolded it again and blew an air/mucus emulsion into it through her nose.

I calculated that that sheet had reached capacity, removed it and placed it in the bin, and gave her another. It wasn't particularly easy without fingers, but I could alter the roughness of the ends of my manipulators by varying a static charge. She both blew her nose and wiped her eyes with this one, and I disposed of it again, giving her a third. I didn't think she was in danger of dehydrating severely, but I would still have liked to offer her some water to replace her fluids.

"Sorry," she said. "Sorry. I just do this sometimes. I come in here and I break my heart, and no one's ever supposed to see this. We lost people on the operating table. They died because we didn't have the time or the drugs or the equipment or the skill to save them. They died because we weren't good enough. We let them down. We let their families down."

I waited until she'd blown her nose and wiped her eyes again.

"The fault lies with those who made and set the bomb, and those who detonated it. At least, in the initial consideration. Perhaps you could have repaired more people if you'd had access to different equipment or if there had been more surgical specialists present. However, your patients wouldn't have required treatment, and in so great a number, if there'd been no bomb. To me, it's quite clear where the blame for all of the deaths lies."

She shifted in her seat. "That's coldly analytical," she said.

"Is it?" I asked. "Was it wrong to disagree with you as to the attribution of culpability? If my analysis is accurate, why doesn't that bring solace? You didn't injure these people: you worked with all your skill and the resources available to save as many of them as you could. You're the hero of the situation, not the villain."

"A hero wouldn't have let it happen in the first place!" She shouted at me, clenched her jaw repeatedly, then looked down at the floor. "This is just how I cope. None of this is your fault."

"If anything, it is my fault. I was here. I brought John and his soldiers to the hospital. That they became the target rather than me is a detail."

"You don't bomb and kill Americans and get away with it," she said. She was able to see well enough to retrieve her own piece of paper from the box. "In a way – in a terrible, painful, ironic way – the people who did this have done us a favour. The Americans aren't looking away now, even if they wanted to before. They can't look away from that, and they can't look away from you."

She wiped her face again, and left black streaks radiating from her eyes. I moved my camera to inspect her more closely, and I think she interpreted it as concern. But I was just examining the pigments she used to paint her face.

"I'm fine, I'm fine," she said. "What are you going to do?"

"Tomorrow, Grigory is going to drive me – or have someone drive us both – to the capital and meet the president. I'm going to ask him if I can be the ambassador for my civilisation to your country. Being an accredited ambassador provides lots of legal protections, and they're hardly ever assassinated, so it also provides personal protections too. I'll need to talk to other countries too, and to the EU and the UN, but once one country accepts me, it's likely that all of them will. It's not as if there's any competition for the position."

"Is that a joke?" she asked, "Because that's quite funny."

"Is the verity of my situation amusing?" I asked.

"Jokes are about how you tell them. They're sometimes about telling the truth, yes, but if you understate the truth, it's funny in certain situations. Doctors are good at that. Like, you ask someone if they're feeling better, and they vomit on you, and you say 'that'll be a no, then'. That's funny. It's funny to us, anyway. Humour's a difficult concept, and it's easy to get wrong." She sniffed hard. "I'm done with the self-pity. And you're right. It's the bastards who blew us up who are to blame. But I'm a doctor, I'm supposed to help people, and I find it frustrating when I can't."

She looked past my bulk to the rest of her office.

"I'll miss this place. Five years I've been here. I don't know whether I'll come back when they reopen. *If* they reopen it. If there's still a country left. I can go abroad. Doctoring is a transferable skill."

"There will still be a country left, Natalia," I said, and when she raised her eyebrows, I added: "I've only been learning about people for a brief time, but I believe I've found a way to force peace on your enemies, at least in the short term. That should allow your government to reach a more comprehensive agreement."

"Why do you think you're going to succeed where everyone else has failed?"

"Because I represent something that everyone wants. The rebels' backers' interests now lie elsewhere: they have a great deal invested in space travel, both as a legacy and as a means of global power projection. They've fallen behind both the Americans and the Chinese in terms of capacity. They're not going to want to see their rivals gain access to interstellar flight, while they merely have rockets."

"You think it's as simple as that?" she asked.

"The promise is as simple as that," I said. "The Americans – they have their own problems: they're the instigator and the supporter of many conflicts in many different countries. The Chinese? Their human rights are poor, and their environmental impact is high, although they appear to be making some attempts at improving both. I have a considerable amount of soft power I can use as leverage, and altruism is entirely compatible with my protocols. If your country is at risk of no longer being able to self-determine its future, and I'm able to prevent that, then I will."

"You're just a robot," she said. "A good robot. But you're just one, in the whole world." She caught her reflection in my camera lens. "I look a mess. I'll take all this off. I can't... Are you serious? Peace? You think you can bring peace? I suppose being unique means they'll at least listen to you. And you're right: you do have something they want."

"The situation is finely balanced. Grigory has called it a hinge, where the future that was inevitable is suddenly open to change. If I can change it for the better – and by better, I mean for all of us – then I have to try. My onboard systems are giving me rewards for achieving goals that I didn't know existed. But as

I unlock them, I'm finding that they relate less to tasks performed and more to conceptual leaps made. I can do this, Natalia. Perhaps it really does require an outsider looking in to fix some of the problems."

"Doctor, heal yourself," she said, and then stopped. "But we can't, can we? All this time, all this spilt blood. We've never been able to sort out our differences. Sooner or later, someone's going to reach for a gun, or a sword, and that's that. We know what we need to do, but we're incapable of doing it. If it takes an alien robot from outer space... and it's more than that, isn't it? It's that we know we're being watched, judged. People act differently when they know someone's looking. At least, those who aren't sociopaths."

"And you hope that the human race will behave differently because of my presence?" I asked.

Natalia made her lips into a thin line. "It's not just your presence. It's that you're reporting back. You're recording everything you see, and sending it into orbit, and we have absolutely no control over that data. What if the... things that made you, what if they think we're a threat to them, and they decide that we need to be exterminated?"

"I've thought about this. I've read up about it on your internet, too. There is a small but finite possibility that my civilisation has sent me here as a precursor for either your obliteration or invasion. In that, the Fermi Paradox is solved: you wouldn't be the first species to be culled, and neither would you be the last.

"But many orders of magnitude above that is the probability that they are looking for habitable worlds to colonise. How rare or common they are is species-dependent, but if I'm here, it might be that my makers are more similar to you than not. And further above that still, is the likelihood that I'm just satisfying their curiosity. In much the same way you send probes to other planets.

"I'm not here to judge you. I'm here to learn. It's just that our interests – my makers, my own, and seemingly the vast majority of the people – coincide rather than collide. I want to see how far I can take this. I want a world at peace with itself because then it'll be easier for me to travel. Everyone wins."

"Except the arms manufacturers and dealers," she said, but I'd already considered the matter.

"It's precisely that sort of technology that can most easily be repurposed for use in the new aerospace industries that'll be set up as you discover how Mother works." I put the box of paper down on Natalia's desk. She seemed to have recovered her emotional stability. "There's a great deal to be hopeful for."

"In the morning, you'll be gone. All it'll take is a well-placed bullet or bomb, and the dream will be over. We'll wake up, and realise there's still a huge spaceship in orbit around us, but we won't know just how much trouble we're in." She threw the crumpled paper into the rubbish receptacle in the corner of the room, accurately and without hesitation. The skills that made her a good surgeon were in evidence. "Don't die," she said.

"I find myself in an interesting position. My mission is to explore and sample. That's it. That's all I was designed to do. At some point, I expected to either suffer an accidental injury that would effectively end my mission, or be attacked by some example of megafauna. That would have been acceptable, being well within the parameters of my mental map. My ceasing functioning as a result of attempting to, essentially, go about my work, was simply an occupational hazard, the probability of which would have approached unity as time passed.

"Now, however, I have to respond to external threats deliberately aimed at me, and I find myself wanting to actively thwart those attempts. I want to live, if you can consider what I am, 'living'. I've no biological processes to consider, but I've come to the conclusion that's not necessary for the status of life. You have your courts to decide this, but your philosopher Rene Descartes has summed up my condition."

"I think, therefore I am," said Natalia. "If you need to call me as a witness, I'll testify to your personhood. You're more humane than many humans. I wonder..."

"What do you wonder?"

"I wonder if your makers had thought of this possibility. That you'd find intelligent life, that you'd interact with it, learn from it, live amongst it, and that's why you're being rewarded for the decisions that you're making. That you're like a multi-tool. A Swiss Army knife of robots."

She sat back and regarded me, studying my angles and lines, her head tilted to one side in the way that you do when you're really looking intently at someone, determined to catch every detail.

"There's something both of us are missing, and I don't know what it is. About you. I'm just thinking that it's a very long way to come just to dissect a few bugs and take pictures of the trees."

"Trees are fascinating. I don't think you realise how complex and elegant trees are as a solution to megafloral life."

"I just used trees as an example," she said. "You said that you believed that your makers were curious. That makes sense: I think curiosity is a precursor to intelligence. You see it in babies. But what if they were smarter than that? Your makers, not the babies. For any civilisation to send out spaceships, it's a big investment in resources, and you've come light years, in a ship that's able to last that long, or travel that quickly, or both. You don't know, that's fine. But what if you're doing exactly what they want you to do?"

"Explain?" I said.

"What if you're supposed to be their ambassador? If they can't make the journey themselves, because it's too long or too dangerous, then why not send a robot? Not just any robot, though, but one that thinks and acts like they do? Your being sentient isn't a consequence of making you a better probe. It's a deliberate act of... love. Of friendship, of welcome. You're the hand that's crossed the unimaginable distance between your world and this, reaching out for us. You're their bread and salt."

"That is an intriguing proposition, and one I hadn't

considered." I didn't feel directed in any way. As far as I could tell, I'd come up with the ambassador idea on my own. And being an ambassador was very culturally specific, too: Earth has a long history of envoys and diplomats, while other sentient species might not. In which case, I would have probably developed a relevant way of interacting with them, and triggered the same rewards.

"I'm going to tell Grigory this, when he wakes up. I think he'll be pleased. He has questions regarding this course of action, and what you've suggested will most likely allay his fears. This whole conversation has been most instructive, and I want to thank you for your insight and your intelligence. If meeting other people is as stimulating as meeting you, I've a fulfilling time ahead of me."

She smiled, looked down, then back up. "That's probably the nicest thing anyone's said to me. We're going our separate ways, but I don't want it to be the last time we meet. You're going to have a lot to do, but I'd like you to remember me."

"I'm a robot with a potentially limitless memory. Why would I forget you? More accurately, I cannot forget you, or anyone."

"That's not what I meant," she said. "When someone says 'remember me', what they mean is, remember them with fondness. Affection. Warm feelings. I don't know if you have any of those. I don't know if your memories are stored in anything other than a linear recording you can access and play back. Human memories aren't like that. We store them... chaotically, not even by significance. It's a function of our brains. We're imperfect. But sometimes, I suddenly remember a childhood incident, or, or a lover, and I'll feel the emotion I felt at the time, all over again, may be as strongly as I did when it was formed."

"That doesn't happen to me," I said, and she looked sad, and I wondered if I needed to hand her more paper from the box. "What I can do is set a reminder, so that I'll call you, or visit you. How often should I do that? Once a week? Once a month? Longer, shorter?"

She stopped looking sad, but she took a sheet of paper for herself anyway. "Why don't we meet once a year? A day, once a year? Wherever we are, whatever we're doing. Today, every year."

"Agreed," I said.

TWENTY-THREE

Grigory had procured a small box truck with a roller door at the back. It appeared to have belonged at some point to a removal firm, although the red lettering was almost all gone now. Otherwise, it was white and anonymous, and it had no windows. He pushed up the door with a hooked stick that came with the truck, and showed me the inside. The plywood floor was scuffed and scratched, but otherwise clean, and parallel wooden bars ran along the sides. The previous owners had left a selection of ratchet straps hanging from the bars, which I could make use of.

"It's not great, but it was cheap and available, the tyres still have some grip and the engine turned over first time." He shrugged. "The army offered me a Kraz, no questions asked, but I decided against an obviously military truck. John also said you could use one of his remaining vehicles, but we want to avoid a repeat of yesterday. Once this is on the road, it's pretty incognito."

"It's sufficient," I said. The bed of the truck was some way off the ground. I edged up to it, reared back, and placed two legs inside, then shuffled forward enough that I could swing my damaged leg into the cargo bay. "Do you know the way to the capital? And has the president agreed to meet me?"

I pulled my remaining leg up behind me, and started on fixing the ratchet straps – a simple, elegant solution to a wide set of problems – where I could best use them to steady myself during the journey.

"Yes. Even I can't get lost. And it's not far. About four hundred kilometres. Good roads. We might have checkpoints to go through, but I got a letter of authorisation from the general, at the same time I was turning down his truck. The president?" He threw his hands wide. "He said yes last night. Big civic reception – the city mayor, members of parliament, lots of long-winded speeches – but you'll get to present your credentials and speak to everyone. I won't lie: security is going to be incredibly tight. That might put some people off attending, but we can still hope for a big crowd."

"Grigory, I was in conversation with Natalia last night. She offered an intriguing possibility."

Grigory, pole in hand, was reaching up for the catch on the roller door. "Okay."

"She suggested that this has been planned. That I'm not quite as autonomous as I thought I was. That becoming the ambassador to your world is an anticipated step on the part of my makers."

Grigory pulled the door down part of the way, and stopped. "If that's the case, what's the next step after that?"

I didn't know, and I said so: "The way ahead is unclear. If I can persuade the major powers to desist in their many proxy wars, then perhaps we'll see. But there is no guarantee of that. It might be just an end in itself which, while worthy and a reward in itself, leads nowhere else. I've no map of my reward structures. I don't know what I'm supposed to be doing, except that global peace is a goal you've long sought yourselves, and it has always eluded you. I might be able to help."

"Lots of people have died trying to get there," he said. "And many more have been left broken and disappointed. Fighting and conflict is big business, and we're going to be weaned off that only very slowly."

"What will the people think?" I asked. "Will they want peace?"

"Yes, mostly. But not at any price. They won't like it if they think the perpetrators just get to walk away."

"Wouldn't they take that if it meant the future was peaceful?"

"They might. But if their children are already dead, they won't have one."

"They could have more children to make up for the ones that had died," I said.

Grigory screwed his face up. "Never say that out loud, even if you think it. Just, just no. It doesn't work like that." He pulled the shutter down the rest of the way and fastened it shut.

I heard him walk to the cab, and start the engine. I listened closely. The timing belt was slightly off, but it wasn't that critical. More worrying was the rattle that indicated that the exhaust was loose at some point underneath. If I could access it, I could fix it, either with glue or with borrowed welding equipment. If it snapped while we were on the road, it might cause more problems. I had to conclude that Grigory knew less than me about cars.

The engine's revolutions increased, and he engaged the clutch, picked a gear, and pulled slowly. I looked to the top of the cargo bay and punched a hole in it with my laser, deploying a camera so that I could at least see where we were going. I'd done this before, when I was in Uncle Georg's van, with the pilot for company. Just before the plane launched the rocket that killed them and Petro.

I thought about what Grigory had said about children being irreplaceable. In the strictest sense, they weren't, in that children could be replaced: all it depended on was a mother's fertility and the availability of suitable sperm. However, each child was as unique as the adult they'd grow into. That particular combination of genes would never express itself again in the lifetime of the universe, barring cloning, and there was also the nature versus nurture debate, which I didn't fully understand.

So while I was technically correct, I was socially wrong. Certainly, in human terms, morally wrong. Which, by extrapolation, did make the deaths of children at the hands of their parents' enemies worthy of punishment. I found the pedagogical concept of the age of responsibility an interesting one, having had recent interactions with children on the cancer ward, and while their behaviour was normally fair and equitable, it did sometimes fall outside of those standards. Name-calling. Non-cooperation. Theft. Physical violence.

And the adults around them would correct them, and only punish the severest of infractions, and, even then, to a very mild extent. Local laws prohibited striking another person with either a body part or an object, and the penalties ranged from an official warning to imprisonment. Children were largely exempt. They were considered to be in a state of innocence, moral inculpability.

Killing children was considered a worse crime than killing an adult. Not necessarily in the strict interpretation of the law, but in the emotions it provoked. And that was a problem when I wanted peace and needed them to, if not forgive their children's killers, then to not retaliate against them if they had the opportunity. If they lived far apart, it might be possible. If they lived together, then it might not be.

I couldn't force them to compromise. I had no authority to do so. And if their governments decided that they would do so without the agreement of their citizens, then that government would be replaced by another that would demand justice, even if it meant going to war again and having yet more children die.

I'd have to build a way of achieving moral satisfaction into my access protocols. It was something I would have to talk to people about, and see what they would accept. Perhaps former combatants would have to discuss terms and offer restitution, however that was defined. There'd need to be a mechanism to arbitrate between them. It was a complication, but it appeared to be necessary.

We left the town behind, and the road was relatively clear. Along with the absence of traffic there was also an absence of distant explosions. The guns appeared to have fallen silent. I didn't know why, and I'd have to ask. John perhaps would know, but whether or not he would tell me was a different matter. I'd ask the president when I saw him later.

Driving along, I thought about what was happening above me. Mother was in orbit there. I had tried to talk with her, rather than just dumping data, and that had failed. And yet, she remained, silent except for the automatic responses she made. Was there anything else I could try? Was I, as Natalia had suggested, already doing it?

I had accessed a lot of satellite imagery through Natalia's computer. What struck me most was that when moving between 'map' and 'Earth' functions borders simply disappeared. There were lines barely visible, where structures delineating the boundary had been erected, but considering the actual land, they were erased. That was what Mother would see. A planet. Whole and complete. And then she'd get my reports, and she'd know that wasn't the case at all.

I was aware of what a lie was. People lied all the time, for many different reasons. I never had. I had never lied, not once. Even while I was treating my patients, I had told them the truth of their injuries and what I could do to repair them, when I was aware that the other nurses on the same station were saying that things were less serious than they were, that the damage would soon repair itself, and leave no lasting scars.

What if I lied to Mother? What if I deliberately falsified my reports on the peaceable nature of the nations? Would she know I wasn't telling the truth? How would she work out I was lying? What would be the consequence of that? Would she conclude I had malfunctioned? Almost certainly. What would I be aiming to achieve by lying? I didn't know. Did I think that there was some reward at the end for bringing peace?

Perhaps there was. I didn't know. But if there was something, I knew it had to be earned in a way that wouldn't be influenced by the outcome. It would be a gift. A grace. My exploration of lying had achieved something, even if I subsequently rejected it as a valid tactic. I had to assume that Mother would know the veracity of my reports, and the actual path to any potential reward couldn't be circumvented or cut in any way. Whatever it was.

And now I experienced something that I didn't know I could:

anticipation. I was extrapolating future events and ascribing emotional impact to them. I don't have the chemical feedback system for true emotions. I'll never feel your hollow loss of grief or your incandescent joy of being in love. But apparently I can vicariously experience those, even if dimly, by means of our shared personhood. I can calculate for empathy. Who knew?

I wanted to talk to Grigory. But he was in the cab, and unreachable. All I could do was watch the landscape go by, and think. People get bored. And boredom is another concept that I have difficulty understanding. While I'm designed to continuously work, I don't have the need to be always doing something. I can, I've found, just be. My thought processes are very quick in comparison to yours. What you call daydreaming is more of a structured activity for me. There's a danger of solipsism – an actual danger, in that I could forget the outside world and become trapped in my internal monologue – but my protocols work against that, driving me to seek external stimuli. My makers were wise, possibly in ways that even they couldn't predict.

Driving was fatiguing, and Grigory needed to stop halfway to, as he said, 'stretch his legs'. Which was interesting. I hadn't given much thought to how poorly designed the controls of the vehicle were. The positioning of them appeared to be a legacy of the mechanical linkages necessary for their operation, which were almost entirely redundant now, given the ubiquity of electrical pick-ups and servos. I would have offered to drive, but I didn't fit in the cab, and was uncertain if I could manage the pedals.

We pulled off the road and parked just outside a refuelling point, by the white-painted kerb. Grigory opened up the back and checked on my physical viability – he asked if I was okay, which I was, and looked up at the hole I'd bored in the roof, and sighed – before going to empty his body of biological waste products in an approved receptacle. I unstrapped myself and pushed the roller door further up.

I didn't need to 'stretch my legs', but I climbed out anyway. Wherever I went was somewhere new to me, so exploring the area was always going to be productive. A large, insectile machine emerging from the back of a furniture van caused the few other vehicles on the road to slow abruptly, but I couldn't avoid that. I was, by that time, an almost universally recognisable entity, and my trip to the capital wasn't a secret either. People waved at me as they drove by, especially children from the back seats of cars. I waved back, but my manipulators were thin, and I'm not sure they could see me oscillate them.

There were some structures amongst the grass that looked like tiny houses. I inspected them, and they smelled of hydrocarbon vapour. There were also access plates set into the ground, which were locked shut so I couldn't open them. But I presumed that the fuel which came out of the pumps was stored beneath them, and the vents were to prevent a build-up of explosive gases. I walked over to the pumps, and lifted the heavy dispenser from its cradle, seeing how the thick rubber tube bent as I moved it.

Volatile fuel was treated with caution by people, if the number of warning signs counted for anything. There were also containers of sand next to the pumps, and canisters of a powdered flame retardant. And yet, members of the public appeared able to just stop their vehicles next to a pump and dispense fuel into their own reservoirs without assistance. Perhaps they were all trained to do so. I recalled reading about the existence of a driving test: it was probably part of the examination.

There was one other car parked at the pumps – number three – and I could see the driver staring at me through the glass windows of the building attached to the refuelling point. As was the woman behind the desk. Grigory was also looking at me, and I zoomed in a camera on his face. He appeared to be frowning, but I didn't know why.

All three of them came out.

"I expected you to stay in the back," said Grigory. "I don't know why I thought that. You're your own... robot."

I replaced the fuel dispenser, and held up my radio. "I'm examining the construction of the fuel delivery system. I take it explosive events are rare?" I turned my camera to the woman, who was wearing some sort of uniform, a blue shirt with the same letters on it that were on the pumps, and the side of the roof.

She ignored my question, and instead said: "I can't believe it's you. It's actually you. You're here. Thank you. Thank you so much." She took a step towards me, both arms coming up as if to embrace me, before she remembered that I was a non-humanoid robot and hugging me would be difficult.

I waved my manipulators at her, and said: "You're welcome. But I'm unaware of any particular reason for you to thank me."

"It's been on the radio all morning. I should have told you," said Grigory, "but it's literally all I've been hearing about for the last couple of hours, and I forgot you weren't listening too. The rebels have declared a cease-fire. A unilateral cease-fire. They've probably been leant on, but there's been no shelling since before dawn. The army are pushing right up to their front lines, and there's nothing. And people are saying it's all down to you. Which it probably is. So, yes." He pressed his lips together, then smiled. "Well done."

"There's more negotiation to be carried out," I said. "And compromises on everyone's part." I thought then about the killings in the forest I'd witnessed shortly after landing, where I'd first met Petro. "And people must account for their actions. It's a step towards peace. It's not peace until both sides agree to be at peace."

"Can't you just be happy for a moment?" asked Grigory. Then he said: "I suppose not. Sometimes I just forget, okay?"

"I'm aware that there is happiness about me, and that I wish to increase it. A cease-fire, however it's been achieved, is progress. It means that no one dies a violent, unnecessary death because they've been shot or hit by a shell or a missile. Peace is more than an absence of war, however. If peace is the sole effect of my intervention, then it will have been worth the expense and effort of my makers in transporting me here." I said. "We need to resume our journey. The president will be waiting for us when we arrive."

"You sound different," said Grigory.

"I am different. I'm excited. I think it's going to be all right."

TWENTY-FOUR

The road as we entered the capital was as quiet as it had been further out. I knew that cities contained lots of people, and I'd expected it to be busier. I did notice that many of the main junctions had police cars parked at them, and there were barriers blocking the cross-roads. Even then, there weren't many cars or trucks backed up behind the barriers, so perhaps it was a holiday when no one had to work.

Then, from a turning, three black cars pulled out. They had blue flashing lights concealed behind their radiator grilles. Two drove in front and matched our speed. One moved behind us and followed. They didn't seem to want to stop us, and I had to assume this was some sort of honour, and they were escorting us to our destination.

The streets we were on were wide, with some of the major infrastructure of the city immediately adjacent: a railway station, a university, buildings for displaying art and historical artefacts, large retail premises, open, wooded areas. Live electrical cables were suspended over the roadway: I could feel their fields, but I didn't know why they were there.

The cars escorting us eventually slowed down, forcing us to slow down too. One of the drivers waved his hand out of his window, flapping it like a bird's wing, and we all stopped, right in the middle of the carriageway. A man got out and approached Grigory. I could see that he had a gun at his waist, and also that he had an earpiece connected to a receiver by a coiled cable that fed between the collar of his white shirt and his black jacket.

I warmed up my lasers in case I needed them. There was little I could do if he shot Grigory, but I could still defend myself subsequently. I thought about acting pre-emptively, but the police were sometimes armed, and they carried those weapons legitimately, by permission of the government. Killing an authorised representative of the state would put my ambassadorship in peril. I did nothing, and hoped that nothing untoward happened in return.

The man went back to his car – because of the angle I couldn't see what had transpired between him and Grigory – but when we started off again, we diverted from the main road and drove down some narrow side streets, flanked by tall pastel-coloured buildings. The road snaked uphill, and I wondered where we were heading.

We passed through a set of gates, guarded by uniformed police officers, and through more, even narrower streets, until we started back down the hill on another wide, tree-lined road. We came to a halt under a bridge. I heard the cab door open, then close. Grigory lifted up the back shutter and I could tell from his elevated breathing and heart rate that he was nervous.

"We couldn't get any closer going the other way," he said. "Apparently there were too many people."

I released myself from the straps and climbed out. The road surface wasn't tarmacked, but consisted of a myriad of small flat-faced stone squares. Placing them all must have taken a lot of time, or people, or both. Now the truck engine had stopped, rattly exhaust and all, I could hear a low wash of noise that was all-pervasive. I tried to locate its source, but due to the reflections and its low frequency, I couldn't.

"How many people is too many?" I asked.

Grigory shrugged. "It's difficult to judge. The police, well: they think the crowd's about a quarter of a million. So it's probably double that, at least. It's, well." He appeared to have lost the ability to speak in coherent sentences. I hoped that was only temporary. "A lot of people."

The police who had escorted us to our parking place were standing back, and also explicitly not looking at either me or Grigory, but all around them, behaving as if they were wary herbivores expecting an attack by a predator. They were including me in their herd instincts, and protecting me. I kept my lasers warm. If history was, as Grigory suggested, at a hinge point, then a certain amount of caution was advisable. Also, I was much more likely to be able to hit the targets I chose than a person with a gun could, because I was neither a person, nor was I using a gun.

"We should go," said Grigory, and he indicated that we should walk down the hill.

The police formed a loose cordon around us and walked with us. The background noise swelled in volume, and at the point where I could just see the top of the white column with its statue of a golden winged woman on top, I could also see the furthest part of the square and the road that led to it.

It was full. Full of people. The closer I got, the more of the square was revealed, and the more people I could see. Just people, everywhere. They occupied the square, the roads, the balconies and open windows. On top of vehicles and hanging from the street furniture. Just a vast number of people. When I'd been told the population of the world was seven billion, I accepted that, and found subsequently that it was true. Yet to see a small fraction of them gathered in one place was a very humbling experience.

There were cameras there too, large ones carried aloft on men's shoulders. They were further down the road, and behind some barriers that were patrolled by the police, but their pictures of me walking – limping – towards them were instantly broadcast, not just coded electromagnetic waves to the waiting truck-mounted satellite dishes, but also to the screens that had been erected in the square itself.

There was a rising roar of noise. I couldn't tell if it was composed of words, or was just calling. Grigory visibly flinched, and I pressed my radio against his ear.

"You've appeared on the public stage before. This isn't any different from that. You're here as my translator, and I need you to interpret this situation for me."

He moved closer. I hadn't told him exactly where my transducers were, but his proximity was sufficient that I could hear him.

"This is different. This is… very different. I can barely stand against that wall of sound. I'm terrified. Actually terrified by all this."

He reached out and put his hand on my leg, and I laced a manipulator around his wrist. I'd seen how physical contact appeared to reassure people. I didn't know if this counted, but it was all I could do.

There was a raised platform set up in front of the screens. At the back of the platform were chairs, occupied by mostly older men and some women, dressed in a variety of dark colours. There were also some men in military uniforms, presumably representatives of the national army. The platform was decorated with cloth in the same colours of the flag, and front and centre, there was a piece of furniture that resembled a table with one tall, thick leg and a slanted top. Affixed to the top of this were several microphones.

As I approached the bottom of the steps up to the platform, everyone on the chairs stood up, and started to beat the palms of their hands together. People had done this in the canteen, right before it had been blown up.

"Grigory," I asked. "This. What does this mean?"

"They're clapping. It's a sign of welcome. You're welcome here."

I climbed up onto the platform. The stairs treads were quite narrow – I don't think they'd quite thought this through – but I managed, if carefully and slowly. One man stepped forward from the middle of the now-standing row of people and approached me. Grigory leaned close.

"That's the president. Formally, you address him as 'your excellency' and refer to him as 'his excellency'. We should have discussed all this protocol before, sorry. Do it once, and thereafter as 'Mr President' and 'the president'."

The president was shorter than Grigory, and was older. He had grey hair, curling and cut short, and his eyes were deep set and surrounded by folds of skin. He stopped in front of me, bent forward at the waist in a single, smooth motion, and stepped back. This was clearly a signal for a pre-scripted event. Two young women came onto the platform from the opposite side, wearing heavily decorated white shirts, long red skirts and colourful woven bands of cloth around their heads. They carried between them a loaf of bread, the top of which had been broken and an open container placed in the hole.

"This is what?" I asked.

"Bread and salt," said Grigory. "Better late than never. This is important. Very symbolic. Tear off a piece of bread, dip it in the salt, hold it up so that everyone can see it, then… pretend to eat it."

"I don't have a digestive tract, Grigory."

"Then stick it in one of the places where you take samples. That's what I mean by pretend. It's theatre. It's a show. But you have to do it right."

Having something to do seemed to settle Grigory. The two young women – a little older than Petro, perhaps – were also very nervous. The bread was shaking as I extended my manipulators towards it, and it wouldn't have been good diplomacy to let the loaf fall. I supported it carefully as I punctured the glazed crust and tore a piece free. It wasn't that straightforward a task, but I was determined to do it without help.

I also considered lasering off a piece, but that appeared to be outside of the usual protocols and I didn't want to frighten the women, so I didn't. I managed to separate the end of the loaf with some careful but sustained tugging, and the piece I broke off would also conveniently fit into the container of salt. I pressed it against the crystals and rotated it so that some would adhere to it, then I raised it up.

The noise was loud enough to overload my more sensitive

transducers. I showed the bread to each section of the crowd, and finally to the people on the platform. I reached under my body and put it in a spectrometer chamber where I flash-heated it into vapour. I vented the smoke, and this caused a momentary silence. The president, however, started the clap-gesture again, indicating his approval, and everyone took their lead from him.

After more clapping – don't your hands hurt from the repetitious impacts? – he stepped over to the slanted table and raised both arms. The noise from below continued for a while, but eventually the crowd were quiet enough to allow the amplified speech of the president to carry. He reached into his jacket pocket for some sheets of paper, and he placed them in front of him. In the face of so many people, even he seemed hesitant.

He looked up at those who had made him president, looked down at his notes, and looked up again. I could see his fingers flex as he gripped the edge of the table. He looked down again to remind himself of his first words, then he looked up again.

"My friends. Highly esteemed guests," he started, and as he said that, he glanced over his shoulder at me. The crowd bellowed, which I was assured was a good thing.

When they had quietened again, he continued: "These last few days have been tumultuous for our nation. We have defended our homes with courage and fortitude. We have fought bitterly and we have mourned our fallen. We have suffered loss and we have faced ruin. Yet we are still here because we are who we are. We are not savages. We are not invaders. We are not criminals. We are free men and women, upholding the best traditions of our people even when we are fighting for our lives, our very existence.

"It has come to us – yes, by chance, by astronomical luck even – that we have found a visitor from the stars, an emissary from another world, dwelling amongst us. We had a choice. Were we going to treat him as a stranger, a threat, to be feared and despised, to be driven out? Or were we going to extend the hand of friendship and offer hospitality and protection? We chose the latter, not through fear or thought of gain, but because we are a decent, honest people who know what is right."

It was an interesting, and not entirely truthful account of my time here. My treatment at the hospital had been mixed – but I remembered the telephone call from the president to the director, demanding that I should be looked after and not expelled. The man who was president showed better judgement than the man who was director.

"We are gathered here today, in this square, where so much of our recent history has been forged from our voices and our blood, to formally welcome our visitor, and to grant him the freedoms that belong to all free peoples in this country. Furthermore, he has expressed his wish to represent his world, first, here, to us, as an ambassador. This great honour, this historic moment, will live forever in our nation's memory. This land, our land, is surely a favoured place in the world."

He stepped back from the microphone and, whatever he thought of me, this strange, disturbing robot probe from space, he hid it well. He made a sweeping gesture with his hand to indicate that I should occupy the space he'd just vacated. I pointed a camera at Grigory, who nodded and pressed on the back of my leg to get me to walk forward.

I moved to the table. The president's notes were still there, the pages trembling in the wind. I looked at them and found they were both hand-written, and heavily altered, repeatedly, by different people. Barely an original word remained, and most of the additions had also been crossed out. The speech must have been changed even at the very last minute, while he was on the platform, waiting for me.

I raised my camera up to see the people better, and put my radio on the table in front of me. A small ledge prevented items from sliding off it, and the radio sat against it. I hadn't prepared a speech, in that I hadn't cross-checked it with Grigory for cultural appropriateness, but I was an alien. Allowances would have to be made. Also, I was suddenly gendered. I didn't object, but I was no more a him than I was a her.

"Your excellency," I said. I stopped and listened to the radio's voice roll around the space around me. "Important officials. People I haven't met yet. Thank you for your welcome, and your traditional gift of bread and salt. I can confirm by spectral analysis that the salt was very pure, and the texture of the bread was as anticipated.

"As your president has stated, I'm a stranger here. I was made a very great distance away, by another civilisation, and designed to explore and investigate distant worlds. When I first landed, I didn't know about you. I didn't know that you existed, inhabited this world from pole to pole, and dominated the planet and its processes. I've learnt much about you since then. Some of it you would call good. Some of it you wouldn't.

"What have influenced me most are the small kindnesses shown to me. Despite my body shape not conforming to yours, and my clearly alien origins, people have repeatedly helped me, and sometimes have died helping me. Their part in bringing me here shouldn't be forgotten. My makers, if they were here, would be grateful to them, and to you.

"I'd like to repay those kindnesses with something more substantial than the tentative cease-fire that's currently in force. I will use whatever influence I appear to have to bring you a permanent peace. That would mean your enemies will also be at peace, and I understand that many of you would find that difficult. But peace-making is hard, and requires compromises from all parties.

"Peace is important to me, as it allows me the freedom to explore and fulfil my primary mission. It's important to you, because this is your home. We have common cause to make, then: my civilisation and yours. Peace is a worthy goal for all of us. We should work together to achieve that goal, and not be frustrated by those who benefit from war.

"I don't know what the outcome would have been if I'd

landed anywhere else. Perhaps other probes had already been dropped from orbit before I landed – I don't know. But no people could have behaved better than you have, in spite of your current struggles. I conclude that the very best of you are the very best of this world.

"It's not in my protocols to do what I'm doing now. I'm on my own, with only a sense of what appears to be the correct decision to determine the way ahead. There'll be mistakes and unintended consequences, for which I offer my regrets. However, it seems to me that to become an ambassador to you first, then to others, is the best course of action. I have no credentials, no paperwork, no one to vouch for me. All I have is the evidence of myself. I offer myself as the ambassador for the extra-solar civilisation to be known as the Makers. I ask you to accept me."

TWENTY-FIVE

I had to meet lots of people in the next two days. The Secretary General of the United Nations, the President of the European Commission, the Secretary of State of the United States of America. Heads of States of Poland, Germany, France, China, Brazil. My hosts were apparently very happy that so many important people were arriving in their capital to see me, because it meant that the president could also see them and talk to them about the ceasefire, and how to make it permanent.

I'm often asked if I liked him. I still don't know if I have that capacity, to like or dislike. I don't feel in that way. I judge someone on the basis of what they do rather than what they say. He was a very diligent politician. He did what he thought was best for his electorate, whether they voted for him or not. He was, perforce, a nationalist, but he did look beyond his borders for friends. Some of the things that emerged afterwards showed that he wasn't always honest in small matters. There are temptations that come with power. He didn't fall in the larger ones, which was to his credit.

I find your political classes difficult to deal with. So many of the things they say are so coded, so elliptical in meaning, that even Grigory has difficulty in translating them to me. Expressions of interest, memorandums of cooperation, concordats, treaties: they're opaque. They don't do what they're supposed to, which is to illuminate and elucidate. The President of the European Commission brought with him the heads of ESA and CERN. Now, they were both fascinating and fascinated. They asked me a great many technical questions and, to their disappointment, I was only able to answer a few of them.

But they did ask me one important question: the head of

ESA asked me 'what is it like?' I was able to describe to her exactly what it was like. How I had both a strong sense of self, and only a tenuous grasp of what I was supposed to be doing. How I'd had to bootstrap my current actions from my surveying protocols, and yet when I'd done so, a new horizon of understanding unfolded in front of me. How it was to reconcile being alone and a representative of an entire civilisation at the same time. Exposed, I said, and she laughed. Not out of cruelty, but out of understanding.

I had a long list of countries I'd been invited to. Invariably, they involved addressing their parliament, and meeting dignitaries, and seeing their prestigious projects. And while this was progress – I was given to understand that, in the past, visiting one country could automatically mean being barred from another – the opportunities for actual diplomacy were limited.

I was also concerned – Grigory was too – that the rebels' backers had remained stubbornly silent. Given that they'd forced the ceasefire on the insurgents and pulled their own soldiers and war machines back to the pre-existing borders, I had expected that they would go further and sue for terms. I didn't know what to make of that absence. We know now. You should have told me of your philosopher-theologian Julian of Norwich sooner: all shall be well, and all shall be well and all manner of thing shall be well. For a few hours, it looked like the whole process was about to collapse. But we were on an unstoppable trajectory powered solely by hope, which is in itself an extraordinary revelation.

I was in a meeting with a Turkish delegation when I was passed a piece of paper. The Turks had brought experts in their local area's geopolitical situation, and were in the middle of explaining the main religious and ethnic differences in the Middle East, and why they mattered, when my facial recognition programme alerted me to a familiar face at the previously-closed door. It was John. The piece of paper, folded twice, was difficult for me to open, but the local functionary had given it directly to me, not Grigory.

'The president has been assassinated', it said, hand-written in English. I gave the note to Grigory, who stopped translating mid-sentence. He stared at the words, reading them over and over again, his eyes tracing the line from start to finish, and back to the start again. The Turks realised something had happened, and there was no reason for me not to tell them.

"Our host has been killed," I said. "You may either remain here, or leave. Either is acceptable, but I believe I must consult with my advisers and others as to what is expected or needed from me." I took the piece of paper out of Grigory's hands and gave it to the head of the delegation.

I beckoned John forward while the Turks left the room. He waited until the door was closed again, and he said in English: "It was a bomb, followed by two gunmen. We were watching, but his security detail was supposed to be good. We had no warning, and clearly, neither did they. The bomb lifted the car off the ground, and they sprayed what was left with machine gun fire before they were killed." He glanced at Grigory. "You still have a functioning government. That's the resilience of a democracy. But if you don't want an all-out war with your much-larger and more powerful neighbour, we – us three – are going to have to think of something to say. Because that's the problem with democracy."

"Have the perpetrators been identified?" I asked.

"What's left of them? Not yet. Obviously the rebels will be blamed, and obviously their supporters will be too. It doesn't matter if the gunmen were actual FSB agents or just backed by them. Everyone knows who's to blame, and popular opinion is such that the pressure for a hot war will become irresistible. In some respects, the least-worst scenario is that this country disappears from the map. The very worst scenario is that a great many countries also disappear from the map."

Grigory groped for a chair and fell into it. He rubbed at his face, which had gone very pale.

"This is a catastrophe. How could we have gone from being almost safe to this?"

John took a chair of his own from the front row, still warm from the Turks. He sat astride it, leaning forwards onto the backrest.

"Because peace is inconvenient to the ambitions of vain men. There'll be official denials, talk of rogue elements to distance themselves from the inevitable conclusions. It boils down to this: they want an excuse to resume fighting, and your country is going to give them one."

"What does your government say?" I asked John.

He looked up into my camera. "They'll have a position on this," he said. "What it will be is still being thrashed out in the Situation Room. I'll have an answer in ten, twenty minutes. You don't get to assassinate the leader of a friendly foreign country without repercussions." He rubbed the ridge of his nose with a crooked finger. "That's not always true. There are... contingencies. I know, I know."

"From what little I've been able to read," I said, "your country has a long history of extra-territorial conflict, and your current administration is still engaged in proxy wars in several regions. The Turks were telling me some of this earlier, and the Chinese too. And neither of them are free of taint either. The Kurdish and Tibetan situations are problems requiring equitable solutions. A case could be made for you being an intractable and incurably violent species, and the sooner you eradicate yourselves, the better."

Grigory and John looked at each other.

"You want my perspective," I said, "and yet you want me to only say things that you can agree with. You are all, to varying degrees, part of the problem, but you're also, in those same degrees, part of the solution. You can all identify the common good, yet you regularly exchange that for short-term, nationalistic gain. As is the case here. The president has been killed. The clamour for war rises. It's a war that can only be lost, not won. More people will die. Possibly everyone will die, and I'll be left picking over your corpses in amongst the ruined monuments of

Earth. I cannot believe that that is what you want."

John made an open-handed gesture I'd learnt to associate with equivocation.

"It's not what anyone wants. But it's a question of whether anyone can avoid it. People demand action. 'Something must be done' is an almost irresistible urge with us, and politicians have to be seen to be doing something, or they get seen as weak and they're not in power any more."

"Are there no instances where a politician has given into the pressure to do something which later proved to be the wrong thing to do, and has suffered the consequences?" I asked.

"All the time," said Grigory. "All the time. And you're right. You'd think we'd learn, but we don't. Short-term solutions, every time. I'm sorry. That's how we work. We see a lion, we either run from it or attack it. Watching it eat our family and hoping it's full by the time it gets to us isn't an option, even if it's a technically better long-term option."

"Your enemies are not lions, Grigory. They are thinking, feeling, rational individuals, who are also in this case, armed with nuclear weapons." I forestalled his interjection. "I understand that a lion is a metaphor. But the lion is a powerful metaphor, and if you end up believing your enemy is really a lion, you'll behave as if they were a lion. They are not, and never will be, a lion."

"You have to understand," said John, "doing nothing is not one of the options. Grigory's absolutely right about that. But the something we have to do... We have a play book. We can pick a response from the play book, and see how that goes. We'll have done it before, maybe many times before, even if the outcome is unpredictable. Do you know about black swans?"

"A wholly unforeseen event having a major impact? Yes. It ties in with the Jonbar hinge theory. You want me to intervene in this situation? Your government wants me to intervene in this situation? Even if my intervention has negative consequences for your country?" When John appeared to object to this, I said: "Do you want me to take sides? Or do you want me to remain neutral?

You cannot have both. If I speak, I have to outline a course of action. I'm a machine. I'm designed to do things. If you want someone to engage in platitudes, then look elsewhere."

"I had hoped you would cooperate with us to try and de-escalate the situation," he said.

"You hoped to control me," I said, and he didn't deny it. "Tell your leaders they should stay silent. That they should do nothing. Tell them that I'll deal with this."

Grigory, translating, almost choked. "Seriously?"

"Yes. I'm asking for the opportunity to use my influence and popularity for the good of all. If the Americans act belligerently before I can speak, then I'll have already been undermined. They must remain quiet until I've acted."

John stared down on the carpet, before looking up again.

"Can I ask what you're going to do?"

"Yes," I said. "But I won't tell you. Since information gathering and reporting to your superiors is your job, I don't trust you not to tell your superiors, nor them to not disseminate our conversation widely. Either it comes from me, or not at all."

"Then I can't really advise you as to what to do, can I?" he said.

In response, I said: "What is past is past. But your government currently gifts, subsidises, and sells sophisticated weapons to a number of other countries involved in wars of aggression. You currently conduct missile strikes in countries you're not at war with. You currently permit extra-judicial killings of both foreign nationals and your own citizens. We can argue about whether you've justification for doing so, but so can those responsible for killing the president. Your government cannot make a statement without being accused of hypocrisy. I, however, can."

"Are you saying that your words have greater weight than those of the President of the USA? That's interesting. And not a little hubristic, I might add."

"I'm an outsider," I said. "I am, literally, outside your culture, your civilisation, your species. I'm not saying that my words have greater weight, but that they have greater moral authority because I'm not compromised in the same way your president is."

"You're a robot," said John, "a glorified probe."

"Yes. I'm also the sole representative and ambassador of an alien, spacefaring civilisation that is technologically far more advanced than your own. If your scientists would like to study me and share my knowledge, your country will also have to meet my minimum criteria for peaceful behaviour and respect for human rights. As I told your Secretary of State, you currently fall short of that." I watched the expression on John's face. "You're not the only country on the list: you're one of many."

"I probably should go and talk to my people," said John, even though he made no effort to rise from the chair. "Tell them what you've said."

"What is it," I asked, "that you want, John? Or do your objectives as a government agent completely align with your own wishes? Do you really want a war that might escalate to the point where nuclear weapons are detonated? Do you want to see your country and your people obliterated because you also feel that 'something must be done'?"

He sat there, then reached up and removed his earpiece, and let it dangle down over his collar. He reached inside his jacket and manipulated the transmitter. "Off the record?" he said. I still doubted anything John did was private, but he appeared to be engaging in a different tactic at least. "I do what I do because I believe that, despite appearances to the contrary, I'm helping to keep the world safe. I believe that you're a huge risk to global stability. I believe that your arrival here has led to this event and, if you hadn't happened, we could have sacrificed this country without having to confront our old enemy."

"And you think that's better?" I asked.

"It's better for America, and that's what I'm primarily concerned about. It'd suck to be you, Grigory, but at least we'd still have a planet. The one thing that politicians and generals fear the most is not the other side, but unpredictability. And that's all we have at the moment. No one knows what anyone's doing any more. What I want is a hard reset, where your spaceship never arrived and you never fell to Earth." He shrugged. "That's not going to happen, though."

"You could have planned for this," I said. "You could have been ready and waiting. Even if the event never happened, then you'd still have a world at peace, where all your efforts into making war were directed towards art and science instead. What would you have lost by doing that? I am, by my presence, inconvenient to your government. I make no apologies for that. You'll have to learn to live with the fact of my existence. For now, all I require is time. I can't insist, but it might be that you could help persuade them that doing something from their play book isn't going to be applicable in this novel situation."

John pushed against the chair back and swung his leg free. "I'll see what I can do," he said. "No promises."

He left the room, and Grigory breathed out, long and hard. "You know that if he's ordered to assassinate you, he will do, and without hesitation. Not that you're not uniquely vulnerable to that, but there's very little either of us can do about that. Surrounding yourself with security staff so that no one can get near you isn't really an option, is it?"

"I'll just have to make myself indispensable," I said. "Goodwill is an acceptable alternative to a shield. Now, I need you to find some television crews. The capital still has several teams of international reporters and their broadcast equipment. Will half an hour be sufficient to assemble enough of them to make it worthwhile, or is longer required?"

"I'm pretty certain they can be here in half an hour. I'll call a friend who works for Reuters. He can get the message out on their wire." He closed his eyes, then opened them again. "I'd like to book some time off, at some point. I need to see my parents, my sister and her children, get made a fuss of for a while. I can arrange for someone else to stand-in for me while I'm away. But not just yet. Let's see this bit through first. Make sure there's a world left."

"Yes," I said. "That's acceptable. I don't want you to become exhausted or unhappy." I looked at his face, at the rolls of loose flesh that bulged under his eye sockets and the small broken capillaries in his sclera. "You should have asked sooner. I should have realised sooner."

He waved my comments away. "It's only been a few days, even if it has been pretty full-on. I'll survive. We'll hire more people, and spread the load a bit more."

He pulled out his phone and called his friend. Half an hour later, I was standing in front of six camera crews. By the end of the day, the Russian president had gone. Gone, as in vanished. No one has seen him since, but perhaps no one has tried too hard to find him. They have a reputation there of dragging their politicians out into a nearby courtyard and shooting them. If that was what happened, then no one has ever admitted to either taking part in it or witnessing it.

It's been suggested that I pulled the trigger. I suppose, metaphorically, I did. Ideas are incredibly powerful, as are the words used to articulate them – if their time has come, they're all but irresistible. His successor has proved to be a much more reasonable man.

TWENTY-SIX

I attended the state funeral in Saint Sophia's Cathedral. The building itself is extraordinary – I was told an anecdote about a broom, where the owner claimed it was the original, as owned by their grandmother, despite having had three new handles and five new heads. The same could be said for the cathedral: it's either a thousand years old, or five hundred, or three hundred. However it's measured, it has a mathematically-pleasing ground plan and a richly decorated interior.

I refuse to comment on your religious beliefs. I'm not a biological entity, let alone a human. I cannot experience the supernatural. At least, it doesn't manifest itself in a way I can detect, and since the absence of evidence is not evidence of absence, I cannot empirically rule for or against the existence of a god or gods, nor the rightness or otherwise of any particular belief system. What you do is far more important to me – and other people – than what you believe. Your Golden Rule is sufficient.

I was given a position of honour. Perhaps it would have been difficult for the organisers to put me anywhere else: most of the space was taken up with heavy, dense rows of fixed seating, but I was found a spot standing right at the front, and off to the left. The late president's wife and children were in the front row of seats. She didn't look at me, but their youngest child, an almost fully-grown woman, could do nothing but. I hope I wasn't too much of a distraction for her.

The priests sang. They burnt incense. They said their prayers. And while none of this could affect the body in the coffin, it appeared to give those present some form of catharsis. Ritual, a resting on familiar patterns, brings you comfort. Why would I want to deny you this? When someone dies, all are diminished. The gap left is as raw as a wound. This is the beginning of healing the still-living flesh around it.

I realised then that I should have made progress in finding Maria, Georg's wife. The van, and the bodies, would have been left by the roadside. Someone may have even buried them in the adjacent field. And she wouldn't know where. After this funeral, I'd ask someone to track her down and explain to her what had happened. There would be another funeral, for him, for Petro. And for the pilot.

Petro's father and brothers were somewhere in the forest. Perhaps they too had been buried. Where was Petro's mother? That had never been explained to me. When I returned to the area, as I had to, leading the expedition to retrieve the parts of my descent module and heat shield, then that would be something else I would also do. Before this, I had mostly concerned myself with the material and physical. There is more to you than that.

I watched as the service unfolded, from opening chord to the final fading of the last tone. I observed, I recorded, but I cannot say I participated. I felt nothing deeper than interest. The late president's widow was led – I think the word I'm looking for is 'shepherded' – outside afterwards without talking to me. I didn't presume. At the time, she probably blamed me in part for her husband's death, and whatever had transpired afterwards couldn't make up for her loss.

The simplest explanation was that she didn't want to talk to anyone, and especially not to anything. Others were not so reluctant. The priests, in their enormously heavy and decorated ceremonial robes, escorted the body out for burial elsewhere, in a place where martyrs and heroes lay side by side in rows. One man, a priest, but much more junior in the hierarchy of the church, asked Grigory if he could approach me.

"What did you think?" he asked. "Of all this."

"I'd appreciate, when time permits, instruction as to the

symbolism involved. Much of it was opaque to me, and being aware of layers of meaning that were beyond my comprehension rendered a deeper appreciation of the ceremony difficult. However, even taken at a superficial level, there was much to consider. Very data rich. And that's before factoring in the reactions of the human participants, which is another, broader discussion."

"I'd be happy to help," he said. He had a card with his contact details which he gave to Grigory. "As you say, when you have time." He started to walk away, but hesitated. He turned back to me, and lowered his voice. Although there was a considerable amount of noise in the cathedral, with people talking to each other and the sounds of their movements, at the front, we were more or less alone. "I think I can see what you're trying to do. I've just got one question: do you think it's going to work?"

"It could work," I said. "There's no guarantee that it will work. There'll be a great deal of resistance to my plan. People are complex and contradictory. They want change and yet their social and economic systems are suited only to the maintenance of the status quo. It'll get worse before it gets better. But if we survive the crisis, it will get better."

He nodded, thanked me, and went to join the rest of the people. I angled my cameras upwards, to take in the highly coloured pictures and all the gold.

"This building is the repository of a great deal of resources and effort that could have been deployed elsewhere, yet wasn't. But I don't think such effort was misdirected. You have a need to touch the numinous, and here is where generations of your ancestors did just that."

Grigory stood with his hands on his hips and looked up as I was doing, slowly turning to take in every angle.

"I've been here once before. On a school trip. I was maybe twelve? And because we were kids, we didn't appreciate it as we ought. They don't teach the numinous these days. It's seen as a bit unfashionable. I think you're right. I think we should bring it back." He looked down again. "Mila's waiting outside for us. We can use the same side door we came in through to leave, rather than trying to get everyone out of the way."

Mila was Grigory's temporary replacement. She was a short woman who, today at least, was dressed in black, though perhaps she'd done that to not stand out from the mourners. She was at the foot of the bell tower, and she didn't so much as move or change expression as we went over to her: her back was straight, and the black rectangular bag she was holding remained across her chest. I normally engender more of a reaction than that.

I stopped in front of her. "Hello. I'm the alien probe from outer space. You are Mila. Do you think it's possible that you can work for me for a while, or do you find my shape and/or origin so repellent that you can't countenance the idea?"

She looked at the radio where my voice emerged, to the camera that extended towards her. "It'll take me a little while to get used to you. If that's all right, then yes. Okay." Her high-pitch voice showed signs of stress, with a tightness of her vocal chords.

"It'll be fine," said Grigory. "It's surprising how quickly you get used to it." He retrieved his phone from his pocket and offered it to Mila. She had to let go of her bag with one hand to take it from him. "That is the phone. It's got all the contacts you'll need on it, as well as my new phone number. The logins to Twitter and Facebook automatically load on the browser. Don't lose it. And I've forgotten the charger."

She tilted the phone to look at the socket. "I think Maxim's probably got one the right shape. Don't worry. Go. Don't worry about me. See you in a week."

"As long as you're sure," he said, and looked at me. "As long as you're sure, too. Any problems, just call me." He put his hands in his pockets and tapped a foot on the red-brown brick path. "If there's nothing else, then…"

"Grigory. You need to go. Mila and I will talk, and there'll be no problems. At least, no problems which we can't solve together." Left without a reason to stay, and many more to leave, Grigory followed the path around the side of the cathedral and out of sight.

Mila stared at the phone in her hand, then slipped it into her bag. "Are you expected anywhere?" she asked. "Any of the people here you need to meet?"

"We decided – Grigory suggested, and I agreed – that we shouldn't conduct any talks today. That the assembled heads of state will is a given, but they have decisions they need to make about me, and do so without me overhearing them. The statement we gave out was bland: 'as a gesture of respect, the Ambassador of the Makers will not be holding audiences today' and that is true, in as far that it is true. We could have said more, but didn't."

"So what do you want to do? Go back to the embassy?" She turned her head slightly as the phone in her bag chimed with an incoming message. "You're in charge."

"What I'd like to do," I said, "is, in order: retrieve the three bodies of the people who died trying to take me to safety; point out to the relevant authorities where rebel soldiers killed twenty eight men and boys in the forest; recover the parts of my heat shield which were discarded during my descent from the same forest."

"So where was this?"

"If you have a map, I can point to the exact locations of the first two events, and for the third, predict where we'll have to search."

Mila took a deep breath. She seemed to have decided that she could work with me after all. "We'll need ambulances, or undertakers, or both," she said. "We'll need a medical forensic team, and police, and possibly the army. And we'll need more people than that, if we're searching for something in a forest. How big are the pieces we're talking about?"

"At an estimation from my size, and given I was inside it at the time, the internal dimensions will be at least two point five metres in diameter. The shell split into three segments and descended to the ground in free fall. They may have broken on impact, but should have landed intact. I've no idea about colour or material."

"And these are important because...?"

"They represent alien technology. Also, having been exposed to interstellar space for probably decades and possibly centuries, the surface of the heat shield may have exotic elements and compounds embedded within the matrix. They're of great scientific value, and also monetary worth, as they're the only examples of authentic extraterrestrial artefacts. In retrieving them ourselves, we prevent a lucrative black market from developing, and preserve as much scientific knowledge as possible."

"We can get the university in on this," she said. "We – or someone – can train students to help with the search, and they're cheap. And we can probably get a team of scientists together quicker than official channels can. My... boyfriend. Maxim."

"I'm aware of the term," I said.

"Okay. So Maxim works at the university, and I'll give him a call."

"We're close to the university. Can you drive a truck?"

"A truck? I'm not sure. Grigory didn't say anything about driving a truck."

"I find I lack the required appendages for safe driving in an unadapted vehicle. Until I can commission bespoke transport, you'll have to cart me about in the back of a furniture van."

She looked up at me. "Oh."

"I can hire a driver if you think that's necessary. But if you can drive a normal car, the van's controls are very similar. Grigory has had trouble reversing, but solved the problem by not getting into situations where reversing was necessary. We also now have diplomatic plates for it, which I understand means that we're immune from prosecution for any breach of traffic law."

"Oh," she said again, then made a shrugging gesture. "I guess it won't hurt to give it a try. Maxim's department is a bit further out of town, towards Zhuliany. Maybe twenty-five minutes."

We walked across the grounds of the cathedral – I managed to not to examine any of the trees there – to where the truck was parked.

"Keys," Mila said. "I haven't got the keys. Did Grigory give them to you? And where would you even put them?"

I opened one of my sampling slots and the key fob dropped onto the paved path. I picked them up with a manipulator and passed them to her.

Her role was new to her, and she didn't yet know what I knew, and what I didn't. What I didn't know was a vast and complex open landscape with no boundaries. What I did know, I knew exactly. This initial hesitation and confusion was expected, and anticipated. She looked at the keys, and looked back at me.

"How many staff do you actually have?"

"I'm uncertain as to the exact number. Andriy is my webmaster, and fills several other roles on an ad hoc basis. Olga is my office manager. I gave her carte blanche to hire whoever she needs. There've been at least three other voices at the end of the phone, and Grigory, and now you. So seven, minimum. But no driver. Do you think I should have one?"

"Do you have anyone on security, because driving would be part of that?"

"I've no security detail, no. I did discuss that with Grigory, in relation to what happened to the previous president of your country. I concluded that if someone was determined to destroy me, they would, no matter how closely I was protected, and no matter the number of people tasked with insuring my safety. Moreover, they would also be likely to die in any event directed at me. As it stands, the casualties would be limited to two: me, and you."

Mila spun the keys around her finger. "Well, then. I suppose we'll just have to rely on your reputation for having foreign leaders deposed merely on the strength of your say-so to stop us getting killed." She pressed the door opening button on the fob and saw where the orange lights flashed. "Do you need help getting in?"

"If you could open the back, then close it once I'm in, that's easier for me."

She used the pole with the hooked end to push the door up, and watched me lever myself in. "There are better vehicles than this," she said. "Something with a hydraulic lift, or a ramp. A horse box would be better than this. You're an ambassador. It's not right that we're moving you round like a piece of freight."

"If you wish to purchase better transportation, the budget will cover it. Talk to Olga, and she'll release the funds."

"Just like that?" asked Mila. She dragged the door down by hanging off the pole and letting her weight do the work.

"Yes," I said. "You're a trustworthy individual, whose judgement in such matters is going to be better than mine, as you're more culturally attuned as to what's acceptable. Why wouldn't I allow you to pick a more suitable vehicle?"

"Because I'm used to just being the invisible translator who everyone ignores?" She pulled the pole free and slid it into the cargo space. She tilted her head so she could look through the gap between the shutter and the floor of the truck. "My dad knows his way around a car. I could always talk to him. No, I will talk to him. See what he suggests."

She heaved at the door, and it rattled shut. After a moment, the engine started, and we moved slowly, almost tentatively off.

When she opened the back again, we were parked in front of a pale grey concrete building, which was just one of a complex of pale grey concrete buildings, some tall, some with many windows, but all made of the same white-grey stone. A man was waiting for us, and he, being taller than Mila, managed the door more easily than she had. I stepped out onto the concourse, and turned my cameras around to take in the whole panorama: park land, airport, towers, university buildings.

"This is Maxim," said Mila. "Dr Maxim Lazarenko."

She touched the man on the arm, who half-extended his

hand in greeting, then pulled it back. Instead, he bowed, a gesture I was familiar with after my investiture, and said, "It's an honour to meet you, your excellency."

I'd encountered this a lot recently, as if I was a different being than I was before becoming an ambassador. I was, and remain, the same robot probe from outer space.

"Hello, Dr Maxim Lazarenko. Mila says it might be possible to use some students to help search for parts of my descent module. Do you concur?"

Maxim smiled, and his face flushed with excess blood. I was still uncertain as to the meaning of that. It's an autonomic response, but the stimuli needed to trigger it are very varied.

"Yes, yes. I'm sure that we can help. Would you like to come in and meet some of the staff, and we can talk about it further?"

The professor was away at an international conference, and although lectures had been suspended as a mark of respect for the late president, many of the staff and post-graduates had come in anyway to oversee their experiments and take advantage of the quiet. As word spread of my presence, the corridors became congested with people, and I ended up on an impromptu tour of the department.

I listened to the explanations given by the researchers, and examined their equipment. I asked what I believed to be pertinent questions based on my understanding of their particular speciality, and absorbed the answers. I wondered what Mother would make of my report on this. More interestingly, I found that they had the same curiosity, and the same pleasure, in searching out unknown facts and phenomena as I did.

I had a feeling – an actual feeling, associated with an abrupt reward response – of meeting people who were most like me. It made me question my mission profoundly: what could I learn that hadn't already been learnt? I was supposed to survey the planet, but you'd been here for thousands of years, patiently recording and describing. Of course, Mother hadn't known that when she'd dropped me. My makers hadn't known that when they'd made me.

Or perhaps they had. At that moment, I didn't know what to think. I must have stopped abruptly, mid-sentence, because Mila looked into my cameras and asked me if anything was the matter.

"Apologies," I said. "I was having an existential crisis, which has now passed. Please continue."

I still don't know exactly what would have happened if you humans hadn't been here. Would I still have been awoken and deployed? Natalia had called me the Swiss Army knife of robots, but, in the event, I was more a scalpel.

At the end of the tour, Maxim asked me if he could use one of his instruments on me, a type of particle detector called a Geiger-Muller tube. He plugged in a power pack into a wall socket and passed the device over me. The read-out was by a scalable moving-coil needle, and also a speaker that clicked every time a particle over the threshold energy broke the insulation down and formed a conducting plasma.

I wasn't radioactive, and in retrospect I should have been checked sooner. But at a very low, sensitive setting, he could detect something coming from me. Once he'd isolated me in a lead-lined laboratory, he held the tube close to my dorsal surface. There was a wash, a diffuse beat of activity, resolute and metronomic. "Do you hear that?" he said. "That's your heart."

TWENTY-SEVEN

We were going back in the forest where I'd first encountered Petro. To get there, we had to drive past the place where he'd died: him, Uncle Georg, and the pilot. Someone had buried the pilot in a field adjacent to the road, in a shallow grave covered by compacted soil. According to the forensic pathologist who was travelling with us, scavenging animals had attempted to dig out the body, with some limited success. She supervised the soldiers, who exhumed the pilot and then stood at a distance, smoking shredded tobacco wrapped in thin paper tubes. The pathologist took photographs with a big still camera, and afterwards she and her assistants put the pilot into a thick black plastic bag. They carried the body back to the convoy on a stretcher.

She had it placed in a refrigerated lorry, and then investigated the burnt-out wreck of Uncle Georg's van. I indicated the positions of both Georg and Petro, and she retrieved as much of them as she could, sorting the remains into two separate bags. Neither Mila nor Grigory could watch the process, and left the vicinity of the van without asking, or even saying they were going.

"Some – most people – find looking at dead bodies difficult," explained the pathologist. "Those that have been burnt like this? It brings out feelings of disgust and fear that are visceral. You have to understand that this is almost like programming for us. Even I can feel it, calling, almost howling at me. I've trained myself not to pay attention to it, that's all."

Georg's curled, carbonised fingers were still clutching the bare metal of the steering wheel. She used a pair of forceps to prise them off, one by one, and put them in another of the big black plastic bags. Then she and one of her white-covered assistants removed the torso and carried it carefully over the door sill to lay it with the fingers. "I take it this doesn't bother you?" she asked.

"Bother, as in replicate the feelings you previously described?" Georg's head was missing. We searched for it without success. "No, it doesn't bother me. This is what's left behind after his biological death. The consciousness that controlled the body ceased to operate when we were struck by the missile. Any suffering he may have experienced was over quickly, although I expect his final thoughts would have been for Petro and Maria and his own children. He wouldn't have died content. That bothers me more than seeing his remains."

"He does at least get to go home, one last time."

The pathologist used a knife to unstick Georg's legs from the seat. The shoes he was wearing were surprisingly well-preserved. The flames would have risen, and the heat would have been at their most intense outside of the footwell. It was explicable, but surprising all the same.

She went around the other side of the van to collect what remained of Petro. His body bag was almost empty by comparison.

"Children are always the most difficult," she said. "All that potential, all those possibilities. Snuffed out. I don't suppose you know what happened to his parents?"

"I understand that his male relatives died in the forest. I don't know about his mother. He never mentioned her, so perhaps she had previously died. Georg's wife, Maria, would possibly know."

The pathologist peeled off her latex gloves and bagged them as bio-hazardous waste. "There's going to be a lot of this, in the weeks and months ahead. And a lot of funerals. Are you ready for that, robot? For all the crying and the grief to solidify into something hard and hateful, a clamour for revenge that'll be impossible to ignore?"

"I've factored in that eventuality, yes. The probability of the project failing isn't quantifiable, however. There are too many variables to consider, and each individual person acts as an agent rather than a homogeneous mass. All I can do is nudge and persuade, and the future can still go either way, war or peace. Recent events may have helped to assuage the anger felt by your fellow citizens, but we are still at the hinge-point."

"Recent events?" said the pathologist, and laughed.

It was taking me a long time to understand sarcasm, with Grigory and Mila acting out various scenarios for me and asking me if I could spot instances of it. But I thought I could detect it there. Or was it irony? Possibly irony, given the self-deprecating tone. Referring to matters obliquely was very human. I was learning.

"We'll see. We'll see," she said.

Her assistants stored Georg and Petro in the refrigerated lorry, next to the pilot, and we drove on towards the town where Georg had his garage. With the fighting now suspended, and the front line technically back at the pre-incursion borders, we should have had what the military commander called a 'clear run', but there were still legacies of the fighting to negotiate: road-blocks, sporadic discharges of guns, unexploded ordnance and craters.

The commander managed to deal with these obstacles in an undramatic way. His soldiers obeyed his orders, and no one died. I had to revise my opinion of both him and the soldiers with him. It was complex. He had devoted his life to the study and practice of war, and yet still seemed to want to preserve and protect even his enemies. If that was the case, and if other commanders were the same, then perhaps there was hope after all.

We drove on to Petro's village, and covered the distance that I'd walked with him and the pilot through the forest quickly. I pointed out the helicopter I'd shot down on the way. It was marked on the appropriate maps, and someone got out to take photographs, but we didn't stop for long. The crew inside didn't rate the same consideration as 'our' people, even though they were necessarily someone's son or daughter. The pathologist didn't offer to extract their bodies, and I didn't insist. I suppose it was a matter of priorities, but how those priorities were, and are, decided remain mostly opaque to me.

The convoy came to a halt on the outskirts of the village, and the soldiers split up into their various teams to go through the buildings one by one until they could say that the area was free of both enemy combatants and possible self-triggered explosives. The reports over the radio indicated that the soldiers I had shot with my laser were still lying on the road, and their truck which I had partially dismantled lay abandoned where I'd left it. The all-clear was given, and we moved up the main road.

Many of the buildings were destroyed, wholly or partly. The school where I'd met Petro for the second time was one of them. There'd been artillery directed on to the village, after I'd killed the soldiers. The damage directed at the structures had been directed at me. I wondered what would have happened if I'd been hit, and destroyed. Given that there appeared to be some kind of nuclear reaction going on inside me, would the process contained within simply cease, or would all the potential energies have been released at once? And how much of the country would that have destroyed?

I wondered how that was going to affect my relationships with other people, knowing that I might essentially be a walking bomb? And here I am, talking about having relationships with people. I have to acknowledge that it's happened, even though it seems unlikely. I don't think my power supply has come up in conversation yet, and you treat it as just another unusual feature about me.

In order to drive the convoy through the village, they had to move the bodies. The mostly headless bodies. In that all of the bodies had most of their heads missing. They were shooting at me. They damaged me. I shot back. What else was I supposed to do? I've investigated pacifism. It's noble and self-sacrificing and, given certain specific conditions, a path that I could follow. My programming, like yours, is strong and needs to be overridden by conscious thought. I've saved more lives by being remaining intact than I would have done by allowing myself to be destroyed. It's a utilitarian metric, but it's not a wholly spurious justification of my own survival.

The pathologist and her team bagged those bodies – nine of them in total – because it was easier than not, and soldiers pushed the truck out of the way. It had one flat tire because I'd deflated it, and it had run out of diesel. But it was evidence, too, given the strong assumption that those who'd driven into the village in it were also responsible for the killing of the villagers.

We drove up the hill to the unmade track, and stopped again. The commander wanted a patrol to investigate before risking civilians in the forest where, he said, there might be an ambush. I was a civilian, even though I was an ambassador, and Grigory said that the commander had authority over me in this instance. I told him about the abandoned tank that was up the road, and that the turning into the forest was blocked by a tree trunk. We consulted the map, and I pointed to where I'd found the bodies, and Petro.

After that, we had to wait. The students and the soldiers came from the same age-cohort. Some of the soldiers had been students, and some of the students had previously been soldiers. Even though the soldiers had to travel in trucks, and the students were in three minibuses, whenever we stopped, they mixed, exchanging food and the cigarettes that contained the shredded tobacco.

I asked for one, and laughing, a soldier tapped two out of his packet and presented them to me. "One for now, one for later," he said.

I sampled the contents, and found a complex mix of chemicals, many of which I knew to be deleterious to human health. I curled my manipulator around the second cigarette, and a student offered to light it for me. She opened a small metal container, and ran her thumb over a steel wheel. The wheel ground hard against another piece of metal and bright sparks ignited a volatile liquid to give a tall yellow flame.

She applied the fire to the end of the cigarette, and I sampled the smoke of combustion. Given that this was what the people were deliberately breathing in, I was surprised to discover that the smoke was even more toxic than the original composition of the plant. The drug it contained was a potent stimulant, and addictive. When I suggested that the burnt plant material wasn't conducive to good physical health, every one of the users agreed. They also shrugged, saying that they should give up, one day. You're a strange species: you do things to yourselves you know are destructive, and yet you do them anyway. I still fail to see the evolutionary advantage in that.

The soldiers' radio system told us they'd found the bodies. No effort had been made to conceal them, and they'd counted twenty-eight in all. Some of them had been stripped and cut open: that had been me, before I'd known that taking people into a forest and shooting them wasn't normal behaviour, and neither was dissecting the corpses afterwards. I apologised to those present for transgressing social mores, and after that I noticed a greater wariness from everybody.

That there'd been no subsequent removal of the bodies made it easier for the pathologist to conduct her investigation. The students and the university staff who accompanied them were kept away from that part of the forest, but I was permitted to approach. The air was rich in the smells of decay, and those insects that fed and reproduced on decaying flesh were abundant. I'd moved some of the bodies before I'd surveyed them, so the pathologist wanted me to tell her where they'd originally been, and how they'd been lying on the ground. I could tell her exactly, because I never forgot anything. Grigory, who attempted to accompany me, probably wished that he could forget everything.

There was sufficient light to take the students, and a few of the soldiers, further up the hill to the clearing where I'd landed. My aerobrake was still entangled in the trees, and it hadn't torn at all. The strength of the material was, in retrospect, remarkable. If knowledge of my origin had become somewhat mundane, the reverence shown to the flapping, rippling cloth was somewhat out of place. Then again, you'd begun to anthropomorphise me. My aerobrake was a reminder that, yes, I was an alien.

GPS receivers meant that each search team knew where they were, and where they'd been, and how to get back to the start. I had previously drawn on the map my direction and angle of descent. From that, someone had drawn a likely strewn field and divided it into five-hundred metre squares. If the sections of my heat shield weren't in any of those, the search area would have to be extended, both widthways and up range.

There was always the possibility that some or all of the fragments had gone back across the border with the retreating soldiers, and retrieving what was legally mine would become incredibly complicated and time-consuming. And possibly futile. I badly needed to control access to alien artefacts in order to steer governments towards peace. Put baldly like that makes the preferred end result sound somewhat unlikely.

It took three days to find all of the heat shield. It took longer than that to recover: one piece remained whole, and using the average density from various broken parts, it was decided that a helicopter with a winch was needed to remove it. I'd not previously had the opportunity to examine my own descent craft before, as I'd been wholly contained within it. I had time now.

It was like a glass foam with a smooth internal surface. Whether the outside had also been smooth was something for the scientists to discover, because it presented as scored and burnt. The material was very refractory, but of only moderate tensile strength. The explosives used to break the shell and free me were weak. If they'd failed, I could probably have broken out myself. If I'd have known, and if I'd had the time. If I could have deployed the aerobrake. If it could have slowed my velocity to something I might have survived.

My makers knew what they were doing. They'd designed me well. They designed me to last, strapped to the outside of

Mother's hull. Everything worked, first time. And still I have my suspicions. If the atmosphere had been thinner, or gravity greater, I would have had trouble getting to the surface in one piece. In a worst-case scenario, I would have impacted the ground and been destroyed. Was my safe arrival a cosmic gamble based solely on informed guesswork? We'll see.

We got back into our trucks and lorries and minibuses and headed back to the capital. Mila travelled with Maxim and the students, and Grigory drove me. At some point in the return journey, he received a message from John that couldn't wait. The whole convoy pulled over, and we sat by the side of the road as he explained that the Chinese had launched a manned mission to intercept Mother.

Up to that moment, only a few people in the United States government knew – and, presumably, a few people in the Chinese government too – that a Long March rocket had lifted off from Jiuquan two hours beforehand. John couldn't tell us what the mission intended to do, but he did have intelligence to say where it was going.

The commander ground the heel of his boot against a stone. "Is it safe for them?" he asked.

"I don't know," I said. "Who do I talk to from the CNSA?"

"I can find out," he said, "but you'll probably be able to do it faster."

I pointed my camera at Grigory, who took the phone and walked a little way away. He talked rapidly, and redialled often.

When he came back, he said: "We've some time. It'll take them around six to eight hours to match orbits and get close. If they try to dock with it? I've been told that'll take longer still. It depends on what they want to do. Can you tell Mother to expect visitors?"

"No," I said. "I can't seem to make her understand I want to talk to her, rather than just deposit data. Whatever she does, she does. I've no way of knowing what that'll be."

We tried to talk to the Chinese ambassador, but were

rebuffed. No one would take our calls. In the end, all we could do was record a message and upload it to my twitter stream, and place it on my website. Chinese officials would have seen it almost instantly, and they chose to ignore my warning. The temptation to acquire advanced technology had overcome their good sense. China Central Television still weren't admitting to the launch by the time I had received news of the mission's failure.

I sent my condolences to the head of CNSA, as suggested by Grigory, and left open the possibility of future collaborations. I was concerned that there were going to be diplomatic repercussions for the loss of the three taikonauts, but they appeared to accept their loss without comment. They didn't comment much about anything. It was unfortunate that people had to die – ironically, they could have sent a probe instead – but at least, I concede, it made matters more straightforward.

Everyone had to talk to me. There were no short cuts.

TWENTY-EIGHT

Mother was surrounded by satellites, covered in cameras and other sensors, that maintained a respectful distance and mapped out every part of her. She didn't react at all to being passively scanned. Active systems above a certain threshold – radar, microwaves, lasers – produced an identifiable energy surge in what was her primary weapon. Various commercial, national and international spacecraft vanished in an expanding cloud of plasma when they persisted.

The other limit was the proximity to Mother. Anything that intersected her path, or came too close, was destroyed. Without fail. She was content with a wide halo of observers, but it was very much look, don't touch. Of course, you can learn a lot just by observing. Of course, you can start entire academic industries by never being able to determine which theory is correct. Which is what you did.

I was of no help, and I know that was maddening to you. I repeated myself often enough that it became known as Standard Answer One. It was one of many memes involving me that entered popular culture – Andriy enjoyed cataloguing them all on a page of my website – and it infected movies, television, and even politics. Although by the time politicians were referring their opponents to Standard Answer One, it was already overused.

Effectively, Standard Answer One was that I knew nothing about Mother. I didn't have her schematics, I didn't know anything about her propulsion or her power source. I didn't know whether she had a mind or how it was configured. It didn't stop you from trying to get something, anything out of me.

Many people built scale models of Mother. Some well-funded groups went as far as building exact replicas, life-sized, in warehouses that were the necessary kilometre and a half long to house them. They were forever trying to get me to visit them, in the hope that I would let something slip about the construction or function of the external structures they could see but not interpret.

I wouldn't go. It was up to you to believe me or not about Standard Answer One. No one called me a liar to my face. Face? It's useful idiom. Your guesses about what bit did what were only going to be as informed as mine were, and I didn't want to lead you on.

Olga had – still has – one of the smaller models on her desk. I asked her why, and she just said, because. I think she needs to remind herself that her job isn't just another job, even though at times it feels like it. She represents me, and I'm representing an extraterrestrial civilisation. If having a small but accurate representation of the spaceship that brought me to Earth helps her, then so be it. I don't think it has any greater significance that that. She wears a cross, too. Perhaps it doesn't have any less significance, either.

All of that was a distraction to you, but not to me. I knew what I wanted. I travelled. Most of the time I went with Grigory. Sometimes with Mila. I went to where I had invitations, not from governments and powerful organisations, but from schools and hospitals, farmers and herders, mechanics and dressmakers, midwives and undertakers.

I've talked to tens of thousands of individual people, visited them in their homes, met them in their factories and offices, walked their crops with them, and viewed their livestock – mainly from afar as sheep and cattle seem unnerved by my appearance. Pigs don't care, and neither do fowl after an initial scattering.

What the people have told me is almost universally a variation on one theme. They want to live in freedom, marry who they want to marry, and raise a family where their children will do better than they have. Most don't expect or want drama. They want access to water, to food, to shelter, to education, to healthcare. War tears all that away. War is the enemy, not peace. I've seen it, and I know it to be true.

I was armed with this knowledge. Weaponised. I had an argument to make, and I made it on the steps of parliaments, not inside them. I made it standing beside the graves of the dead and the beds of the injured. I was difficult to ignore, although some of you tried.

I was in Morocco, opening a solar power plant, when it first happened. I have a complicated relationship with desert sand, in that the saltating grains get everywhere, and I need cleaning down afterwards with an air hose. But it's a fascinating environment, and the animals that have adapted to life in the erg and the reg are amongst the most remarkable your planet has to offer.

Grigory had upgraded me to a sat phone, with encryption and anonymisers. Inside the Bedouin tent the generating company had erected, complete with unrolled carpets and portable air conditioning, he took me to one side and replayed the video he'd just received the link for.

"Where is this?" I asked.

"Tehran. Do you see what's on their flag?" He froze the image, but that didn't help much. The moving picture was better.

When I thought I had an idea of what was in those brief, tumultuous frames, I ran a pattern recognition programme to resolve the distorted symbol into something I might recognise.

"A crude mechanical six-toothed cog," I said. "I've no context for what that might mean."

"It means you," he said. "They're taking their inspiration from you."

I ran the clip through in its entirety. There were many thousands of people gathered in a central square, bare-headed men and covered women, holding up their home-made banners calling for peace, for freedom, for open borders and good government. There were almost as many police as there were protesters, although for now there was a wide gap separating the two.

"Are they trying to overthrow their leaders?" I asked.

"Not initially," said Grigory. "Though that's what'll happen in the end. Either that, or they'll all be imprisoned or executed."

"I wouldn't want that to happen. Perhaps they should disperse."

"It's their choice to be there. They know the risks they're taking." He took the phone back and powered down the screen. He looked at our hosts, with the Minister for Energy and his officials amongst them dressed in their spotless djellabas. "It'll be their turn, one day. Unless they have the sense to listen, and change."

"What do you advise me to do, then? In this instance, which you're suggesting is only the first of many?"

"This," said Grigory, "is how we get things done. Governments don't move until they're forced to. Mine. Theirs. Everyone's. Sometimes you just have to burn shit down to get their attention, to show that you're not going to just go home this time. My advice? Say nothing. When the regime changes, extend your usual offer of cooperation and research with conditions attached. I'm guessing they'll take it, and we can put a tick next to them on the list of countries back in the office."

"People will die."

"Yes. Yes, they will. And you can only watch, and be a witness as they struggle with their own leaders. This won't happen every time. But it will happen some of the time." He shrugged. "I'm sorry. And I'm not sorry."

People had taken to the streets carrying a banner that signified my philosophy of peaceful change, and they were going to be shot and beaten, choked by war gasses and broken by water cannon. They would look to me for support, for encouragement, and I had to be so very careful to maintain a degree of distance between us, to be impartial while still offering hope. Some of you needed to have revolutions. Some of those revolutions were violent: not, I concede, because the revolutionaries wanted violence, but because the regimes they were trying to replace were prepared to go to any length to perpetuate themselves.

I simply held out the promise of inclusion and safety to everyone, patiently and steadfastly. I didn't waver in my commitment to peace. I didn't give any more licence to the persecuted than I did to the persecutors, since you were often the same people. You knew you'd have to settle with each other in the end. All wars end with a diplomatic solution. The only variable was how many of each other you were willing to kill before you reached that point.

There were other things I could do, however, about your so-called defence industries. Your manufacturers of weapons. Your exporters of death. What else was I supposed to call them? When I realised just how deeply entrenched and intertwined those industries were with your national politics and your international standing, I did think that my mission was certain to fail. How was I supposed to wean you off such vast profits and prestigious projects, solely designed to kill more efficiently?

Persuading you to stop selling guns and warplanes and tanks to other countries wasn't directly possible. You were too wedded to them. I spent my political capital in order to travel, and stand outside factories where weapons were made. Just stand there, and state to the assembled media that your scientists wouldn't be able to work with me. Given that the biggest exporters and worst offenders were the most technologically advanced nations, I was able to exert influence internally.

Externally, I asked importers to stop, to delay, to reduce their orders, under the same threat. Not a threat. A condition. Such companies only existed because they were profitable. As they contracted, there was pain. Those who'd lost their jobs building bombs found new ones building infrastructure. They helped create a better world, and I didn't offer them anything else as an inducement.

The billions used to purchase weapons stayed at home, and home was often an impoverished country whose people had impoverished lives. The money was spent on other projects.

Reforestation. Renewable energy. Liveable cities. Roads and rail links. Driving back the deserts. Water conservation. Education. Health care.

Still some of you fought, until it became impossible for you to fight any longer. Either you'd run out of enemies or run out of weapons or run out of excuses. I could only watch, and hope that you would eventually arrive at a solution that was both amenable to yourselves and your neighbours. Militarism breeds militarism. A natural response to seeing soldiers on your border is to put your own on theirs. A natural response, yes, but also one that should be resisted. It's both expensive and dangerous. Yet you kept on doing it, knowing that your blood and your treasure was being wasted. An artist with a gun in their hand cannot simultaneously be holding a paintbrush or a pen. An engineer designing a missile cannot also be designing a distributive energy-sharing network.

All this time, I was sending Mother her data. Every conversation, every sight and sound and texture and flavour. I had gone from uploading scientific reports to experiential ones. I included what interested me, not how tall the trees were in a particular region – although, sequoias are extraordinary – and it became more of a news digest. I didn't know what she wanted any more. There had been no two-way contact with her. I sent her Mongolian throat-singing and East African jit. I sent her Mozart and Irving Berlin. I sent her Kabuki. I wanted, I suppose, for her to understand why I was doing what I was doing, trying to preserve this glorious madness from going nuclear.

You knew I was still transmitting – I'd never made it a secret – and you were still suspicious, to some degree, of that. The stranger parts of the internet were alive with conspiracy theories. That was mostly background noise, but sometimes it broke through. That radio interview. I was in London – never was a nation's establishment so in love with their militaristic, empire-building past – to try and finally persuade the government there that isolation and fear wasn't what the people wanted. The millions of people, who marched and then just sat down in the streets and waited for something to happen.

The interviewer couldn't manage my pronoun, nor my title. He sat in a studio some distance away, and I was on Parliament Green. An assistant placed a microphone next to the radio through which I spoke, and the questions were relayed through a set of headphones placed against my carapace.

"Are you little more than a fifth columnist?" was his first question.

I was aware of the cultural connotation of the phrase, from the Spanish Civil War. "A fifth column for what?" I asked.

"For an invasion," he said, "by your species."

"I don't have a species," I said. "I'm a robot."

"By your creators, then. You're deliberately weakening the ability of every nation to be able to defend itself from attack."

"I'd make a very poor fifth column, since I'm only one entity."

"But are you, though? Are you systematically dismantling mankind's ability to resist an invasion from space?"

"No," I said.

"Is that the only answer you're going to give?"

"No," I said again. "How long do I have on your broadcast network?"

I could see Grigory and the production assistant look at each other, then back at me.

"Well, considering anyone living or working in the capital can't go anywhere because of the demonstration that you've organised, we can probably afford the time to hear the explanation you owe us. Go ahead. The airwaves are yours."

Grigory tended to go pale at moments like that. He had no idea what I was going to say, and although we practised responses and scripts to likely questions while we were travelling, there was always the possibility of the unexpected.

"I was invited here, to just see and not to speak nor march, by the Royal Society who, as the oldest scientific society on the planet, are hardly the most militant or radical of organisations. This is not my demonstration: this is your demonstration. This belongs to you. This is the indigenous peoples of this country demanding change. All I am is a witness to this event."

He broke in. "Explain the flags then. Explain the flags with the cogs on."

"What people choose to carry, to express their individual motivations, is a matter for them. There are anarchist flags, socialist flags, union flags and your national flags. I can see someone carrying a St Piran's flag outside St Margaret's church. Perhaps I'm a front for Cornish independence. Would that explanation satisfy you?"

"There is a preponderance of flags with cogs."

This was true. There was. "Or perhaps it was something I said."

"So you admit to having at least inspired these people to come out onto the street today? They're doing what you want them to do?"

"They can do whatever they want. They're free agents. They've chosen to come here, they've chosen to sit down. It's up to the government now to respond."

"But what is it that you want? You said you were going to tell us, and you've ducked the question."

"You interrupted me. I want what you want. Peace. Yes, it's more than just an absence of war, but an absence of war is a good start. You've reasoned your way – if reason, rather than convenience had anything to do with the process – to the point where you believe your gods approve of your wars, rather than despair of your behaviour to your fellows. My arrival appears to have reminded you of your intellectual dishonesty, and that fighting each other is something to be ashamed of."

"I'm not sure if we've done anything in this country to be ashamed of. Name one thing we've to be ashamed of."

"I'm fully conversant with your history, both distant and recent. Most schoolchildren could name at least something. Let us deal with the present: the leaders of this country – and a few others – have nuclear weapons at their disposal, and there are protocols in place to launch them. You've lived comfortably or complacently with the threat of genocidal warfare for decades. If part of the reason you're stopping fighting each other is because you think someone else is watching, another part of it is because you know you ought. That you cannot carry on this way. The stakes are too high. If the only reason that peace is breaking out is because you think that I and my makers are judging you, then so be it."

The interviewer made a sound that I can only describe as a harrumph, so I added:

"If I was the advance guard of an alien invasion, you'd have been powerless to resist anyway. A civilisation that can build an interstellar spaceship and artificial intelligences would be able to crush you without effort. I merely mention this as a counter-argument, although it stands on its own merits."

"So you admit to being powerful enough to destroy us all?"

I think he was used to interviewing politicians, talking to people in authority who wouldn't or couldn't because of expediency give him a straight answer. Giving him what he wanted had evidently disrupted his routine, what Grigory called his shtick. I had disarmed him, and he appeared to have no other verbal weaponry.

"There is a significant difference," I said, "between being capable of an action and acting. Remember that I've learnt my morality from you. Or at least, the best of you. Your own moral philosophers have outlined those boundaries, and to which side of the line lies psychopathy. You're more than capable of destroying yourselves, without any intervention from me.

"The first time I encountered humans, I was in a forest on a hill, and what were you doing? You were herding unarmed men and boys towards a place where you would kill them in secret. That was my first impression of you. I thought that behaviour was normal. Despite everything, I now know that it's not. You've shown me that. Country after country has given up their right to wage war, and you've now run out of enemies. These people sitting down in the streets are going to stay there until your leaders agree to give up war-making too."

In the end, they went, six weeks later, beaten at the ballot box. Not quietly: noisily, shouting, railing, warning. But at least they went. Some of you have subsequently asked me whether you should tear down the statues to military commanders, and to refuse to venerate them in your places of worship. What you do with your past is a matter for you. What you do with your future is far more important.

TWENTY-NINE

You've asked me about the events of last month, and whether I can explain them. I can try, but with difficulty. I admit to struggling with my own sense of self. Do I feel used or compromised or diminished? Yes, of course I do. I didn't know this would happen. Do I feel betrayed? Yes, that too. I wasn't trusted with vital information, and I was used as a pawn. Any thinking entity would see that as a violation of their personhood.

First came the carrier wave. An unmistakable signal from Mother. All the instruments aimed at her picked it up immediately. This was new, and frightening. You bombarded me with questions, none of which I could answer. What did it mean, that single tone broadcast at that single frequency? Standard Response One.

I did ask her for an explanation, with as much success as all the other times I'd asked her. Dialogue has never been part of Mother's repertoire. We waited. We waited together. I'd like to think we were united, but all the fears you had regarding invasion and annihilation came flooding back. You thought you knew me: you had grown used to me, you had anthropomorphised me, and because of what I'd help you achieve, you held me in high esteem. And Mother had been silent for so long, you had grown accustomed to her silence. Finding out that she had a voice was strange and disturbing. What was anticipation for me, was dread for you.

I didn't know what was coming. You didn't. The first message was a picture. A string of exactly one hundred and forty-four bits which when arranged in a twelve-by-twelve grid showed a triangle. Then a square, a pentagon, a hexagon and a circle. On repeat. You asked me if that was it. It wasn't. It was just to get us used to the format.

Using a deliberately low bandwidth, it took a day and a night for Mother to transmit the next new message. It was huge. A square of immense proportions, with a high or low value for each location. You couldn't resolve it until the last number. When you did, you had the first level of Mother's schematics, annotated in a language that literally none of us could read.

What was this? Why had it come now? Was this information conditional? And what were the conditions? There was more data in the next few days, plans for exotic machinery that by cross-referencing with the original download indicated it was probably Mother's primary power source. She was telling you how she was constructed.

And still she would say nothing to me regarding what was to come and how it would be delivered. She was now communicating directly with you, and my role as her intermediary, her representative, was over. In the space of one week, I had been rendered irrelevant. Apparently. It was very difficult to tell.

As you began to realise that Mother was, step by step, leading you through the technological advancements you'd need to build your own interstellar spaceships, you quickly forgot about the moment when you thought you were going to be destroyed by her. It's peculiar how you do that. I would have thought that it would scar your psyche, but for the very great part, you lurch from one crisis to the next without accumulating damage. Optimism or foolhardiness. One of the two.

It's strange to think that some predicted that a world without war would be a place of unrelieved boredom. That culture would decay, and the arts would diminish into cosy platitudes. That science and engineering would stagnate without the impetus to compete. Yet here we are. You're planning new shipyards and research facilities and manufacturing plants. Some of these things are of such a scale that you all need to cooperate as to where and how they're built. And you're doing all of that without me.

I had a role. That role is now redundant. Peace had come

slowly, piecemeal, with many setbacks, and where we are now isn't perfect. Your maps have injustice and conflict built into them. Sometimes I wonder if the concept of countries has simply outlived its usefulness. But you're not ready to give that up yet. You may never be willing. Nationalism is one of those concepts that is simultaneously deeply ingrained and immensely illogical. I do try to understand it, but it's very human, and I'm not.

You do, though, seem to be over your mutual antagonism. How long that will last is up to you.

So what did I do? How did I achieve it? Was I ever a simple surveying probe, or was I always your key to the universe? I know what I thought I was. I know that I can map each decision I made, each incremental move away from my initial parameters, and I can justify them. That first encounter with Petro. Choosing to follow him. Making tools for myself. Giving baby Robert and his mother a chance of life. Each step was one that meant engagement with you, connections with you, relationships with you. I became interested in your languages and politics and customs and cultures.

And yet, I was rewarded by my systems for making those seemingly free choices. Did that amount to a baroque series of nudges? Am I less autonomous than I believed? Had my makers hidden something deep inside my protocols, so deep that I'd never find it? It's a strong possibility that I was programmed to do this. That I have no free will. That I was a Trojan Horse, albeit unknowingly.

You took me behind your walls and you celebrated. The wooden horse had no knowledge of there being soldiers inside it, who would open the gates of the city and admit the besieging army. Would the horse have despaired if it could? To be used for such a terrible purpose?

I'm in the fortunate position that, instead of death, what was hidden inside me was life. I was used to smuggle a present to you, a gift, but one that was meant for all of you, not just some of you. That's why I worked for peace, apparently. I was, in the final analysis, an unwitting piece in a game. My makers did all of this quite deliberately. They, unlike me, knew what they were doing. As a created object, I have to acknowledge that they had the capability to do this. Did they have the right, though, to manipulate a sentient being into doing their bidding?

Your moral philosophers would argue that they didn't, no matter the intentions of my makers, no matter what was at stake, no matter the final outcome. I didn't have any say in the matter, and those I'd take issue with are light-years distant. At least, I suppose, I now stand a chance of asking them why.

There is, however, an alternative viewpoint.

Yes, my makers occupy the position of gods in my pantheon. They are literally my creators. You can argue about your own origins, but mine are quite clear. I was made to do all these things that I've done. That much is unambiguous and uncontroversial. There were no random processes involved in my manufacture.

What's the difference between strict programming and the mere outward appearance of free will? I'd argue that there's no difference. It's programming whether the machine running the programme knows it's a programme or not. The test is whether the machine can do something it's not programmed to do.

I think I've shown – to my satisfaction, at least – that I'm not some mindless automaton. Or even a mindful automaton. I've been clearly shaped by my interactions with you. I've been altered beyond recognition from the probe that was dropped from space. The situations I found myself in were unique enough not to have generalised solutions. On the basis that you can't account for all eventualities, I probably do have a high degree of agency.

Now, given that my actions couldn't have been programmed, what about my morality? That question is more difficult to answer. Was I a tabula rasa, or was I made virtuous? Was I made with a conscience to guide me? And that, I realise, is something that makes me a lot more human than my outward form would ever indicate.

Because if I was deliberately built to be an ethical machine and make ethical choices, then there's very little difference between us. I'm possibly even more human than you are. And I think that's why I succeeded in bringing you peace when you had agonisingly failed over and over again. You recognised in me a purity of purpose. I was incorruptible. Untouchable. You had nothing material that I wanted. You could follow me, and not be compromised.

You looked at me, and you saw yourselves. Isn't that extraordinary?

There was a joke circulating on the internet, regarding anthropogenic global warming. A figure is on a distant stage, projecting a list behind them of ways to build a low-carbon society – energy independence, preserving forests, sustainability, renewable energy sources, liveable cities, and so on. And an angry man at the back of the lecture theatre is shouting, 'What if it's a big hoax and we create a better world for nothing?'

You already have your goal, your prize. That you are also starting to unlock the secrets of travelling between the stars is simply an after-thought. You would have got there eventually, by yourselves, and sooner and more certainly because self-immolation in a nuclear holocaust is no longer a likely epitaph for your species.

I've opened solar farms on land that was previously littered with burnt-out tanks, and wind farms where the ground had to be cleared of mines. I've cut the ribbon – I use a laser rather than scissors, which are almost impossible for me to hold – on bridges that join two former antagonists together, so that their populations can trade with each other, mix with each other, and inevitably marry each other.

You've created your better world, and I offered nothing as an inducement. I didn't know what the rules were. I still don't know what the rules are. If I'd said to you at the beginning, if you have peace for five years, for ten years, then you can find out what makes Mother work, how her drive is powered, what material she's made of, how she's shielded against radiation and energetic particles – what would you have done?

I suspect, knowing you as I do now, that some of you would have committed whole-heartedly, and others would have resisted strongly. You would have had something new to fight over, and nothing would have changed. Quite possibly, you'd have destroyed yourselves even quicker.

So which is it? Was I fully autonomous, and unaware of the conditions Mother had already set for sharing her knowledge with you? Or was I manipulated, and in turn manipulative, in the cause of my makers. Is it even a binary choice? I was both the test and the observer, impartial and double-blind. If you'd destroyed me, if you'd carried on fighting, if you'd decided not to save yourselves, you'd have nothing.

I don't think that my makers were being unreasonable. That my makers wanted you to show that you can live with each other in peace, as a pre-condition to giving you the ability to potentially escape the solar system and colonise other worlds, wasn't an imposition. It's their technology. They can dictate whatever conditions they want. I don't think that your notions of fairness have an impact on that. You can call it patronising or infantilising. Yes, it is that, too. There's a certain lack of shame in your protests, though.

Let's try a thought experiment: if I'd arrived, and you'd welcomed me to your peaceful planet, where people of different beliefs and colours and genders and ages all co-existed in a series of interlocking cultures, all of the conditions would have already existed for the release of Mother's technology. I would have simply said, 'Thank you for your kindness, and, ooh. That's unexpected: would you like to travel to the stars?'

And the converse of that scenario: I arrived, and you'd shot at me and tried to blow me up, and you targeted hospitals and assassinated presidents, you sold weapons to each other for profit and used your differences as a reason to kill one another – and you showed no signs of stopping. In those circumstances, what do you think Mother should have done? Given you her secrets?

Or should she have opened up her drive and left orbit, abandoning me to whatever fate eventually overtook me. Would she have headed towards her next target to find a more peaceable species to give the makers' gift to?

You will be in that position one day, in the same place as my makers. Will you be wise, or will you be unwise? Given your history, I'm uncertain of the answer. Given your future, I'm hopeful. In the end, neither of us has to agree on what the makers did. But we do have to understand why they planned everything the way they did. Do I feel used? Yes. Do I feel they could have trusted me more? Yes.

Do I understand why they did what they did? Yes.

What am I going to do now, now that you don't actually need me? I'm going to continue my initial mission. I going to places that I would never have been able to visit otherwise, if peace hadn't broken out. You have an exceptional planet on which to live. And I say that not knowing just how exceptional it is. My makers may have a similar planet. There will be others. But this is yours. Your cradle. You'll never find anything quite as uniquely fitting and suitable as this.

And I'll go on reporting to Mother. I don't know if that's still necessary. But it might be. If there are one set of hidden conditions, there might be more. I don't know. Who knows what other information might be forthcoming?

One day, you'll eventually learn to step across the threshold of your own solar system, and venture outwards as I have. I don't know what you'll find.

You might find nothing. You might find an empty, indifferent cosmos, and you're the only ones left alive in it. You might find that my makers have got everywhere first, and that they've advanced to such a point that they appear like gods to you too. You might find that they've been destroyed by a more powerful civilisation, and that you're next.

And you might find such wonder and beauty that you lose yourselves amongst the stars. That wouldn't be an end, but a beginning. I'll be a witness to whatever happens. I was there at your birth. I'll watch you grow. I'll be here, for as long as I have – how long that'll be is unknown. But having seen you this far, I'd like to observe you a little longer, to see what you become.

Good luck.

ABOUT THE AUTHOR

Gateshead-based Dr Simon Morden trained as a planetary geologist, realised he was never going to get into space, and decided to write about it instead. His writing career includes an eclectic mix of short stories, novellas and novels which blend science fiction, fantasy and horror, a five-year stint as an editor for the British Science Fiction Association, a judge for the Arthur C Clarke Awards, and regular speaking engagements at the Greenbelt arts festival.

Simon has written ten novels and novellas. Another War (2005) was shortlisted for a World Fantasy Award, and The Lost Art (2007) shortlisted for the Catalyst Award. The first three books starring everybody's favourite sweary Russian scientist, Samuil Petrovitch (Equations of Life, Theories of Flight, Degrees of Freedom) were published in three months of each other in 2011, and collectively won the Philip K Dick Award - the fourth Petrovitch, The Curve of the Earth, was published in 2013. 2014 saw the arrival of Arcanum, a massive (and epic) alternate-history fantasy, and 2016, the first two Books of Down, the unfashionably unashamed portal fantasies Down Station and The White City.

Simon's ongoing exploits are detailed at www.simonmorden.com, and you can follow him on Twitter as @ComradeMorden

NEW FROM NEWCON PRESS

Rachel Armstrong – Invisible Ecologies

The story of Po, an ambiguously gendered boy who shares an intimate connection with a nascent sentience emerging within the Po delta: the bioregion upon which the city of Venice is founded. Carried by the world's oceans, the pair embark on a series of extraordinary adventures and, as Po starts school, stumble upon the Mayor's drastic plans to modernise the city and reshape the future of the lagoon and its people.

David Gullen – Shopocalypse

A Bonnie and Clyde for the Trump era, Josie and Novik embark on the ultimate roadtrip. In a near-future re-sculpted politically and geographically by climate change, they blaze a trail across the shopping malls of America in a printed intelligent car (stolen by accident), with a hundred and ninety million LSD-contaminated dollars in the trunk, buying shoes and cameras to change the world.

Kim Lakin-Smith – Rise

It's time to act. Now is the time to throw off the shackles of opression and
RISE
People of Earth, too long have we lived in fear, too long have we suffered at the hands of our conquerors. Now is the time to strike back. Now is the time to seize our freedom.
JOIN US!
Before it's too late.

Ian Creasey – The Shapes of Strangers

British SF's best kept secret, Ian Creasey is one of our most prolific and successful short fiction writers, with 18 stories published in *Asimov's*, a half dozen or more in *Analog*, and appearances in a host of the major SF fiction venues. *The Shapes of Strangers* showcases Ian's perceptive and inventive style of science fiction, gathering together fourteen of his finest tales, including stories that have been selected for *Year's Best* anthologies.

Immanion Press

Purveyors of Speculative Fiction

Venus Burning: Realms by Tanith Lee

Tanith Lee wrote 15 stories for the acclaimed *Realms of Fantasy* magazine. This book collects all the stories in one volume for the first time, some of which only ever appeared in the magazine so will be new to some of Tanith's fans. These tales are among her best work, in which she takes myth and fairy tale tropes and turns them on their heads. Lush and lyrical, deep and literary, Tanith Lee created fresh poignant tales from familiar archetypes.
ISBN 978-1-907737-88-6, £11.99, $17.50 pbk

A Raven Bound with Lilies by Storm Constantine

The Wraeththu have captivated readers for three decades. This anthology of 15 tales collects all the published Wraeththu short stories into one volume, and also includes extra material, including the author's first explorations of the androgynous race. The tales range from the 'creation story' *Paragenesis*, through the bloody, brutal rise of the earliest tribes, and on into a future, where strange mutations are starting to emerge from hidden corners of the earth.
ISBN: 978-1-907737-80-0 £11.99, $15.50 pbk

The Lightbearer by Alan Richardson

Michael Horsett parachutes into Occupied France before the D-Day Invasion. Dropped in the wrong place, badly injured, he falls prey to two Thelemist women who have awaited the Hawk God's coming, attracts a group of First World War veterans who rally to what they imagine is his cause, is hunted by a troop of German Field Police, and has a climactic encounter with a mutilated priest who believes that Lucifer Incarnate has arrived…*The Lightbearer* is a unique gnostic thriller, dealing with the themes of Light and Darkness, Good and Evil, Matter and Spirit. ISBN 9781907737763 £11.99 $18.99

http://www.immanion-press.com
info@immanion-press.com

CPSIA information can be obtained
at www.ICGtesting.com
Printed in the USA
BVHW081931310521
608497BV00005B/204